THE ROOTS OF DRAYTON

TONY BERTAUSKI

Life and death.

One cannot be without the other.

Life and death.

One cannot be without the other.

PROLOGUE

He will feed her.

Brenda Gallagher had bent over to retrieve a hand trowel, the red handle buried in dollarweed, when a red tide filled her vision. She woke to a peculiar point of view. Yellow buttercups dangling in her face and the earth at her back.

She had been gardening when an old woman stopped to admire a patch of coreopsis near the road and asked Brenda what they were. There was a peculiar smell as she neared, a spicy fragrance the old woman must have picked up at the market. Cloves, perhaps.

"He will feed her," the old woman had said.

"Pardon?"

The old woman had moved on, and Brenda, perplexed and slightly nauseous, went back to the garden. Then the world was above her—the crape myrtles, the blue canvas of sky, a honeybee laden with fertile lamps of pollen. The smell of cloves in her sinuses.

Somewhere a bird sang.

The morning was tinted with pluff mud, earth muck saturating the Lowcountry, a fetid blanket exposed during low tide along with delicacies for spoonbills to discover. Her grandfather used to take her fishing, her yellow boots sinking in the soft mud, the stink filling her pores and impossible to wash off. She was born of the Lowcountry, of sunsets and lively wetlands.

Her breath was the tide.

A sleepy sensation collapsed her left side. She reached out with her right hand, fingers crawling through the mulch and fallen leaves, between clumps of perennials that she had planted years ago. The beds that served as her morning therapy now were a place to lay her head. She wasn't thinking of the old woman anymore—didn't remember her, the memory fading like images from sun-drenched paper—but only her daughter.

Her phone was in her pocket. It might as well be buried. She panted quietly, snatching each precious breath from the Lowcountry breeze. What would she do with her phone if she could reach it? Call her daughter to say goodbye, to hear her mother's last breath?

When is death convenient?

It was rarely greeted as a friend but rather an enemy, spit upon and cursed. No one welcomed the sadness of a funeral and the grief destined to never lift. Once she had been so happy that she wished for immortality, but no more. There was a beginning and an end. The best a person could wish for was a good death, one that satisfied. One without fear. Welcomed.

In the bed she tended, she could imagine no other.

Foliage crinkled beneath her, dried bits stuck in her hair. Between stalks of farfugium, the front lawn came into view. A slice of the old house was beyond, the shutters painted Charleston green. The trim in need of a coat. The front door, tinted with the growth of algae, was charmingly crooked in its frame and swelled in the summer.

The plaque next to it was tarnished and grungy with lichen. *James* was etched into a plate, a memorial to his passing. His former clients had presented it to her a month after his death. This was where he practiced, an old house passed down through the family, a house Brenda watched over until this day. Friends said she should sell it, she should move on with her life. Instead, she allowed someone else to practice therapy while she kept the lawn trimmed and the flowers in bloom. It was a quaint Charleston niche where tourists sometimes stopped in horse-drawn carriages. A place preserving history, that weathered storms and war alike. A place that grew out of dark times and smiled and welcomed its guests.

A place to lay her head.

No one would see where she had fallen. Only the black beetle struggling up a blade of grass would witness her death, and the spider dangling from a thread. Flakes of fallen leaves were pasted to her cheeks. Her tongue had swelled like the crooked door in its frame. James had died of a massive stroke near the Battery. Her death would be in a bed of flowers.

Witnesses said he'd passed with a smile, muttering gratitude to no one in particular. Pure Jimmy Gallagher, always seeing light where darkness gathered. He wasn't perfect, had his peccadilloes like every man, but he'd always managed to smile at the right time—when she was mad, when she was sad, when there was no reason to be happy. He smiled. All the way to the very end, he smiled.

He will feed her, she thought, wondering what that meant. And who said it.

A swallowtail landed on a flower, the weight of such a soft touch pulling it closer to Brenda's lips, where half a smile was born. She would pass beneath the flutter of wings with mulch at her back and dirt beneath her fingernails. She would transition to what was beyond, if there was anything out there.

She did not subscribe to the notion of heaven or hell. There would be no line awaiting her arrival, no loved ones floating in clouds with wings or dancing on hot coals. Whatever was there was there, whether she believed it to be or not. She had lived a good life, the best she could. Heaven, she reasoned, could not be out there waiting for death to carry her to it. It was not hovering out of sight or testing how far her faith could leap. Heaven and hell were quite simple.

They were here.

Her lack of belief did not give her comfort. Did life owe her that? Was the point of a good life to feel good when the cold hand of death found her? She believed a life worth living was a life striving for truth, to see what was there, to pull back the curtain regardless of what was behind it. If that meant a lonesome death, then she would accept that as well.

Jimmy smiled.

A rogue breeze danced with the trees. The swallowtail fluttered off, a pattern of black and yellow into the blue beyond. She looked to the old house once more and noticed the bike. Brenda closed her eyes. The bike her late husband had rode to work each morning was leaning against the stoop. It couldn't be.

It was in storage.

When she opened her eyes, the smell of cloves had vanished, and a different warmth filled her. It wasn't paralyzing, wasn't tingling. Tears pooled in the recesses of her eyes.

James was sitting next to the bike.

His jeans were worn, the sleeves of his shirt long. A clutch of yellow flowers was in his hands. She imagined the white whiskers on his chin, the way his eyes crinkled. The way he whistled when he focused on a project and the tight pucker of his lips. The comforting embrace when he came home.

She clawed the weeds. His name was on her lips but never passed through them. His name remained a silent petal resting on her tongue.

Her late husband stood.

The smell of perspiration, of an old shirt with dirt ground into the elbows and rubbed across the front, was near. She closed her eyes because she would pass from the world as he did.

Was my name on his lips, too?

A shadow silently passed over her, a cloud resting on the blue backdrop. She was lucid enough to know that wasn't Jimmy sitting on the porch. There was no bike against the stoop. She was imagining that because, in the end, she didn't want to be alone. She hoped there was an afterlife.

But someone was there.

It wasn't her late husband returning from death, not his spirit descending from heaven to welcome her to everlasting peace. A young man stood silently over her. His scalp was clean, his flesh as dark as fertile soil and as smooth as a newborn. His footsteps had not crushed a twig or wrinkled leaf. He felt as ancient as a Lowcountry live oak, as if he were the very fabric of the South. He wore the hardworking fragrance of her late husband.

A breath shuddered through her lips.

Perhaps her imagination had conjured this image of death, a polite young man to still her heart. Jimmy had spoken of this person before he died. He was the client who had appeared in the days before his death. And now he was here.

Perhaps there were angels.

His eyes were deep holes that absorbed all that was wrong and all that kept her from letting go. Her daughter would be just fine without her. A smile grew upon her to lighten this lonesome moment.

He will feed her.

The young man reached for her, a slow motion that seemed to jitter in fractured space. He took her hand. She felt the pressure, felt his presence in her chest.

Jason, the therapist now working in the old house, would find her the next day. He would arrive early in the morning with shadows still cast over the house and see her yellow boots. She would be on her back, hands folded over her stomach.

Yellow flowers tucked between her fingers.

A cool essence condensed in her chest. A thick white cloud seeped from her nostrils. Brenda Gallagher drifted through the branches of the live oaks, the curly silver strands of Spanish moss guiding her upward. She wafted on the breeze to birdsong, carried by the fetid smell of pluff mud.

She was home.

PART I

When I let go of what I am, I become what I might be.
— *Lao Tzu*

1

The pencil was a nub.

Amber cupped it to the page, applying soft strokes beneath the dark eyes of her subject, the stubbled scalp and whiskered cheeks, the ponytail braid hanging from his chin that he stroked lovingly with one hand while swiping a tablet with the other. She captured the beaded necklaces and the large holes in his earlobes—a man who would preach the sanctity of nature ensnared by technology's lure. He looked up only once, but it was enough for her to grasp the icy cold irises.

These were the moments she travelled outside her body, so absorbed in the dashed lines and the sweeping curve of a neck or collar, the pinched wrinkles across a forehead. When the world cast a long shadow of demands, she disappeared into her sketchbook.

The man suddenly stood up, stretching, yawning, rubbing his tired face, and tugging the chin braid. Amber lifted her knee and hooded the page. Never looking her way, he walked off without a glance or clue she had copied his conflicted soul. That was the tingling she felt when she sketched an unknowing subject, as if she absorbed the true essence of someone with a stroke of her hand. She attributed it to bringing his presence to life, making it breathe on her page.

It was cool and electric.

She grabbed a pink eraser and swiped across his face, beams of light obscuring a few of the details. She had been taught never to erase, that every line had a purpose. Art included all the marks, even the ones outside the lines. The first time she used an eraser was out of frustration. But then she liked it. It reminded her of sunlight, each beam a pure manifestation of energy—forgiving, loving. Beautiful.

I am the light, she told herself on days like this.

She dropped her phone on the bench and swiped through a dozen photos she'd snapped of him while pretending to text. She'd sketch him at least one more time before she was done, as if he were a dishrag to be wrung out.

She returned to sketching the birthmark on the left side of his neck, a strawberry likeness of Texas stamped just below his jawbone, when her phone went off. She ignored the call, hardly noticing the nearby conversations or the broken shadows across the pavement, lost in a niche she had carved in her mind when she was very young. It was a place she could hide, a safe room.

Because the world was dangerous.

Life was uncertain. All that was beautiful would one day decay. Perhaps there was beauty in that, too.

Rarely did she sketch in public. Today was beneath a live oak on campus. Her drawings weren't secret, not really of interest to anyone. She preferred the model didn't know what she was doing. It spoiled the rawness when they did. The mask went up and the rules engaged. When people were in their heads, sitting alone in a café or on a bench, they were exposed, and Amber captured their essence on a blank page.

I'm an idiot.

It wasn't fair to think such things. Could she be blamed for her attraction to the wrong people, her fascination with damaged goods, boys with fractured lives that mirrored her own? They were these dark rooms that she could somehow revitalize, throw open the curtains and beam brightly on their lives, lift them higher. Turned out she was as lost as they were. How many times had she chastised herself for mingling with a shady crowd and waking up next to cigarette butts in a Solo cup?

Why am I like this?

Her parents had taught her different. They walked a road that was straight and narrow and productive, but crooked tracks had been carved in her DNA. The legacy of her genetic roadmap crackled in her veins. She was lost.

Is there light without dark?

A shadow blotted out dappled sunlight. A pair of Timberlands met the toes of her flip-flops. She closed the sketchbook and slid it under her book bag.

"I texted," Macon said.

"Sorry. I was distracted."

"Where have you been?"

She watched her fingers tie knots. He stepped on the orange patches of nail polish chipping off her toenails. She slid her foot back.

"Look," he said, "if this is about the other night, I said I was sorry. You know how it is."

The knots in her stomach pulled tighter. God, she hated this. People like Macon knew she would rather lie down than throw swings. He could wipe his boots on her and she would apologize for getting them dirty.

"Don't blame me, Amber. I barely remember anything. Don't believe what anyone says."

The beauty of social media was that everyone's mistakes lived in public. Someone had tagged her on the photo, the harsh light of a flash and his face buried between fleshy thighs. He had been too fucked up to even know that whoever owned that pussy had taken his picture while he was French-kissing it.

"I need to study, Macon—"

"Don't do this." He squeezed her hand hard. "I promise it won't happen again. That's all behind me, I told you. Christ, Amber, it was just a party. Maybe if you were there, things wouldn't have gotten out of hand. You should think about that. Get out of the apartment every once in a while. Put the fucking pencil down."

"Don't blame me."

"It takes two, that's all I'm saying."

She tried to yank out of his grip. This wasn't a discussion between them. It never was. If she said something, he would bat it back and she'd catch it where it hurt. Another promise. Another lie.

Stop, she thought.

"It's got nothing to do with… any of that," she said. "I've got to study—"

"You're jealous."

"What?"

"This isn't all *my* fault." He paced around people walking past. "It takes two, Amber. It takes two. You think you're the good guy in relationships when you're really waiting around for someone to blame. You hold back until the other person has had enough, and then you can explain why you're the victim, and that's why you are the way you are."

"You're right, Macon. I suck, you suck. So why are we doing this?"

"If you didn't bury your nose up every professor's ass, you might see what's in front of you. I mean, can you just relax for one fucking second? Christ, it's like you're still trying to make daddy love you."

"Stop it."

"Admit it. It's all about you, every person you ever dated. Neatly disguised and hidden from you and the other person, it's all about Amber. All day, all night, Ambrogina Scion Gallagher eight days a week."

This was why she chose the middle of campus. He wouldn't break things with everyone around them, wouldn't toss the apartment with people watching. Nothing survived Hurricane Macon. It wasn't his fault God made him this way, he'd once said. He just made landfall and things happened. People got hurt in storms. That was just the way it was.

He was sort of right.

She felt the urge to hide in her mind, go blank until the storm passed, ignore what he was saying and go numb. The strategy that worked when she was little. The strategy she was outgrowing like tap shoes.

"Fuck me!"

Macon slammed his book bag on the pavers. Things broke inside it; glass rattled. Now people were looking. Cowardice ate a hole in her stomach. She was lying down again, ready to lick his boots if he just didn't sweep everything out to water.

Don't take this shit, a voice told her.

"What's this?" He snatched the sketchbook. Her laptop slid out of her book bag when he did. The corner cracked on the pavers. "Who you drawing now?"

"Give it back."

"I am the light." He frowned at the inscription. She didn't remember scribbling that. "You fucking this guy?"

"Jesus, Macon."

He backed into someone, absorbed by the pages. One by one, he began ripping them out, dropping loosely crumpled snowballs on the sidewalk. Frayed tags fluttered from the coiled binder.

She didn't stop him.

They were just drawings. He could burn every notebook she ever had, but he could never touch the safe room in her mind that spawned them, the only thing that kept her from running off the cliff in this mad world. She didn't move, even when he tossed the book straight up. It fluttered like an animated creature flapping doomed wings.

"Is everything all right?" A balding man stopped between them, a faculty ID around his neck.

"It's fine," Amber said.

The professor set his briefcase on the bench and picked up the loose pages. Two people stopped to help. Macon just watched.

"I can call Public Safety."

She shook her head. She didn't want to fix the situation, just wanted it to be over. She wasn't going back to the apartment. Everything she needed was in the back of her Jeep. Her clothes, the toothpaste, the towels in the bathroom and dishes in the sink were all his now. It was a small price.

"Call me when you get lonely."

Macon strolled off with his backpack on one shoulder. If she could just erase his tracks and rearrange the pieces of her life, then everything would be all right. But she couldn't be a kid again.

Some pieces stayed broke.

2

The work study didn't look old enough to be in high school, let alone college. Maybe it was the braces or the acne. Or the eighty-pound frame. Her companion was thumb-deep in his phone.

"Can someone help me?" Amber said.

"What do you need?"

Amber cradled her laptop and explained how it wasn't working right. She could take it to a repair shop, but then she'd have to pay for it. That would bring up questions when her grandma saw her statement, like why her computer was broken again. At which point her grandma would guess it had something to do with Macon, at which point Amber would lie.

"We don't do repair," the work study said.

"Can someone just look at it?"

"We just do tutoring and desk time."

"Is there, I don't know, an undergrad that could look at it, just to see if it's serious?"

The girl shrugged. "If you want to leave it, I can ask the professor."

Most of Amber's schoolwork was in the cloud, but ever since the campus breakup episode, the laptop hadn't been working right. She'd been living out of her Jeep, showering at the gym and studying in the library. She switched parking garages daily, never sleeping in the same one two nights in a row.

Her acceptance into the Medical University of South Carolina seemed like a mistake now. She'd always wanted to go to MUSC, but that was before her mom was found in the flower bed. But there was no backup plan for two dead parents.

Her phone buzzed.

She reached blindly for the mute. She would have to change her number. Macon was using someone else's phone now. The worst texts came late at night. There was usually a photo attached, some that would make a stripper cringe. Could she go to the police, show them her phone?

She glanced at the text. *Call me when you have a chance,* Grandma had sent.

Mom's death had imparted her grandma with a sixth sense that was finely tuned to Amber's sympathetic system. The day after Macon's departure, she had called three times just to see how she was doing. In the weeks following, it was every day. Maybe the tone in Amber's voice was giving it away. Or the echoes of a parking garage.

Macon wasn't paying the rent or utilities. Booze and weed, he had covered. Amber needed to break the lease, pay the fees, and come clean. Start over. Summer semester was a month away. She was beginning to feel homeless. Her skin was tired, her legs cramped up from sleeping in a fetal position, and her hair felt like yarn dipped in oil.

The lab was mostly empty. A wheelchair was in the back corner with saddlebags spackled with stickers. The long-hair was slouched over a keyboard in surfer shorts and a T-shirt, his thick arms a canvas of tattoos that went past the knuckles.

Amber stood at his side, a middle schooler with a laptop clutched to her chest, and watched his fingers speed over the keys. He was talking to the monitor in singsong rhythm.

"You work here?" she asked.

He glanced up without breaking rhythm. Hands levitating above the keyboard, he reached through his long, stringy hair and pulled out a speaker pod. The music leaking out was a pickax of ear violence.

"Do you work here?" Amber repeated.

"No."

"Could you look at this?"

He paused with the speaker pod rolling between his fingers, then plugged his ear and returned to jamming the keyboard. Arteries bulged on the backs of his hands, the intricate patterns of ink writhing over tendons. Scars were etched between the knuckles, raised tissue interweaving with tattoos—the kind of past wounds that looked intentional.

He pushed his hair over several hooped piercings and snatched the pod out. "This is going to sound rude, but what do you want?"

"I'm sorry, I don't mean to pry."

"Okay."

"It's been a shitty… month." She was thinking year. Then life. "I'm in Maymester biochem, and my crazy ex-boyfriend just—I mean, never mind. My laptop hit the ground a few weeks ago, and it's been acting weird. I just want someone to look at it."

He was staring like she was the one covered in tattoos.

"I could take it somewhere, I know. I'd rather my grandma not find out; she's been through enough. It's a whole thing."

She didn't lay down the dead parents rap. She wasn't above it; it just didn't seem relevant. It wasn't going to work on him anyway. He leaned back, looked at her shoes then the top of her head.

"Trust-fund problems?"

"Excuse me?"

"Let me guess, if your grandmother finds out you broke your laptop, she'll take away your Prius."

"Why would you say that?"

His eyes took another walk. "You got any tattoos?"

"None of your business."

"I'll bet you have a little butterfly on your ankle. You want to be tough, but not ruined. Maybe your sorority sisters dared you to get inked, and one night you drank too many cabernets and just went for it. You ever been arrested? Got a speeding ticket? Ever skipped a class? I'll bet you've never gotten anything less than an A your entire life. Not even a quiz."

"I'll bet you're an asshole."

"Want my help? Go down the street, swipe your credit card, and stop wasting time."

He plugged his ear and went back to work. The work studies were staring. They had spun their chairs around to watch the show. The little shits could've warned her. She was a bunny who'd stumbled onto the train tracks, eyes wide and locked on the high beams barreling toward her.

But he wasn't wrong.

It was a smiling sun, not a butterfly. And it was on her hip, not her ankle. Tequila, not cabernet. The rest was dead-on. She had all the advantages—raised in a loving family, given a home and money and love and support. She was white.

She was a fuckup.

That was the worst part. She was on her way to med school, so she seemed together on the surface. The truth lurked a scratch away. Even with that head start in life, she was an utter mess.

She backed up, squared the phone, and began tapping the button as she circled behind him, capturing shots of his right arm and left, shooting the sticker graffiti on the back of the chair and the ratty ponytail falling out of the hair band. He sensed her crouching down for a profile photo—his hair still tucked behind his jeweled ear—and rolled away from the table, exposing a colorful thigh. Gnarly roots and thorny vines wrapped around his legs where, on the right thigh, was an exquisite portrait of a bald black man. The eyes were hypnotic.

"Oh hell no. The fuck you think you're doing?"

"You just took my inventory. I'm taking pictures. Tit for tat."

"Tit for bullshit."

She swiped the photos and showed him the best one, a full frontal with all the ink on display. These were good. They made her fingers twitch. She was a mess and the world wasn't fair, but she had fodder for a new sketch. She left her laptop on the table and walked past the work studies with her book bag over her shoulder.

"I'm not fixing that." He pointed at it.

"Consider it payment for the photo shoot."

Wheelchair or not, he was an asshole. And she would draw him.

* * *

THE EMAIL SAID to park on the side street near the back.

There were two forest green gates alongside the historic home. Eight-foot walls hemmed in the property. Fig ivy was trimmed along the columns in precise lines. Beige, almost peach-colored stucco was visible through gaps in the thicket. Tiny white flowers had sprinkled down from the overhead crape myrtle, its tan mottled trunk twisted and knobby. Beyond the walls was a private garden on the largest residential property in downtown Charleston.

The Garden House.

The email also stated that someone would meet her at noon. It was twenty minutes past.

She debated bailing and probably would have if the Jeep hadn't taken on the smell of post-marathon running shoes. The funk was in her hair. Summer brought a suntan and a respite from schoolwork. It also delivered sweltering heat that had turned the back of the Jeep into an Easy-Bake Oven. She couldn't run the air-conditioner all night.

She had looked at a few apartments, none with roommates. There was a cute one off Rutledge, an upstairs bedroom in a retired couple's house. It was safe, but weird. She didn't want a family. She wanted the exact opposite. Showering and pooping with an old man downstairs wasn't in her top ten.

There were hundreds of Craigslist ads for sublets. She didn't remember seeing one at the Garden House or even applying for it. Maybe her name had ended up on a list, or someone had recommended her. The email had showed up one morning with a vacancy in the guesthouse.

If this didn't work out, she'd poop with the old people.

Med school started in a month. In the meantime, she turned off, spent her days on Folly Beach, and stayed away from downtown, the bars, the scene. She was off social media. Macon couldn't tag her on photos, couldn't post on her account, or even message her. Occasionally, he texted a photo. She needed a new phone number, but then she'd have to explain that to her grandma. Eventually, he would get bored. As soon as he met someone else, he'd forget her.

That would be good.

She swiped through her collection of photographs—the lone fisherman on the pier, the naked baby in the sand, the young man with a sleeping dog and a cardboard sign, a fallen ice cream cone half-melted and covered in ants, an attractive middle-aged woman smoking a cigar. Amber's hand ached to capture their essence. Her fingers twitched to channel their soul onto paper, to lock their spirit in the safe room of her mind and decorate the walls. She had a new sketchbook and a fresh set of pencils. The last one was her obsession.

Tattooed in a wheelchair.

She never got tired of sketching it, absorbed by the details of his tattoos, disappearing for hours—the dark tones and dim shading, like a black hole sucking light from the page. What had possessed her to take them? She wasn't angry. He was an asshole but, judging by the work studies gawking, there was nothing new about the way he was acting. He treated everyone that way, she was nothing special. He wanted to be left alone, and she was asking a stupid favor.

What he'd said, that inventory he'd taken had somehow freed her from the recent past. She left the laptop behind. It was the last vestige of her stupidity, her ignorance. Her last act of brazen rudeness a series of photos taken without permission. Forty of them. She could easily have taken three times that many. *What was his life? How did he end up in the chair? What did the tattoos mean?*

She could spend at least another three weeks drawing him, savoring each stroke, capturing every little detail of ink-stained flesh, every glimmer of jewelry.

The back gate cracked open.

They began a slow, mechanic swing. A young man stood inside, hands latched behind his back. A ripple galloped up her arms. It had the feel of showmanship, like an epic tour was about to begin and Amber had the golden ticket.

His hair was short and proper and damp with—probably, most likely—comb tracks starting at the part. A collared white shirt was tucked into pastel yellow shorts with a narrow belt cinched around his waist. He looked like a cabin boy for one of the cruise lines. Probably a College of Charleston graduate who had taken six years to complete a degree in tourism and spent a couple of years bartending on Sullivan's Island until his parents wanted to know how he was using their eighty-thousand-dollar college debt.

Or he was a nice guy who treated his girlfriend with respect and attention, brought her flowers, and cooked dinner while she was studying for finals. *Totally not my type.*

Amber rolled the window down. "I'm supposed to meet someone about a room?"

He stepped aside and waved, pointing at the Jeep then pointing inside. She eased through the tight opening, the gates automatically closing behind her. He guided her next to a refurbished horse barn with corkscrew topiaries on the corners and a large window. This was how kidnappings began. First, get the car off the street. Next, invite her into the cellar.

He's not that kind of guy, she thought. As if proper hygiene and etiquette expunged naughty behavior.

"Welcome." He opened the door. "Sorry for keeping you."

His cologne was potent, capable of subduing a seven-day-old corpse. It was clean, expensive. Blunted her senses. Beneath it, though, there was another smell. Like a long draught of cinnamon tea.

Even though the walls were only eight feet tall, the noise of traffic didn't seem to get past them. Birdsong and hidden fountains were sealed inside the property; an undercurrent of peace and equanimity radiated from the ground. Would the neighbors hear her scream?

Stop the crazy thoughts.

The main house was yellow and three stories tall. Actually, it was three and a half stories if the squatty attic was included—an arcing window that overlooked them. Porches wrapped around all three levels with a spiraling staircase.

Between the main house and the refurbished horse barn was the guesthouse. At one time it was likely the servants' quarters, or slave quarters, depending on how far back in history you looked. It could suit a family with three children and a couple of pets but was now rented out to college kids. The stucco walls were beige-peach like the border walls. A metal roof swooped over the front porch.

"I like your necklace."

She was absently rubbing the pendant around her neck. "Thank you."

"Is that an insect?"

"It's a fly. I know, weird."

Her mom had given it to her. She'd found it in her dad's study shortly after he had passed away, sitting on his calendar as if he'd recently picked it up at the market. He often did that, cruising the local stands to find something interesting, not so much the T-shirts and hats but the bowls carved from long-leaf pine or fragrances in little corked bottles.

"It's amber," her mom had said. "It captured a bug."

"I don't think I can afford this."

"We typically lease to MUSC students. It's a place to study, a break from the outside world." His accent was Southern country. His teeth, perfect. "The guesthouse is restored and converted into four efficiency apartments. Currently, it's unoccupied. You'll have it all to yourself."

He pointed at a second-story window.

"I haven't signed anything."

"We don't have a contract. You stay as long as you need and leave when you want. We're very old-fashioned."

He offered his hand. It looked like he smelled: clean and smooth, unaccustomed to manual labor. She shook it a few times. It was surprisingly cold, as if he'd been fishing drinks from a cooler.

"You live here?"

"In some ways." He chuckled. "The owners are currently unavailable."

"How do you know I'm a med student?"

"We do a very thorough background check, Ms. Gallagher. We invite those best suited for the property."

"I'm sorry, but I don't remember seeing an ad. Did we email each other?"

"We were in contact, yes. There's only one rule. When you're on the property, you can go anywhere you wish, but the main house is off-limits. Really, that's it. The rest of the garden is for you."

For me? "Maybe I should see the room first."

"A room is a room and nothing more without a view. I think you'll like what you see."

"And what will I see?"

"That's up to you, Ms. Gallagher."

His eyes were sharp. The gray irises contained a dark ring around the perimeter. His cologne was not cloying or intoxicating; it was the kind of fragrance that was hiding something rather than enhancing it. Or maybe she was imagining that.

Instead of going to the guesthouse, he walked behind it. Hesitantly, she followed, wondering if there was a back door. Instead, an old brick path was around the corner, hemmed in by a blooming wall of hydrangea that led to a small fountain. He'd already turned that corner, the bread crumbs of his fragrance drawing her to follow. She looked back once, straining for a hint of the outside world—a car horn or clopping horses—then continued. Her fingers began to itch as she neared the end of the shrubbery where the brick path turned sharply left.

A room is nothing without a view.

Hand tense with anticipation, she craved the unyielding weight of a drawing pencil. This was where she would fill her safe room with the oddities of the world, where she would get lost in her mind and change.

The young man—she didn't know his name—had disappeared along one of the many narrow paths. But at the end of a long brick path, where junipers spilled over a stone wall and spikes of agapan-thus exploded in celebration, an old man shuffled. He was wearing a long-sleeved beige shirt, the breathable type with a vent along the back. He bent over to cut a stem from a rosebush and glanced in Amber's direction before resuming his walk. She would come to know him as Mr. Eilif. He lived in the Garden House with his wife.

But he wouldn't be around long.

3

The incoming tide slapped the pier.

A barge heavy with containers eased beneath the cable-stay bridge. Traffic passed over it, high beams winking through the supports.

The couple at the end of the pier hardly noticed, too polluted to appreciate the anaerobic odor that clung to the cordgrass, the silent sailboats sliding through the dark. Crabs that skittered through the reeds.

They certainly didn't notice the young man to their left, hands on the thick rail, his flesh as dark as a new moon. His T-shirt captured the evening breeze and billowed like a sail. Drayton closed his eyes, nostrils flaring. The essence of the South swirled through his head, but failed to extinguish the annoyance that nibbled at his thoughts.

He was unaccustomed to annoyance.

It wasn't the groping couple's sloppy thoughts that poked at his mind. He'd dined on a thousand such victims without a care, filling his lust to the brim with essence. In the old days, the savage dark days, he'd drunk it directly from an artery, his appetite satiated. Derelicts and upstanding citizens all tasted the same.

And satisfied alike.

But Drayton was not accustomed to emotions—the base elements of human experience, the intangible experience of thoughts linked to sensations. At that moment, he was feeling annoyed by his annoyance, a vicious cycle feeding on itself. Even though he looked human, he was anything but.

To some, he looked to be a descendent from the Horn of Africa. His ancestry, though, was an unknown. His flesh was once lighter, if his memory was correct. He had no reason to doubt his ability to recollect, but memories tended to fade and distort with time. Several thousand years exposed to the sun had changed his appearance. Several thousand years had changed him.

The couple fell over each other. The woman's laugh was piercing. His was messy. This irritated Drayton further. He didn't care for the niggle in his stomach or the irrational reaction that tossed him about like a sunfish sailboat caught in a rogue gust.

Drayton understood the human experience. It was a benefit of immortality. Several thousand years bred understanding. It put forth the pillars of wisdom on which to build. Boredom had been peeled away beneath the scorching heat of awareness and fell away in the endless desert of wandering.

There is just this moment. There is no other. How could that be boring?

The annoyance had nothing to do with the inebriated couple whose tongues now tangled. He could no more feel agitated by their ignorance than one could blame a flame for heat or curse water for drowning. They were exactly who they were, both from broken families, cockroach-infested apartments, and little education. They sought the thrill of flesh, the richness of endorphins. They knew no other way. He did not pity their existence.

The annoyance started with Brenda Gallagher.

He had guided her from this world, eased her mind as she lay in a bed of flowers. There was little suffering despite the massive stroke and certainty of her end. She was quite content when he took her hand. The annoyance had begun shortly after. He couldn't understand why.

The agitated noose tightened.

Her thoughts had pressed upon him like braille beneath the fingertips. Drayton had visited her husband, James Gallagher, five days before his death and told him he was going to die, that an artery would burst in his brain and the result would take his life.

Perhaps telling someone the exact day of their ending would not be compassionate, but he sensed the man would find peace in it and take the opportunity to mend a few relationships. To know his own mortality would give him the opportunity to invite death when it arrived. Despite Drayton's presence and premonition, he was not death incarnate.

Merely a witness.

There was a time he'd delivered death with the vengeance of the reaper's curved blade, but now he was simply present when the essence of life slipped from the body, there to inhale it, to fill his coffers with its brilliance.

He had done so with James Gallagher not too far from where he now stood. Ten years was an outstanding period of time for him to remain in one location. Five hundred years ago, he could stay in a village for decades at a time, perhaps take up a cottage and a servant, assume a practice to hone a skill in blacksmithing or carpentry while slipping through cobbled alleys to inhale the escape of a man or woman's silky essence, to assuage his hunger. Sometimes, a child.

But not in today's world.

There were no angry townsfolk and torch-driven manhunts. It wasn't stories or mythos that would identify him, nor paintings on cave walls that foretold of the death angel. Today's world would know him from coast to coast and across the seas in the moments it took to post a photo. He preferred that not happen, but the longer he stayed, the greater the possibility he would become an urban legend. Why had he not left the Lowcountry, then?

Therein lay the annoyance.

The sloppy couple was done petting. Bra strap hanging from one shoulder, the woman leaned into the guy as they weaved their way down the boardwalk. They would climb into a car and drive to his apartment. In the morning, their failures would bleakly stare at each other, and the current of their lives would toss them onto unforgiving shores. It was irrational, what they did. It was a hole they were born into, a path carved for them to wobble upon. They would physically abuse each other. He would apologize. A week later, they would do it again.

That was their lives.

In their wayward escape, they stumbled into a family and accidentally knocked an ice cream cone to the boards. The father cursed with a Jersey accent. The couple hurried along without apologizing. Drayton watched them hustle past the swings where tourists sat and watched the cargo ships and counted the bridge lights.

Someone was watching them.

Drayton couldn't see who was in the shadows. Ordinarily, it would not pique his interest. Humans were a curious sort. He could reach into their minds and pluck their thoughts like blossoms from a peach tree, consume their memories like ripened fruit.

There were always anomalies.

Evolution relied on such mutations. Occasionally, a man or woman would be difficult to read. Their thoughts were sometimes dimly hidden behind layers of static and a mixture of deceit. Drayton found it a challenge to solve such a mystery.

So he watched this person leave the swing and move out from beneath the shelter. A female stepped into the yellow glow of a streetlamp, slender, almost petite. Her boots rang off the boardwalk in a delicious rhythm that tailed the swerving couple.

She dropped something.

Drayton reached for her and threw a net to gather her thoughts like minnows, only to find them slipping through the fabric of his mind. Instincts told him to remain still and let this mystery pass. She was of no significance.

There were always others to harvest.

He picked up the object that she had dropped. It was a beige strip of a palmetto leaf expertly folded into a rose, something kids sold to tourists. The stem was bent. His intuition screamed for him to leave the Lowcountry, and that was annoying.

And curious.

4

"Help!"

Drayton drank the panoramic view of Holy City's Southern flavor—the spires adorned with crosses pointing heavenward. On the far side of the rooftop bar, an urgency swayed the crowd. It was more than a college student vomiting in a corner.

These situations seemed to find Drayton.

He no more brought inevitable death to humans than he lifted the sun above the morning horizon. He simply intuited such opportunities as a shark sensed blood.

A waitress emerged from the crowd.

He took the teacup and saucer from her and let it hover beneath his nose, inhaling the aroma of black tea. Earl Grey his preference, he had taken to a local blend grown on Wadmalaw Island. He had even toured the plantation to sample the product of neatly clipped camellias.

"Anything else?"

"No. Thank you."

He expressed this without looking up. Her name was Trish. A single mother stuck with children and a lack of ambition. She leaned deeper into his periphery, subconsciously seeking the lovely endorphin kick she'd gotten when he first sat down, that first submersion into his depthless pupils that submitted those that peered inside.

The wind carried the sour smell of an overripe dumpster mixed with the receding tide. Buckling bluestone sidewalks were clogged with flip-flop-wearing tourists, the kind that licked ice cream while staring at their phones; ants going about their petty concerns, days limited by minutes to be filled with full stomachs and satiated desires, continually pushing their daily boulder up the slope with no concern for the inevitable crush of God's boot.

Drayton sorted through their thoughts and tasted the tang of their lives—the accumulation of emotions and thoughts, memories and desires, the essence that made them something they believed mattered in the universe. His mind was a cast net that filter-fed on their hopes, a mental technique he had honed throughout the ages. Nothing was secret to him, no sin or dream. The light of his vision induced the purest form of confession, exposing those that looked upon him, compelling them to give up their skeletons.

"911!"

Drayton drew a breath from the cup. Legs crossed, the proper young man allowed the subtleties of the tea's complex aroma to scintillate his senses and followed with a short sip. He required no food or drink to continue his immortality, none of the usual fare reserved for warm-blooded mammals, or anything organic for that matter. He imbibed occasionally for the pleasure, a habit that had followed him the past few centuries. It cleared his mind when he drank. It sharpened his senses.

He searched the ant farm for the woman.

It had been months since that evening on the boardwalk when she'd slipped from the shadows. Her awareness was a whisper slipping on the ocean breeze, an ungraspable hint of presence. A ghost, perhaps. He imagined that might be how he would experience himself. Statistics suggested that, given his extensive travel and penetrating presence, a chance encounter with an immortal such as himself was inevitable.

Hope? Is that it?

Questions followed him always—if he was the only such immortal among the human population. It mattered not, really, but the question was always with him no matter how many times he came to answer it.

There were few surprises on the fabric of immortality. When they appeared, he preferred to watch them unfold from a distance. He was not opposed to change, the very engine that drove evolution, the very reason, he proposed, his existence had developed—a predator to cull the human herd.

Do I choose the direction in which to grow? Is there free will with which to guide this world?

"His medication is at home," a woman cried. "Please… someone…"

Drayton summoned the waitress. No one would see him raise a hand or call a name. Bystanders would not feel the thought he pressed into the woman who was born and raised in Charleston, a woman with hopes of finishing a floundering college degree in order to escape the long nights of food and bev.

A moment later, the waitress appeared.

Drayton creased a hundred-dollar bill lengthwise. She accepted it kindly, returning to the chaos that had drawn the crowd's attention. Drayton watched the city. Help had still not arrived on the rooftop. Sobbing had begun; reality clenched those closest to death's choice.

He took the remainder of the tea—now cold but aromatic—to the upper deck with the intention of finding a quiet space along the harbor. Perhaps he would walk out to Edisto Beach and wander the countryside. The wetlands always calmed his mind.

The annoyance still lurked.

The crowd parted upon his approach, a subconscious willingness to step aside for something that, paradoxically, compelled them to forget his very presence. He was a cutter that split waves. A man eighty-two years of age with thinning white hair and a roadmap of veins upon cheeks of olive was on his back. Lips turning blue and collar unbuttoned, his wife of the same age cradled his head. Her cheeks were smudged with emotion.

They had come to the rooftop for a glass of wine and a view of a city they called home. He was a retired attorney. She was an art collector. Nothing out of the ordinary, just another conclusion to human life. The impressions he gathered from them—age and occupation and affection—were somewhat hollow.

They felt like cardboard cutouts.

Drayton was familiar with the varied expressions of death. Most life, Drayton had witnessed, ended with terrified agony as the prey was rendered helpless by the predator and eaten while still breathing —the parasite that lays the egg inside its host, the snake that swallows hatchlings. The bear that runs down the fawn. This man was about to die in the arms of a loving wife.

It seemed normal.

The man had turned his glance in Drayton's direction, half-lidded eyes hazy and unfocused. Drayton wasn't interested in taking the man's essence. His hunger was satiated. His intention to investigate, though, was driven by the curiosity of the strangeness hiding behind normality, the feeling he was imitating life.

His name was Mors Eilif.

His bluish lips hardly moved as his words soared like a spear through the haze of battle. Drayton stepped into the circle of death, the space cleared around the man and his wife, a wall of sticky bodies watching the drama unfold in real life. His wife looked up.

Her name was Umi.

Drayton was accustomed to sweeping a man's or woman's name from the holdings of their awareness, learning their secrets as easily as pressing cotton to a well of ink. But her name, as the old man's name, seemed to well up from inside him, like the hot brand on the hide of an animal seething beneath the nap of fur.

No one noticed Drayton take a knee. No one objected as he dropped his ear next to the old man's cheek. Saliva glistened on his lips, pockets of white spittle gathering in the corners. He had seen the angel of death and wanted something in return—a final purchase in exchange for his mortal coil. For that he beckoned Drayton closer. His final breath heaved the words forward.

"Protect her."

The cold draft of Mors's essence would drift in an ethereal stream and a cool vapor would seep through Drayton's pores and fall upon his tongue.

But it never came.

The lightness of Mors's death was apparent. The sudden vacancy of his empty form was held tightly by his grieving wife, but the release of essence was not there. Never had Drayton experienced such an absence. There were moments on battlegrounds when the earth was buried beneath a landslide of bodies. A cloud of silvery essence hung like fog so dense he could cup it in his palms. Essence was always released upon death. It was the distillation of a human being.

Paramedics arrived. Drayton remained unnoticed with the old man's eyes upon him. Still half-lidded, his request was upon parted lips. The crowd was ushered back, room given, Mors plied to a stretcher.

The meandering crowd returned to their social purpose, the memory of what had happened strangely disappearing from the mind fog. Not a word uttered, not a hand to mouth or video uploaded or quip tweeted.

It was dark. The sky was spattered with stars and the city streaked with lights. First the woman on the boardwalk and now this. And something else.

Drayton was suddenly ravenous.

5

Many tourists had been to Magnolia Cemetery.

Guides told stories of long-dead relatives stalking a full moon, some wearing confederate gray uniforms, others sweat-stained tunics. Those tales were tall among the tombstones. In the back corner, far from the burial plots for the general public, was a large lot of land.

Beyond those gates, locals told a different story.

The black iron bars were crusty with lichen and a dusting of algae. Rusty hinges were anchored to columns of old plantation brick, the mortar chipping from the seams. Wrought-iron fencing was attached to either side of the columns, stabbing into a thicket of overhanging privet, the black spires dulled with age.

The driver stepped out of a Mercedes Benz, careful to avoid an ant mound. Seeds stuck to his pressed slacks. He bent over the rustic padlock, something as dated as the gates themselves, and slid a large key into the slot and turned it with a fist. The tumblers released the shackle.

He yanked the gate through clumps of weeds. The hinges resisted at first. The grass had been trampled by an earlier procession that had delivered a casket deep into the woods. They were barely able to clear the narrow opening. The pillars had been built at a time when cars weren't as wide and the tires not as thick. The road beyond, once a sandy lane, had been paved with tumbled stone, a one-car path that curved beneath dense canopies. Ferns populated the live oaks that appeared to wither in summer and reemerge when the rain returned.

Resurrection fern.

The driver knocked dirt off his shoes and stared into the shadows. It was a cloudy day, but even on the brightest of afternoons, it was dim and humid past the gate. The anaerobic odor of the wetland lingered in the undergrowth; only a dappled blanket of diffuse sunlight pushed back the shadows.

Unlike the earlier procession that had delivered Mors Eilif, the driver didn't hesitate. He wasn't a superstitious sort, never paid the haunted stories much attention. The funeral director and others, however, had never been through the gates. Very few had.

Mrs. Eilif was in the backseat, composed and fearless. Dry-eyed, she awaited the driver's return. The car eased into the shadows of the family cemetery, a ten-acre lot that bordered the Cooper River. Local fables declared that even spirits from the local cemetery stayed out.

Drayton followed the Mercedes, his skin the color of old blood in the brake lights. The road turned toward the river and disappeared from sight. Drayton was tempted to remove his boots and feel the soil beneath his bare feet. This was why it was so difficult to leave the Lowcountry. There was no other place on Earth he felt this connection, as if his body had been sculpted from pluff mud.

Since witnessing the death of Mors Eilif, Drayton had spent a week wandering the hospital hallways of MUSC, where death was frequent and essence ran on tap. He gorged until the hunger subsided, and even then he was still not completely satisfied. He had arrived at the cemetery the night before and stood at the gate. The night passed in the sirens of treefrogs and the occasional boat trawling the Cooper. The moments were troubling. Never had the hunger been so insistent, so desperate.

Protect her.

Mors Eilif had charged him with the protection of Umi's life. This was a request he did not have to honor, but how could he deny the old man who felt as Southern as the soil beneath his boots—the earth that felt so much like home?

A marble cross towered next to the parked Mercedes. It reached into the trees, its arms wrapped in vines and laden with moss. The surface, dim with algae, was fissured. It had been rooted to the land long before the live oaks claimed it as their own. It faced a stone mausoleum cloaked in shadows, an avenue kept clear of tree and vine so that the muddy water of the Cooper River would always be in view.

Drayton watched Umi approach the stone building where her husband's body rested. A barred door had been propped open. The inner door, a marble slab bolted with heavy metal straps, was ajar. Above it, inscribed in stone, was a string of symbols and the head of a gargoyle, the tongue hanging thickly.

लिफ़े अन्द् डेअथ्

Drayton dug deep into memory to translate. It was Sanskrit, one of the oldest languages in the world, a language spoken long before a Southern drawl.

Life and Death.

Mrs. Eilif held the driver's crooked arm and paused before taking the first step. She allowed him to lean into the heavy door before the darkness welcomed her.

There were two final resting places inside the tomb. Umi would be standing next to hers as she paid her respects. Such traditions among cultures varied. Drayton had witnessed bodies burned in flaming pyres or sent out to sea. He had attended thousands upon thousands of such rituals, the deaths of many for which he was personally responsible. Some were followed by celebration; others inconsolable grief.

Mrs. Eilif did neither.

The driver stepped out and lit a cigarette. His eyes were on the imposing cross. He saw the symbol staring back, the crucifix that saw the sins he was hiding. Raised Catholic, he was deeply etched with a vein of guilt and fed that belief with a string of failures. The crucifix reminded him that sins could be forgiven, but not forgotten.

Even though Drayton knew this about the driver, he did not see his name. The young man seemed mostly blank with a cursory history and little motivation. Perhaps his past was drug-addled, although that rarely barred Drayton from seeing one's true nature. Again, something was off, ever so slightly—the cardboard-cutout feeling when he'd first encountered the Eilifs. This wouldn't concern Drayton had he not experienced the complete absence of the woman on the swing.

Move on, he reminded himself without heeding. *Leave.*

Drayton was familiar with the power of symbols. The crucifix was arguably the most authoritative of the current era, representing a man known as the savior. Drayton had been somewhere in the Orient at the time of Jesus of Nazareth's life. Those were still Drayton's dark years, although not as savage as the old days.

But savage enough.

It was a time when he craved the spill of warm blood, a time when he would stay with his victims before taking their lives. Sometimes he bathed in their blood. The locals claimed a demon was among them, although they could never identify him. But he was no more demon than a bear that feeds upon a fawn, or the wolf that takes the rabbit.

Drayton had learned of Jesus of Nazareth's sacrifice many years after his death. Shortly thereafter, he'd joined the church around the turn of the twelfth century. His flesh hadn't taken the tone it now possessed. Instead, he was known as Mediterranean. An exotic priest, he'd joined the inquisition and converted the nonbelievers, heartily. The depths of humanity's cruelty nearly matched his own predilections. What they called the Holy Spirit, Drayton knew as essence.

He basked in it often.

Umi Eilif was still inside the crypt. *Protect her,* Mors had said. Drayton did not know what protection she needed, but mystery often shrouded the dying's request. People spilled thoughts as they drifted away, sometimes leaving only crumbs for Drayton to follow. Oftentimes even they didn't know the nature of their request, a confession of guilt and wrongs to be righted. Drayton would have to unravel the request before he could provide true help.

The driver flicked the cigarette into the trees, a red streak followed by a splash of embers. Hands in his pockets, he stared at the cross. Drayton willed him not to see him standing at the foot of the religious relic. He would see nothing more than an object in the forest, no more interesting than a distorted tree trunk or stump. Drayton was invisible to those he wished not to see him, a trick of the mind he had employed most of his life. A trick he could play on recording devices as well, distorting the atmosphere around him and projecting the background. It served him well and was the only way he survived in this century. No one saw him coming.

Or remembered him if they did.

The mausoleum door was still closed. It occurred to Drayton she had not taken a light, nor did the driver offer her one. Perhaps she was using her phone. She was still in there, he could sense her, but her movements had diminished.

The Sanskrit inscription seemed to pay tribute to ancient wisdom, but the architecture appeared to go back several generations. Crypts such as these had been plundered in the Civil War. Drayton had done such things himself, posing as a freed slave. The irony was rich as he stalked the very people wishing to put him in chains, feasting on soldiers from both sides of the battlefield. He held no prejudice for man or woman, black or white.

He took them all.

The driver lit another cigarette, but Drayton saw the white cloth of a tent, the flaps thrown open, beds arranged side by side. The sulfur of gunpowder brought pangs of hunger, a Pavlovian salvation for an open throat, a time when he'd strolled through the middle of battles, impervious to the muskets and bayonets that shattered his bones and flayed his flesh—injuries that healed instantaneously. Having mastered his nervous system, pain was a needless evolutionary trait, one he sometimes chose to feel just to remind himself of the human experience. He allowed a knife wound to sear or his organs to hemorrhage.

A scream rose from the tent.

The sound of a saw being drawn over bone. It tore through muscle and tissue, amputation the only recourse to infection. A nurse delivered a stack of recent amputations to a pile outside the tents. Arms and legs tumbled like firewood to the frozen ground. Fingers curled, bones exposed. Some nights, Drayton would sit bedside and send the soldiers off with a gentle hand upon their shoulder, his touch as cold as water drawn from a winter well.

Some nights he feasted.

He shook his head, stepping away from the cross. Drayton did not sleep, did not dream. Every moment of the past several centuries was etched in his mind and catalogued for instant recall—a perfect predator, a finely tuned organism, physically dominant, intellectually deadly, never once failing to anticipate or analyze. But just now he was lost in the memory of the Civil War.

The car was gone.

A single breath sharply drawn—only one, not a second or third— was held deep before it slowly released. He returned to the smooth draw once again, fully present and completely aware. Senses engaged, he merged with the sound of chirping treefrogs and song of crickets, the distant flap of a passing sailboat, the transpirational vapor wafting from sprawling trees. Mosquito wings and the scurry of anoles. He absorbed the Lowcountry through his pores.

For the first time in centuries, he had lost time.

An item lay crooked upon the stone steps. Drayton paused before kneeling. The stem was cocked at ninety degrees. He'd seen this before, on the boardwalk.

A palmetto rose.

PART II

The trouble is, you think you have time.
— *Buddha*

EDWIN AND MARGARET PLATT

The crossword puzzle was unfinished.

Margaret Platt came back to the front room with her glasses. When she had gone to the bathroom, Edwin had just sat down to work on it. Now it was on his chair. Only three words had been answered.

She called his name and searched the house. He wasn't in the back-yard, either. The car was not in the driveway. It was unusual for him to leave so suddenly and not say goodbye. In forty years of marriage, he had never done so, even if they were fighting.

A carriage had stopped in front of the house. The draft horse danced nervously. His ears were pinned back. Margaret swore he was looking at her. A silver car waited for the carriage to pull ahead before swinging into the driveway. Margaret sat on the front porch and waited for her husband.

Pots and pans clanged in the kitchen.

Edwin had gone through the back door instead of coming around to the front. That was unusual, too. She stopped in the kitchen to see him on his hands and knees. He was still wearing his slippers and robe.

"Edwin?"

He stood up with a yellow teapot and began filling it with water. His hearing aid wasn't in. Margaret called again and approached warily as he put the teapot on the stove.

"Oh!" He jumped back. "You surprised me."

"Where have you been?"

"I went for tea."

"We have tea, hon."

A gray plastic bag was on the table. She pulled out a box and scowled. They didn't drink this kind of tea.

"What was so urgent?"

He was staring intently at the teapot, as if waiting for it to whistle.

"Edwin?"

"I'm making tea, Margaret."

She searched for her phone and found it in the bedroom. Her daughter was at work. This was a sign. They were both very healthy and coherent. But this was how it started.

A high-pitched whistle blew from the kitchen. It abruptly went silent. Margaret texted their daughter. *I'm concerned about your father.* She waited to send it. She didn't want her daughter to be worried if this was nothing. So he was making tea, what was the big deal?

When she returned to the kitchen, he was staring at a teacup. A tag hung over the rim. When the oven timer went off, Edwin quickly pulled the teabag out and balanced the cup on a saucer. He did this with the intensity of a master servant preparing a tea ceremony. His focus tuning out the outside world, he carried his offering to the front room. Then he did something even stranger.

He put it on the front porch.

When he came back inside, he began working on his puzzle with legs crossed and reading glasses balanced on his nose. There was definitely something wrong, but she hesitated before sending the text. And then, oddly enough, lost complete interest in it.

That night, she went to the kitchen and made a cup of tea. She wasn't sure why. She steeped it exactly four minutes and took it to the porch.

An empty teacup waited for her.

6

Heavy shoes struck the pavement.

Wood spokes slowly pinwheeled to a standstill. The guide, sitting with his back to the draft horse, held the reins lightly and described the Garden House to his captive audience. Beyond the fig vine and pierced brick walls were oyster-shell paths and old brick sidewalks, where secret niches and knot gardens and fountains delighted.

The horse strained against the bit. The guide absently tugged on the reins as he continued on about the architecture with an emphasis on wide porches and cool breezes, the way the old glass appeared distorted in the panes. Tourists sat beneath the shade of the carriage's fringed awning. They consumed the history of the Old South as the sand fleas found their arms and sunburned necks. The horse turned a large eye on the opposite side of the street to a narrow blue house.

Drayton sat in a wicker chair.

Neither mosquitoes nor sand fleas landed upon his exposed arms or bare scalp. His eyes were as dark as the horse's hindquarters, a Percheron draft horse, bred in France. Drayton had ridden this breed in times of conquest. Originally bred for battle, they'd drawn wagons of artillery or carried soldiers upon their backs. Now they clopped down summer streets and shit in sacks strung from their hindquarters.

The horse's ears turned back, hair bristling. A predator was near.

The tourists sensed nothing but boredom. This was the great human delusion, that they were safe, that there was justice. That predatory beasts only ran down helpless fawns. They believed they were above the messiness of that, that they had evolved out of the food chain. Their happiness was predicated on ignorance, looking away from their vulnerability when death walked step for step. This was the great deception that brought them peace, to forget they were prey.

Every ecosystem had a predator.

With a thought, without a blink, he soothed the horse's agitation. Drayton convinced him that he was not waiting in ambush and no harm would fall upon him. The ears relaxed. He stopped scuffling. To the guide's pleasure, he remained still long enough to finish his well-worn speech.

An empty teacup was on the wicker table, the contents long drawn between his lips. The elderly couple that resided in the blue house had been compelled to deliver tea each morning for the past week, and again in the evening. They drank sweet tea, never Earl Grey. Neither of them knew why they were compelled to purchase a box of Earl Grey and bring a kettle of water almost to boil. They warmed the teacup before pouring the hot water and steeping a teabag for precisely four minutes—the gentleman and his wife standing over the cup as the timer counted down.

Drayton could feel their breathing at night and the aches that possessed them in the morning. The old man cut his chin while shaving on the third morning of Drayton's arrival.

The iron tang of blood flared in his nostrils.

A truck stopped beneath a large street oak where roots buckled the sidewalk. The gardener entered the formal gates of an intricate inlay of wrought iron that allowed passersby a snapshot of the formal gardens if they stood on their toes. A patch of perspiration spread between his shoulders. He closed the gates behind him, yet Drayton could feel his pulse as if his tongue lay on his throat and tasted the salt of his perspiration.

Drayton raised a thought.

Ten minutes later, a cup of Earl Grey was delivered. It was the old man this time. He took the empty cup back inside and washed it before returning to reading a book. Drayton inhaled the aroma before drawing a sip over his tongue and around his cheeks. It soothed the clenching of his throat.

It had only been seven days since feeding.

He had considered taking the Palmetto Trail through Columbia toward the Blue Ridge of North Carolina, perhaps continue up to Ontario and into the Arctic Circle where a cooler climate awaited. Unaffected by temperature, his body was as adept in subzero weather as it was on the equator. He often found the hunger decreased in extreme cold. Once buried in an avalanche, he'd emerged nearly a year later in the summer melt with barely an urge. But curiosity had brought him to the front porch of the blue house.

Protect her.

His sense of duty kept him there, insisted he understand exactly why she needed protection. There was also the incident at the cemetery and the loss of time. Just as the universe had limitations, so did he. He was not a god, not a super-being that could fly or lift a mountain. What he could do was recall every moment of the last five hundred years. Yet he had experienced a gap for the first time at the cemetery.

The Civil War memories were captivating, but it was more than that, more than a vivid recall—more like a spirit of the past that reached out for him. If his past were ever to do such a thing, to come for him and demand retribution, there would be a long line of atonement awaiting him.

These were the reasons he served the requests of the dying, the reason he sat upon the porch of the blue house and sought a way to uphold Mors's request—to stave off the demands of the past and the cries of atonement. *How many suffered from my ignorance?*

The gardener returned with a blower on his back, dusty clouds billowing from the marble steps that checkered the dual staircases climbing toward the front doors. His pulse beat upon his neck and echoed on Drayton's tongue. Sweat clung to his brow.

Drayton inhaled the discomfort of the hunger. There was no stopping it; he could only make room for it. That was the shortcoming of human understanding. They mishandled their obsessions, either indulging them or repressing them. They rarely said yes to their discomfort. There would always be fear to resist, violence to deny. These elements were an inconvenience, a pebble that chafed their lives. But just as a pebble placed in a thimble was an obstruction, the very same pebble was inconsequential in a barrel.

Humans needed to be bigger.

That was what Drayton had become—a bigger container for experience. He had the luxury of immortality to become such. Still, even the barrel had limits. The hunger was no longer a pebble but a stone. It would soon fill him and not be denied attention. It had only been a week on the porch, yet he debated going in search of a meal to buy more time. *Time.* Something he seemed to have an excess of yet still found a need to purchase.

Immortality dragged a deep and heavy net.

The blower went quiet. The garden gate clinked shut. Drayton returned to the dark quietude behind his eyelids and the shudder of a fetid breeze, the song of mourning doves, and the scurry of green-scaled anoles.

The doors to the Garden House swung open.

Drayton opened his eyes. The crosshairs of his focus fell upon a lithe young woman. The house was empty—he was certain of it—yet he watched her float down the stairwell, her choppy steps chattering down checkered steps. Her hair, black as her flesh. Rows of piercings glittered along the cartilage of her ears. Her blouse was sleeveless, her pants loose, and boots just below the knees. She swung her willowy arms, bracelets singing on her wrists, tendons springing from her forearms.

Her.

She was an absent presence, a formless form that stopped at the corner to watch a young couple. She touched the corner of her mouth. Her posture was dangerous. It lurked in the reeds, yet her intentions eluded Drayton's grasp, particles too small or delicate to snare.

Or absent altogether.

Drayton trembled, the first hint of rising from the wicker chair since he sat down, curiosity piqued as she rounded the corner. A car, however, arrived from the opposite direction and nosed into the intersection. The driver of the Mercedes Benz glanced in Drayton's direction.

The car continued straight and around the corner where the mystery woman had gone. He felt it stop in the road, waiting for the automatic gate to open along the fig-vine walls, and park inside the confines of the Garden House property.

Umi's presence was firmly present in space and time, a form that moved within Drayton's mind. Her thoughts were faint. They did not disclose where she had been. The driver's mind suggested scenes of sand and water, swaying palms and swards of cordgrass at an isolated dwelling on one of the nearby islands. Perhaps she had spent a week away to mourn her husband, although no sadness possessed her.

The gardener had left.

Drayton considered a position as his assistant. He would enter the gates with the man one morning. The man would accept him, would work alongside him as long as Drayton wished to do so. He would insert himself into Umi's life and become a shadow she would not recognize from the rooftop bar. He would be nothing more than a vague recollection, the face of a stranger that resembled a friend or family member.

Drayton would begin his atonement.

The front doors of the Garden House opened. This time it was not the young woman. The driver slid his hand down the curved railing as he descended the steps. He crossed the black and white granite threshold and allowed a car to pass before crossing the street.

Drayton passively watched him approach, cradling the teacup on his lap. The unexpected swirl of surprise swung through him when the driver climbed onto the porch of the blue house and looked directly at him.

"Mrs. Eilif requests your presence."

* * *

THE FOYER WAS SPOTLESS, the floors shined. Cobwebs dutifully swept from the corners of the Adamesque plaster design. A smell of adrenaline and perspiration, desperation, as if the plaster pulsed with flight-or-fight.

A small ancient sculpture was on display.

Drayton detoured from the driver's lead to examine the stone sculpture of a lion and bull. It appeared to be a fragment of Archaic art, a marble relief with no tag or identification. Drayton searched the annals of his memory and estimated the piece to be from an era before Christ.

His reflection looked back from an antique mirror.

His appearance had not changed—the black flesh, dark irises, and smooth scalp. But the driver had seen him, had walked across the street to find him. And Drayton hadn't wished to be seen.

Behind him, an oil painting appeared to be from the Renaissance era. It had the elements and composition of the work known as School of Athens. The building in the shape of the Greek cross was filled with ancient philosophers with two central figures. Only, in this painting, the figures were not Plato and Aristotle, but a man and woman dressed in the flowing robes of the 1500s. The surrounding men and women were gathered on the steps in various positions of supplication.

Drayton wasn't familiar with this piece. He wasn't an expert in art history, but he knew the classics and then some. Perhaps it was the work of an enthusiastic hobbyist. But quite a good one.

"Here."

A voice called from the balcony, one with a female edge anchored to a strong foundation.

The adjoining room held a long dining table with several high-backed chairs. More artifacts were on the walls—a sheathed Civil War sword with decorative knucklebow, a curved Roman war shield, and clay pots upon shelves. A humid breeze rippled the frayed edges of a banner above the fireplace. French doors led to the second-story veranda.

Umi sat at a small round table.

Despite the heat, a thin scarf fluttered around her neck, framing the sagging jowls and loose flesh beneath her chin. A lazy fan sagged above her. She was facing the elaborate gardens below, the parterres lined with sheared boxwoods and anchored with spires of Italian cypress. A bone-white espresso cup was balanced on her thigh.

"Have a seat."

Drayton considered the chair. A sense of emptiness was all around, but a thousand years of hunting had honed his senses and told him when to be still and when to prick his ears and sharpen his wits. The same instincts built into a fawn caught in the open.

A scone was on a plate, a bowl of jam with a short knife balanced on it. Next to them was a brass bell. She looked at the setting—her eyes the gray of descending skies—before resting her gaze on him.

"Your name?"

"Drayton."

His name slipped between his teeth. This was not his birth name—a birth he could not remember—but rather a name he'd adopted to put others at ease.

"Drayton." The old woman grunted with amusement. Her expression, however, did not change. "Do you know Edwin and Margaret Platt, Drayton?"

He remained impassive, unblinking.

"Edwin and Margaret have lived in their house for thirty-eight years. They raised three children and five cocker spaniels during that time. And you have been on their porch for the last seven and a half days. I'll ask you again, Mr. Drayton, do you know Edwin and Margaret Platt?"

His eyelids grew heavy. The old woman was playing a game.

"I have security cameras. They are my eyes on this property and the surroundings. In my absence, you appear to be enjoying an overdue respite at the expense of my neighbors. Now, ordinarily, I would summon the police in such an event. But my kindly neighbors have appeared to cater to your needs. Now that seems to be a bit unusual, I admit. Not that they don't have company from time to time, but I have not seen company of your kind."

Your kind. He was accustomed to various reactions to his skin color. Tribalism was nothing new to the human race. Preference for one's own *kind* was inherent. But that wasn't what she meant. Neither of them had yet to blink.

He had felt the electronic eyes of her security system, that much of what she was saying was true. But he had eluded them, as he did every surveillance system. It was getting difficult to stay ahead of technology—his ability to project a background aura had served him well —and he suspected it might eventually surpass him.

Perhaps it already had.

Without breaking eye contact, she placed the espresso cup on an empty saucer and reached for the brass bell. The demanding melody cut through the garden. She struck the clapper for a full five seconds and let the tone fade before placing it on the tablecloth. The driver appeared in the doorway.

"Terrible." She nudged the espresso cup toward him.

He fetched the saucer and cup, nodding with an agreeable frown. Umi never lifted her gaze to him.

"Some people are born to serve, Mr. Drayton. Despite the constitution and other wishful decrees, we are not created equal." Expressionless amusement haunted her gray eyes. "Animals are not socialists. It is not an even playing field. It never was. Even the lowly order of insects knows there are queens and there are workers."

A coffee grinder noise rose from the kitchen. Beans were crushed into dust. The aroma made its way through the French doors. Umi placed her attention on the large fountain below. When silence returned and only birdsong surrounded them, she brought her limp gaze back to him.

"You witnessed my husband's death." A visible grin broke her ashen cheeks. "You were there, Mr. Drayton. And now you are on the front porch of my neighbors' house. Why is that?"

"Concern."

"Concern? I see. You sit on a porch and do not move for seven days. There is no evidence of you getting up to relieve yourself, you understand. And you appear to be drinking tea. There is no explanation for this, Mr. Drayton. Now, I am a patient woman. There are things in this universe that I do not understand. And I am certain there is no one on this earth besides yourself that understands what I have witnessed."

He remained poised and vigilant.

Her thoughts were suddenly nonexistent. Her motivations hid beneath the seemingly obvious questions she posed, yet the lack of panic in response to his illogical behavior exposed her feint. How could a man sit for seven days? How could the occupants become unwitting servants? Why would she not call the police?

And how did she see me?

Deception was at play. Drayton was not the only guilty party.

The driver appeared. He stood with arm bent, saucer and cup in his palm. Umi held up her hand. Large rings decorated her fingers, holding him at bay as her gray eyes searched Drayton's unyielding expression. A game was afoot, and he was holding none of the cards, yet he yielded no ground.

When she dropped her hand, the espresso was placed in front of her. The driver waited for her to sample the fresh drip. She did so without taking her eyes from Drayton. A single nod released him.

"In the South, we drink sweet tea. I am sure you are aware of that. I prefer coffee on a day like today, hot as it is, humid as expected, but you can find most people in the Lowcountry with a tall glass sweating in their hand and a slice of lemon on the rim. It's all very storybook, I realize, but I call the South my home, and I am not opposed to such cliché. It was how we were raised, but I prefer to indulge my own whims." She sipped the espresso. "Your name is Southern. Perhaps your roots run deep and wide, but your namesake was born in the South. Are you from here, Mr. Drayton?"

A wry grin no longer hid her deceit, openly mocking the game she was playing. It wasn't the name he was born with. He'd taken it from a soldier. Still, it was fitting.

She closed her eyes and breathed deep. The harbor was a mile from the porch, but the breeze carried the salty reminder of Southern heritage as if there were a tall glass sweating between them.

"There is meaning in names. My husband was Greek, his name will tell you that. He was a demanding man, a fair man. A difficult, complex man. All long-term relationships are difficult, Mr. Drayton, and they are demanding."

She looked to the garden, this time appearing nostalgic, perhaps forgetting the game for a moment. She spread jam across a scone, plying it with the repetition of tradition and ritual before placing the knife diagonally over the container. Taking a bite, she wiped her mouth with a cloth napkin and resumed her reminiscent gaze.

"Why are you here, Mr. Drayton?"

"To protect you."

"Is that what you do?" She took another bite. "Who are you?"

"No one of consequence."

"Aren't we all?"

She finished the last three bites in silence then cast her gaze to the table and swiftly rang the bell. The driver came to her side and scraped the crumbs from the tablecloth with a six-inch blade. She allowed him to do his duty, appearing quiet and meditative. When he took his leave, she stood with a bit of effort. Drayton reflexively leaned in to help. She stopped him with an adamant hand and reached for the iron railing.

"You need a place to stay, Mr. Drayton."

He didn't respond. Her statement sounded genuine, almost desperate. She had adeptly kept him off balance. Now she appeared to express her doubts. More of the game, he suspected.

"Do not mistake this as pity or my behavior as racist. I understand there is precedence given the color of your skin and length of my tenure in this home, but I assure you this is nothing of the sort. I can look into one's soul and see its place in the world, you understand, whether that be society or nature in general. Everyone has a place, Mr. Drayton. Of that, I am certain. Do you want to know what I see in you?"

She turned to him, hands delicately perched on the railing. For a moment, he wished to open up and allow her access to his past so that she might gaze deep into his soul and tell him who he was and from where he came and why. His soul, if he had one, was indeed dark. He had yet to know it.

Yet he felt she did.

"I am not offering you food. Perhaps we can sit for tea when the time comes, but for now I am only offering a room. I am charitable, despite what those who meet me believe. True compassion does not always feed you, you understand. And neither shall I. There is a room; it is not free. I will be firing the gardener in the morning. His incompetence has brought him to this point, not you. I am in need of assistance. The garden will need to be fed. You may do so to pay for your room."

She paused.

"And if you wish to protect me, as my husband has requested, this will suit your needs."

She didn't wait for an answer. She held his gaze a beat longer and reached for the bell. It was settled. Drayton remained on the veranda after she left. Despite the breeze, Umi's scent lingered in the blades of the ceiling fan.

He was escorted to a refurbished barn, where there was a room that was sparse but adequate. It featured a large window. He stood there until morning came, fading into a meditative state where thoughts settled like grains of sand. As the sun rose on the garden, he had come to a few conclusions. Immortality had not only washed away the experience of fear but nearly all emotions. Now the quiver of fear and uncertainty hummed inside him. He wasn't going to leave the Lowcountry.

In the broad scope of immortality, even a trap was interesting.

7

4:00 a.m.

The wood floor was cool on her feet. Endorphins dripped into her bloodstream like syrup. It would take some moving around to kick-start the cerebral cortex.

Neuropeptide orexin and coffee.

She put a pot of water in the kitchenette and took a speed shower. Since there were no other tenants in the guesthouse, the bathroom was all hers. She carried the coffee press up to her room, where the walls were covered in loose leafs of thick paper. It was a jigsaw pattern of rectangular pieces, the corners taped in place and the bottoms waving beneath the breath of a window unit. She observed her work while the coffee steeped, assessing the doodles and sketches, the gesture drawings and shaded portraits.

Her fingers twitched.

It was a restless syndrome of the heart, a jumpy sensation that tugged at the tendons. Creative energy bubbled beneath the surface.

Sunlight.

The release valve was at the tips of her fingers. If she had a pencil and piece of paper, sunbeams would fire out like searchlights. The margins of her class notes were murals of ink, as were the backs of notecards, napkins and empty coffee cups. Her knee bounced if she didn't let it out. The creative essence needed to flow.

I am the light.

If she drew in the morning, she could focus for the rest of the day. She could hear the professor and take in the information. If she allowed these creative spirits to run wild, gave wings to these imaginative demons, then she would have more space to soak in the world around her. She could hear and see and feel. She didn't have to study the equations, didn't have to memorize terminology or fret over analysis. These things found a rightful place in the spaciousness of her mind.

As long as the creativity flowed.

She poured a mug of coffee and slung an art bag over her shoulder. It was red and yellow with spatters of colors thrown from a paintbrush. Inside were the tools of her addiction.

The garden was still dark. Patches of low-voltage light spilled on the narrow paths. Sunrise was still a few hours away when the early morning would glitter on dewdrops and hover in thick clouds of humidity like ghosts of the South.

The garden song of treefrogs greeted her at the bottom step. The streetlight splashed ragged shadows over the perimeter wall. It was odd that sound didn't seem to make it inside, although streetlights made their way across the cobblestones. The silhouette of fig vines fell on the old brick driveway.

The Garden House was dark, the windows black rectangles on the yellow walls. Candlelight flickered in the attic window, a half-circle jutting from the roof.

Mrs. Eilif was home.

The old woman didn't speak much. Her husband had just recently passed away. Amber had been there almost four months, and she rarely saw them. In fact, the only time she'd seen the old man was on the first day. The old woman she'd seen only once.

It was a week ago.

Her sketch pad had been propped on her lap when she felt the prickly heat rash of August fall over her neck. The swelter had seemed a little early in the day, even for the Lowcountry. When she had looked up, the old woman was standing there. Shadows had fallen through her wide brim hat.

"Good morning," Amber had said.

"Yes."

That had been it. No chance to say she was sorry for her loss. There had been a slight smile and then she'd walked off.

Mr. Eilif's passing didn't make the garden feel any more haunted than it already did, and his ghost wouldn't dissuade her from staying. Lowcountry spirits were known for their polite disposition. They were Southern, after all.

She took the brick path behind the guesthouse.

The wall of hydrangeas blooming large mops of blue had already turned tan. A hairpin turn at the fountain and she looped around to where a narrow path veered beneath gnarly wax myrtles. She was on the other side of the hydrangeas, walking in the other direction. If she parted the branches, she could see the back of the guesthouse.

A shortcut would be nice.

Yellow light glowed up ahead. She entered the kitchen garden—a small niche of herbs hemmed in by boxwoods. Coneflowers and black-eyed Susans bloomed in a center square. A bench was tucked beneath a gaslight.

Amber set her mug on a small table and unpacked her art bag. A stone-faced lion was spitting water on the far wall. She took a moment to settle in, to feel the gravel beneath her feet, the weight of dewdrops on the narrow tips of grass, the dense air and morning's promise. Then she set her phone for two hours and opened her iPad.

Dull gray light clashed with the yellow gaslight. Thumbnails of her latest photographs fell in place—an off-duty waiter crying over his cigarette, a bored bicycle taxi driver, a homeless man in a wheelchair reaching for a tourist.

She swiped into the archives and found a photo she'd snapped from the corner window of her room. She had been looking down into the garden early one morning. The moon was full and the garden iridescent. She had shot it through streaked glass. It was only later that she noticed Mrs. Eilif in her white hat.

She pulled the view closer and cropped her pixelated profile. The details were hardly human, but the proportions were enough. She wondered if she walked the garden every night thinking of her husband. Was that what they had done, holding hands as they journeyed the brick paths, soaking in the sounds of the garden and fragrance of its blooms? She imagined the looks they'd given each other, happy with their lives together.

She closed her eyes and breathed the details of her imagination, let it mold, crystalize, and clarify. Until her imagination breathed back.

The iPad was dark. It would only hinder her now. The pencil fit between her fingers like a missing part of her body, the edges rolling on her fingertips, massaging the nerve endings, tingling up her shoulder.

The blank page absorbed her.

She felt its texture, its nothingness. *Life and Death,* she thought.

Her imagination poured forth—the old couple's love, their comforting smiles, their familiar smells. No separation between paper, pencil and hand.

When life meets death, there is Flow.

Lines sweeping along their necks, wispy curls around their ears, bushy strokes of an eyebrow, the folds of skin along their necks. Lead scratched the rough surface. Light smudged beneath her fingertips, a dark line pulled into a path of gray tones. She tingled in the symphony, transported into a timeless place where anything was possible, titillating every sense—eyes and ears and nose and throat. She was the conduit between her mind and the outside world, pulling something from nothing.

Form is emptiness. Emptiness is form. When life meets death, something comes from nothing. There is flow.

The phone buzzed.

The bench slats were hard. The treefrogs silent. Dusky light filtered through the trees, beams swirling with rising strands of evaporating vapor. The sketch pad crooked across her thigh. Two old faces looked across from each other with a narrow slice of space between them, their gray eyes rising sharply to meet each other.

Their expressions had arisen from her mind and breathed upon the paper. She sat empty and alone, revitalized and breathless. Her fingers twitched. Two hours passed. She panted in postcoital exhaustion, a smile blooming and droplets of sweat upon her brow.

Her coffee cold.

She rushed to her room to beat traffic. In class, she would soak in the information while counting the minutes of her return to the garden, doodling in the margins to satisfy her craving, smiling during study group with a secret on her lips. She was changing her life, finally. All she needed was the right place to do it. The soil to set her roots. She'd finally found it.

And something came from nothing.

* * *

AMBER ROLLED THE WINDOW DOWN.

She was averaging three hours a night of sleep. Twice she got up at three in the morning to squeeze in an extra hour of drawing. Once she woke on the sketch pad when the alarm buzzed. And fall semester midterms still weren't over.

A full moon dropped shadows over the Garden House. Mrs. Eilif had been home earlier in the week, but Amber had hardly been around to notice. A pile of tree trimmings were inside the gate.

Someone had been busy.

She climbed the stairs to her room and made chamomile tea. She would be asleep before hitting the covers. The garden exhaled autumn breath through her window. She just wanted fifteen minutes to listen to its song before passing out.

Paper rustled on the walls.

Drawings fidgeted to get her attention. They were taped over each other, five deep for some subjects. There were at least twenty of the Eilifs, most of them solo imaginings of Mr. Eilif. She didn't have a single photo of him, but his likeness had been set loose in her mind.

She was seeing him in various arrangements, sometimes in the wetlands, sometimes in an urban setting or other parts of the world. It was strange the way her imagination worked, as if it found him in real places rather than dreams.

He was younger in the last portrait, by at least twenty years. His hair was slicked back. This one was in the garden; she recognized the fountain. Only there was an unusual tree behind it, a Japanese maple weeping to the ground.

Where did that come from?

She didn't know where her imagination pulled the imagery from. Once set loose, she watched it unfold and followed the current, letting it take her to where it wished to be. She recorded the journey.

A chorus of treefrogs soon dragged her off to where her dreams spun random images of multicolored strands, where flowers bloomed and the earth unfolded and walls fell down, bricks clattered in dull clunks and slid down a chunky slope that churned in a volcanic birth. It was as if the space inside the garden had begun to unfold and expand, giving birth to a new dimension made of something essential and basic—the fundamental essence that made the heart beat and the universe sing. It sprang from inside her, the well tapped and gushing. She rolled into its warm embrace and sank into the earthy compost—

Her lap was wet.

She leaped up and the mug tumbled on the floor. The handle broke off, a jagged letter *C* looking up at her. A soggy teabag slapped the floor. She'd fallen asleep and spilled the tea. She stripped everything off.

It was October but still muggy. Tacky with perspiration, her necklace stuck between her breasts. She flipped on the window unit and reached up to close the window. The full moon filled the garden.

Someone was out there.

She covered herself and ducked. If they were looking up, they caught the Amber Gallagher late show. They were near the reflection pond. It was only a silhouette, not enough to distinguish gender, age or even if it was human. Or a ghost.

She dropped into bed, pulled the sheet up to her chin, and began drifting back to sleep. A wrinkle of agitation went with her. It wasn't that there was a person in the garden at that hour, or that she'd flashed her tits.

It was the reflection pond.

She could never see it from her window before. Maybe a gardener had taken down a tree or pruned back some overgrown shrubs. There was debris near the gate. But that wasn't it, either.

Why did the reflection pond seem so far away?

8

The bedroom was bright.

A rectangle of sunlight stretched across the floor. She'd never noticed it before because she'd never been in bed when the sun was that high in the sky. She grabbed her phone.

Three missed calls and half a dozen texts.

A weekend study group was meeting at the library. She was the one who organized it. Her head swam awake. It had been years since she'd slept past seven o'clock.

It was 10:15 a.m.

They would have started without her and were probably still there. No one would miss her. She'd rather stay anyway, find a place in the garden to spread out her notes, and binge PowerPoints. She started a press of coffee and stared out the window as the timer counted down. Her dreams felt like an eternity of sleep, but she couldn't pull a single detail back into real life. There was a kaleidoscope of colors and images unfolding into more colors and more images, over and over again. And beneath it ran a current of agitation.

The reflection pond.

There had been someone out there last night. It could've been a shrub shaped like a person—it was late, and she was naked and half asleep and smelled like chamomile—but that wasn't what disturbed her. She couldn't see the reflection pond from her room before last night and now she could. It was full daylight, and she was staring right at it.

It's farther away.

This was no illusion. The reflection pond was just past the fountain behind the guesthouse. Now it was a hundred yards away, like the garden had doubled in size. Pouring her coffee, she slid her flip-flops on. Caffeine was already lighting up her synapses when she followed the brick path behind the guesthouse.

She stopped.

The hydrangeas had grown halfway across the path, heavy globs of senescing inflorescences bobbing at the end of the branches. One of them was missing. The ground wasn't dug up or disturbed. There was an opening in the shrubbery.

Gravel crunching underfoot, she expected to see the kitchen garden, but there were no wax myrtles on the other side and no curving path. It was a shortcut to another part of the garden.

How did I miss this?

There was a tunnel of crape myrtles, their branches interlacing overhead. In the past several months, she'd explored the entire property. Even a commercial landscape crew couldn't pull off an installation like this.

"Amber?"

She cocked her head and listened. It occurred to her she'd never heard anyone in the garden. She still hadn't seen the young man who had met her on the first day, the one who worked for the Eilifs.

Something ricocheted off the guesthouse. She returned to the barn in time to see a second rock come arching over the gate. It bounced once before clanging off the Jeep's bumper. Amber peered through the pierced brick wall. A narrow space sliced in the fig vine allowed her to see the sidewalk.

Macon.

He was in the road. A car came to a complete stop before he got out of the way, still searching the wall and shouting through cupped hands. It sounded so far away. He went to the house across the street, explored a pile of construction debris, and came back with a half brick.

"Drop it, Macon."

"Amber?" He hustled across the street. "Where are you?"

"Drop the brick."

"I need to talk. Open up."

He knocked on the gate like a motivated salesman. This chapter was over. She moved on, he moved on, the end. But he was clinging to the last page with a brick in the other hand.

"Please, I just want to talk."

His cheeks were flush and his eyes half-lidded. His moppish hair matted on one side. She'd seen this act before, starred in a supporting role for over a year. The ending was so predictable.

"I've been texting. You changed your number."

"You sent me a pic of your asshole, Macon." *Goddamnit.* She bit her lip. She was reciting her lines just like the fucking script called for.

"That wasn't me, Amber."

"There's nothing to say, Macon. Go home. I wish you the best, really. Just go."

He backed up to the curb and scanned the wall. "I want to say sorry. That's all. I'll go away after that. If you want."

She could practically mouth his lines word for word.

"I got your stuff from the apartment. I didn't throw it away. I got all your pencils, the sketchbooks, your drawings and clothes. I just want you to have them."

He was pointing down the street. She didn't see his car.

"I can bring them over here if you want. I know you spent a lot of time on them, how you feel about them. I just want you to have them. That's all, that's it."

"Leave them on the sidewalk."

"Hey, there you are." He tripped on the curb and stumbled toward her voice. "Oh, man, I miss you. I need my Ambrogina fix. You know what I mean? I need to see you."

"You're drunk, Macon. Go home."

"Hey, hey, no. I'm thinking clearly for the first time. I just... I want you to be happy, that's all. That's all I ever wanted. I'm a... I'm a mess. I'm an idiot, an asshole. You were right. I had a good thing and blew it. I'm, I'm sorry. Listen, the party's over. I'm tired of all the trouble. I've changed, Amber. You were the best thing about me."

He leaned into the wall and searched the vines like she was hiding in the foliage. The words were coming straight from a manual of abuse: what you say when the bitch leaves you.

"I have to go, Macon. I need to study. I'm sorry."

I'm sorry? Jesus, Amber.

She backed up on her toes, careful not to scuff the pavement or kick a pebble. She would sneak into the guesthouse and watch from the second floor. If he chucked the brick over the wall, she'd call the police. But only if it hit something. Hopefully, a neighbor would come out or a car would run him over.

"Who's Simon?"

A chill seized her. Simon, her lab partner, a Jewish boy from New York with an accent as thick as his neck. They were in study group and sometimes ate lunch on the lawn. They parked in the same garage and walked to class.

Shit.

"That one time you gave him a ride, did he try anything? Or did you thank him? Did you thank him, Amber? Give him a big thank-you while he was driving?"

Of course he was following her. What did she think would happen, that he'd go on with his life? That shit wasn't in the script. This movie didn't have an ending. It just circled round and round forever and ever because he was a sick fuck. He was an abusive, mentally ill sadist who would flunk out of college with nothing else to do but stalk an ex-girlfriend.

"Open the gate, Amber. Tell me you didn't thank him. Just look me in the eye and tell the truth, and I swear to fucking God I'll leave."

Good or bad, the story needed an ending.

"Please." The gate was thumping. He was banging his head. "Please, please, please. I'll leave you alone if that's what you want."

A low growl slowly turned into a painful howl. His grief would emerge as a ruddy-faced demon who would begin pounding the gate and begging forgiveness as he kicked and screamed and hurt everything around him.

There was a loud thump. The brick had been hurled into the gate and clunked across the sidewalk. It came again, the edge biting into one of the wood planks. He was going to chisel through the gate one brick at a time, break down every board if he had to. Mrs. Eilif would see it and ask what happened. Maybe kick her out of the apartment. If she was smart, she would.

And she'd never see the garden again.

"All right!" she shouted. "Macon, all right. Put the brick down. Calm down, please. Just take a breath, okay? Relax and breathe a second."

"Will you open up?"

"If you calm down, please. Don't make a scene."

"That's all I want."

She snuck back to the crevice in the wall and spied him pacing in the road, looking up at the gate like she would come bounding into his arms. He was clenching and unclenching his hands. Cheeks fiery, lips wet.

If the police arrived, his head would explode. Even if she didn't call them, he would blame her for how he was feeling because he knew she had every right to call them. A normal human being would have called them months ago, would have gotten a restraining order, would've explained her fuckups to her grandma.

She just wanted to click her heels. If she didn't look under the bed, the boogeyman would go away. She was Macon's perfect target. The hole was too deep. The path, too steep.

Just this one time.

He would calm him down; then she would call her grandma and get a restraining order. She would explain it was the best for both of them; they could start over. There was no future for them. He had to see that. If he would just go away, get out of her life forever, stalk someone else, and they could both live happily ever after.

See? Everyone wins, you get that, don't you, Macon? Of course you do. That's why you're trying to pickax your way through a historic gate, so you can have a happy ending. I love you, too, baby.

Tendrils ripped from the wall, the tiny suction cups of fig vine pulled away. A hand came over the top of the wall, grabbed the ropey foliage and threw a leg up. A dirty flip-flop sought leverage. Macon heaved his weight toward the other side, overcompensating and tumbling all arms and legs. He hit the pavers with a wet crack and rolled onto his back with his hands buckled around his shin. Silent agony on his face.

Amber stifled a scream, a reaction she couldn't stop. He was inside. The Garden House was silent and dark.

"There you are." He squatted on the good foot, the other one already blood-streaked and swollen. The nail on the big toe was peeled back. "Just open the fucking gate, Amber. Is that asking too much? Fuck."

She mirrored his advance in the opposite direction. She should run for the guesthouse and slam the door. Scream until the neighbors heard her. Open the gate and then run down the street. Anything but stand there. Anything at all. This was what he did when he came home looking for a fight, pale-faced and glassy-eyed with dog-shit breath and pussy on his goatee. The asshole piece of shit. She should run, that was the sensible thing to do. The right thing. The normal thing.

Fuck this.

"It's over, Macon. You and me are over. You get it? We don't have a future, we don't have a now, we got a past and that's it. And God willing I'll forget that, too."

He shuffled to a stop, head floating back on his shoulders, eyes tracking her general direction.

"Get the fuck out." She pointed. "The same way you came in. Get help or keep doing whatever you're doing, I don't care. This is your free pass to get out of my life. Next time I see you or hear you or even smell you, I'm calling the police. I'll tell them where you keep your weed and who you sell to and all the shit you steal from your friends. I'll pull the whole curtain back on you, Macon. You know what's behind it? Nothing, Macon. You're empty. That's why you keep coming back. You're sore from your pathetic life, and you need someone to go down that sad rabbit hole with you."

She advanced a step. "I'm done with you. I'm not going down that path anymore. So get up and get the fuck out."

He didn't move on her. They stood like silent gunslingers waiting for someone to flinch. She'd just torn all the pages out of the script, and this dipshit didn't know his lines.

She didn't give up ground, didn't offer a step back. The ground was firmly beneath her, a foundation that struck a solid chord in her spine. The words came to her effortlessly, loaded and aimed to cut him down at the knees. She tried to be the conscientious observer, the peaceful victim who understood why he was the way he was—his abusive father, absent mother, wealthy overcompensating grandparents, all the ingredients to make the cake. She understood his deficiencies, why he was such a mess, how his dysfunction matched hers, how they had been two jagged pieces that made one giant mess.

"Is that what you think?" He took a tender step. "All I did for you, Amber? I cared for you. I loved you."

A fog preceded his advance, a toxic mix of whiskey and weed. The stench seeped from his pores, sweating through his shirt. He hesitated. She still hadn't backed up. Another step and she was going to add a new twist to the storyline: knee to balls. He was bigger, and he would hurt her. Maybe even kill her, the idiot. But he'd go through life with one exploded nut.

Because fuck this.

"I followed you to watch out for you, Amber. Can you get that through your thick fucking skull? I'm not a stalker. And you with your fucking uppity doctor friends and the white coats have turned you into one of them. This is your fault."

His hand came up. Sluggishly he waved a finger, accusing her. One more step and his inability to have children would happen.

But his reach was long and deceptive.

He hit her in the throat, a jolt that wrapped darkness around her vision and a dull cloak over her senses. She stumbled back and caught her heel. Her momentum wrenched her from his grip and slammed her with teeth-jarring impact on the pavement.

He dragged his bad foot, blood dripping from the big toe.

Color flooded his cheeks, light returning to his foggy eyes. His shadow dropped over her. She dug her elbows between the pavers, cocked her knee back and held it there. Again, he hesitated. This was the part where she would begin weeping, the part where she would apologize. The part where she would fall apart, and he, the sick fuck that he was, would grin triumphant, and she would let him take a victory lap as long as she didn't get hurt.

Something changed.

Not her. It was him. The rosy flush of perverse joy drained from his cheeks, and his eyes widened in shock. He wasn't looking at her. There was no way he was afraid of her painted toenails and tender foot.

Urine ran down his legs.

It dripped from the cuffs of his denims and filled the indentions of his flip-flops. He convulsed once, hard and breath-taking, like a fist was buried in his solar plexus. He folded up and dropped to his knees. A string of saliva jiggled from his lip as he searched for air.

His eyes as round as coins, he was suddenly jerked onto his feet as if yoked by an invisible harness. A life-sized marionette tossed about by a puppeteer, his jaws worked mechanically for tiny gulps of air.

The gates began opening.

The electric motors hummed, the empty road slowly revealed. No car was waiting to pull inside. Macon was shoved toward the opening, the world a tilted floor that dumped him on the sidewalk. A patch of skin stripped from his elbow as he skidded on the concrete. The hanging toenail hung like a tooth that wouldn't let go, a crimson trail all the way to the road.

Amber suddenly felt the person behind her. Standing near the barn doors, between the topiaries. *The puppeteer.*

Amber watched his liquid steps silently glide over the stones. Jeans and a T-shirt, a shovel in his hand, his work in the garden interrupted, as if this assault was nothing more than a sand flea he flicked off his arm.

His lazy eyes didn't meet Amber's stare. He picked up the abandoned flip-flop, laid the shovel down, and delivered it onto the sidewalk, bending near Macon to mutter something. Her ex-boyfriend turned bloodlessly pale after the gardener helped him stand.

The gardener retrieved the shovel and leaned on it, eyes cast slightly left of Amber, his scalp smooth and without perspiration despite dirt on his knees and knuckles.

His gaze flickered up. For an instant, warmth flooded through her, filling her with calm reassurance that everything was exactly as it was supposed to be. He inspected the gate where Macon had thrown the brick. The boards were splintered.

"I'll pay for that. He's not supposed to come around. I'll call the police if he does."

The gardener propped the shovel over his shoulders and strolled back toward the garden with the same effortlessness. It was like watching wheat move in a gentle breeze or a cargo ship cut through choppy water.

"What did you do to him?"

He stopped when she called out, the long wooden handle yoked over his shoulders. Without turning, he nodded again like he'd already answered the question.

"I wished him away."

Macon was in the fourth dimension of a pharmaceutical mind fuck, and then he had been yanked onto his feet and shoved onto the sidewalk in a way that defied the laws of physics. She'd seen it.

I wished him away?

She got up and followed him. The gap in the hydrangea hedge she had discovered before Macon started launching brick and mortar was still there. The stately crape myrtles invited her to discover a new part of the garden. She followed the path, but he was gone. Confused and slightly numb, she returned to her room. That was the first time she'd met the gardener.

I've seen him before.

* * *

A TEXT ARRIVED SUNDAY NIGHT. It was someone from study group.

Nearly a day and a half since Macon had crashed the wall. No calls or texts. No posts on social media, either. Perhaps he'd blacked out that morning's details. There were entire weekends he had erased from memory; waking up with piss pants and a missing toenail wouldn't be anything new. It would be hard to explain, but wouldn't slow him down. She expected business as usual.

He was missing in action.

She would have to tell Simon and the other men in her study group to back off. No big deal, just crazy ex stuff. Everyone had one, right? Macon's blackouts lacked repercussions because he couldn't remember them. At some point, he would fall back on old habits.

I'll have to tell Grandma. Tell her everything.

The sound of metal striking metal echoed in the garden. Amber saw a dark figure swinging a hammer at a green T-post, the sound lagging behind the impact of each swing. He disappeared behind a conifer and returned with a strap, his movements efficient and steady, like meditation in action.

Strangely chilling.

He was dressed the same as the day before, when Macon had defied the laws of gravity. *I wished him away.*

Autumn was beginning to cool. She itched to capture him in action, maybe snap a shot for later, lose herself in this beautiful swinging of the hammer. *Driving the Stake,* she would name it.

She held her phone against the window and tapped a few photos that would prove to be grainy once cropped. She rushed to fit her Canon with a telescopic lens. No time for a tripod. She stepped on the bed to shoot through the upper part of the window.

Drayton began tying the post. Amber leaned against the

windowsill, her breath still and quiet, a hunter spotting her prey. The artificial sound of the shutter clicked—the simulation that made photography so satisfying.

Click, click, click.

He bent out of frame. She remained frozen, weapon poised. When he returned to finish a knot, she fired off a burst of fifty shots before he stopped. Her heart thumped; her chest began to burn. Finger hovering over the button, she didn't make a sound.

He was observing something or thinking or remembering. She didn't move the camera to see what had grabbed his attention, kept trained on her target, waiting for him to return to those effortless strokes. When he turned his head, she prepared to grab a few more shots, hoping he might move farther out to give her a full-body photograph.

He looked right at her.

She ducked out of view, but not before she was caught in the ill net of embarrassment. His eyes dialed right through the camera lens—the muddy brown of fertile silt where the lotus bloomed.

The camera was uploading to the cloud. She only had a few minutes to edit them before needing to leave for study group. The last few had captured the crosshairs of his penetrating stare. She cropped the final one and left it on the screen.

She made it halfway down the stairs when the question that had been nagging her for days clicked like a deadbolt sliding open. It was an odd feeling that she'd already drawn him.

I've seen him before.

She had the distinct memory of detailing his eyes and outlining his face. Had she taken photos of him somewhere? There were thousands of them on her laptop waiting to be drawn. When she reached the Jeep, she decided she would just have to be late for group. As it would turn out, she wouldn't make it at all.

Amber returned to her room and scanned through layers of drawings, lifting corners, pulling off tape, examining layouts. Perhaps it was from one of the sketchbooks back in the apartment, which Macon, she was certain, had already burned. But this felt like something recent. The obsession would follow her the rest of the night if she didn't figure it out.

And then she hit it.

The very first drawings she'd done in the garden were buried under a dozen subsequent works. It wasn't the gardener that she had drawn. It was someone else.

A tattoo on his thigh.

9

The house was the only one without Christmas lights.

A few blocks from the Citadel, it was an old neighborhood on Rutledge Avenue. She checked her email. This had to be the place. It matched the address. A ramp led up to a two-story brick house with a deep porch. A secondary staircase was attached to the side of the house and led to the second floor.

It was signed Young Barnes.

Amber crossed the street. The smell of flavored tobacco grew stronger as she approached the steps. An old-fashioned pipe was on a small table beside the door. A dog watched from a window.

Music bled through the door, the hard-driving kind with machine-gun bass drums and relentless guitars. When no one appeared, she rang the doorbell. The dog went to the glass door, tail mopping the hardwood.

A wheelchair appeared at the end of a hallway.

Young was wearing long sleeves and sweatpants. The leafy tips of vines peeked from the cuffs of his sleeves and wrapped around his fingers. His hair tied back, split ends created a halo around his head. He waved her in. The golden retriever stood next to the wheelchair.

Amber opened the door. "Hi."

He stared. The dog danced next to him but obeyed. He pulled back on the wheels and nodded. Amber took that as an invitation. She stepped inside, and they stared awkwardly.

"What's her name?" When he didn't answer, she read the collar. "Samu."

He looked constipated. Metal music still played from the end of the hall.

"Festive," she said. "Is that 'Jingle Bells'?"

"How'd you find me?"

Amber stepped back and frowned. The abruptness slapped her silent. Then she gathered herself and boldly closed the door.

"I'm guessing you don't get a lot of guests." She crossed her arms. "Let me walk you through this. When you respond to an email and invite someone over, you offer them a chair, maybe even ask if they'd like a drink. Water would be great, thank you."

He rocked back and forth, the corner of his mouth twitching like a fish on a hook. "So you're thirsty."

"No. But water would be nice."

He nodded thoughtfully, then clicked his tongue. Samu turned around, ears perked. "Water, please."

The dog trotted down the hall.

"Is it him?"

She nodded at his thigh, the tattoo hidden. But he knew what she meant. She'd attached a photo of the gardener to the email. He'd replied within minutes.

"You met him?"

"Once. He sort of helped me."

Amber told him about Macon, the way he'd thrown himself over the wall, pissing himself before he'd doubled over like a fist had been buried in his stomach. The way he'd tumbled out of her life and hadn't returned.

The confidence she felt from that day forward.

How could she describe that before she'd met the man tattooed on his leg, she wouldn't have had the courage to come to this house. She would have apologized as soon as he snapped at her, and left.

Samu returned with the water and brought it over and went back to Young for a treat.

"What's his name?" he asked.

"You tell me."

He spun around and went down the hall. Samu followed. The music died a few seconds later. Amber stood in the silence, unsure if she was supposed to follow him or leave.

A dining room was to the left. The table was buried beneath papers and laptops, some open with screensavers running. There were no chairs for someone to sit. She was right, he didn't get a lot of company. Or any.

To the right, what would normally be a sitting room was a wonderful disaster of acrylics. Canvases were stacked against a colorful streak-spattered wall. The floor was lined with tire tracks of every color in the bucket. Tripods held ongoing paintings, each an abstract arrangement of paint-slinging brushes and knife swipes.

She wasn't a fan of this style, it seemed much too easy from her perspective, but was drawn by the raw interplay of colors, the emotion they captured in a still frame. None of the work resembled anything concrete or objectified. That seemed to be the point—one painting more abstract than the next.

There was one in the corner that was different than all the rest, the paint thick and textured, a mash-up of colors that funneled around a white and black vortex, as if this center was drawing everything toward it—a thousand colors swirling together, impossible to separate.

Light and dark, she thought. *One cannot be without the other.* She didn't know where that thought came from. The hairs on her arms stood up. *Was it something I read?*

The painting behind it had the curvature of a skull and the lobes of ears. She slid it to the front. Adrenaline dumped into her veins.

The eyes.

He'd captured the face with a montage of pastels, a collection of slashes and smears—the proportions accurate, the expression she saw in the garden. The work was fixed with a glossy lacquer.

"Do you believe in vampires?" He eased into the studio.

"What?"

He stared at her as if waiting for an answer. She wasn't sure she heard the question.

"Vampires?"

"Not Hollywood bullshit. More like a supernatural, an evolved being who helps others, one who has powers over the mind, can influence people with a thought, even fool surveillance. Someone who doesn't sleep or eat, just walks the earth."

She shook her head. "Are you talking about him?"

Young nodded when she held up the painting. So they were on the same page. The man in the garden was the man on his leg and the man in the painting.

"How can he not eat?" she asked.

He took the painting from her and slid it to the back of the pile. The black and white, color-swallowing vortex was back in front.

"Can you take another picture?"

"I don't know. Why?"

"Do you know where he is?"

She hesitated. "Yes."

He backed into the hall. "No offense, but I need another picture."

"Are you serious? What I sent you is exactly what you painted." She dug the painting out and pointed at the eyes. "He's on your fucking leg."

"You could've downloaded that off the internet."

"Why would I do that?"

He shrugged, expressionless. As if he intentionally emptied out his emotions to keep from feeling anything.

"If I did download it, which I didn't, why wouldn't I just do it again? Look, I know you have a line of people dying to meet you, but I'm not one of them. The guy you tattooed on your leg is working at the place I'm living. You're painting him. Why would you want another photo?"

"I need to be sure."

"Why is he on your leg?"

"Get me another picture and I'll tell you."

"I don't get you."

A smile darted into his cheek, the kind that was more amused than cruel. He backed into the dark part of the hallway. Samu's toenails clicked on the floor. They waited for her to leave.

She considered taking the painting or never coming back. Instead, she tugged the door with a heavy sigh, regretting she was making a dramatic exit. It probably wasn't the first time somebody had left him like that.

"Where are you staying?" he said.

"If I get you another picture," she said, "I'll tell you."

* * *

It was early morning.

She had ignored Young's request. It wasn't worth the hassle. He had a face on his leg, so what? But then every morning she woke up and kept wondering why. Every morning she felt someone watching.

She tossed a handful of acorns at the barn window. Nothing moved. She stepped between the topiaries and rapped on the door. No one had ever come out of the barn. She turned the latch.

"Hello?"

It opened to a common room with a sink and kitchen. Efficiency apartments on the left and right. A stairwell double-backed to the hayloft apartment, where the window overlooked the parking area. Her footsteps echoed in the closed quarters. It smelled of grass and old wood. She climbed the steps.

"Anyone home?"

If the gardener lived there, he might be sleeping. And if he was sleeping, he wasn't a vampire. And if he was eating breakfast, he wasn't the guy tattooed on Young's leg, because when she thought about it, that was what he'd meant. All that talk about vampires had something to do with the tattoo. It might explain what had happened to Macon, but the problem with that theory was that vampires didn't exist. Hollywood bullshit or not.

She turned the knob very slowly.

Dust floated through a beam of light, highlighting an empty bed, the covers pulled up and tucked in, the pillow fluffed. Her heart racing, the floor creaked under her feet. The place was spotless. The top of the dresser empty. Nothing in the corners or hanging in the closet. No luggage, no dirty socks or empty cups.

No vampires here.

In the mornings, she swore someone was watching from the window. From this vantage point, she looked down at the guesthouse. If she ever saw someone, it was a reflection. Maybe he'd moved out.

Or never lived here in the first place.

Someone moved on the third-floor balcony of the Garden House. Amber dug her camera out of her bag and zoomed in. The young man was wearing shorts and a collared shirt, like the first day she saw him. It was a little chilly for summer wear. Someone was with him, a woman with short black hair. Her skin was as black as his was white, the contrast as stark as the checkered walkway in front of the house. They were leaning on the railing.

Their shoulders touching.

Amber had never seen the woman on the property. She moved to the edge of the window for a better angle. Their details dialed into focus, her finger on the button when he looked right at her. She jumped back half a step, her breath caught somewhere at the back of her throat.

She packed up the camera and hustled down the stairs, quietly closing the upstairs door. There was a narrow hallway along the back of the common room that led to a side door. She rushed down it, bag scraping along the wall, and burst onto a gravel path. She hurried into the garden, laughing as she entered the allee of crape myrtles.

Why the hell am I running?

It was the way he looked at her. No, more like the way he knew she was looking at them.

And who was she?

Amber darted down her newest shortcut, a dewy pathway that cut between the crape myrtles. She'd been sitting at the fire pit for the past few months when this shortcut seemed to show up one day. The gardener might have cut it for her, but the trail seemed established.

Bamboo canes draped overhead. She moved sideways to avoid getting soaked, her bag brushing the underbrush. Her new nook was a live oak—maybe the largest live oak she'd ever seen in the Lowcountry. Even bigger than the famed Angel Oak.

A soft bed of moss covered the ground. A bench was tucked between massive root flares, the trunk hugging the armrests. It exuded inspiration when she sat against it with the pad on one knee. The tree seemed to breathe through her fingers until the cold morning stole sensation from her hands. It made more sense to return to the fire pit.

She just couldn't leave this spot.

She sketched an exaggerated view of the live oak standing alone and a decayed opening along its trunk, a doorway that would lead into its girth like a hobbit hole. Then she drew the gardener from memory, adding texture and emotion without the advantage of using color like Young had done. Still, she captured the complexity of the mystery, the depth and wisdom in the eyes.

Who is he?

It was midmorning, and her fingers were aching, the paper smooth and frigid. It was Christmas break. Without the interruption of class, she would draw until she couldn't feel the pencil. But her coffee was ice cold. She stood to stretch, joints stiff and slow. Her stomach barked. She slipped down the shortcut, the foliage gently stroking her cheeks.

"What are you doing?"

The young man was on the bluestone with his arms crossed. Short-sleeved shirt and shorts, his hair streaked with comb lines. That strange concoction of odor preceded him, this time an earthy scent mingled with crushed cinnamon sticks.

"You startled me." She caught her breath. "I was drawing."

He held his ground as she stepped out. She moved into his personal space, and still he didn't budge.

"What were you doing in the barn?"

A cold twist wrung fear into her legs. "Looking for the gardener. There was a situation with my ex-boyfriend. He helped me, and I wanted to say thank you. I thought he lived in the barn. Is he still here?"

"You had your camera."

"I always do."

He fixed a grin, looked down, and shuffled back a step. Arms still buckled, his eyes yet to blink. Eyes so light blue they looked silver in this light.

"I don't mean to be rude—"

"You're not being rude," Amber said, "but you're looking a little aggressive. Did I do something wrong? You said I could use the garden."

"You went into the man's apartment."

"The door was open. He still lives there?"

"Were you invited?"

"I didn't take anything."

"You took pictures."

She moved back into his personal space. Cords flexed on his forearms. He was a few inches taller than her. She met his unblinking stare while digging her camera out of her bag. She flipped through the snaps, showing him there were no photos of the young woman and him on the balcony.

"Drayton is a private man," he said. "I don't think he'd care for you walking through his room uninvited."

"That's his name?"

"You can go wherever you wish, Ambrogina, except where you're not invited. I made that quite clear on day one."

She flinched. *Did I tell him my birth name?* "For the record, you only said stay out of the Garden House. Nothing about the barn. The door was open."

He flashed a well-rehearsed smile, one reserved for customers and bordering on creepy. She put her camera away and moved to go around him.

"Forgive me," he said. "I forget my manners sometimes. I'm still acclimating to this job."

"Okay." She kept from apologizing because she'd done nothing wrong.

He held out his hand, his smile fading closer to something a little more normal. When he didn't let go, the creep factor turned all the way up. She pulled her hand away.

"My name is Mors."

"Mr. Eilif was your grandfather?"

He smiled and winked. Her stomach turned. "I should've introduced myself earlier."

"I'm sorry about his passing. I didn't know."

"Death is nothing to fear. You'll see."

He left her alone on the bluestone, walking off in his short-sleeved shirt and knee-length shorts. This was the South. The summers were hot, but the winters brisk. He needed a better wardrobe for the off-season. He was ice cold.

She needed a hot shower to warm up and wash off the creepiness.

* * *

OUTSIDE HER WINDOW, the trees were wrapped in strands of white lights. Lanterns were strung over the reflection pond that still seemed so far away. Ornaments glittered from limbs.

Christmas in full swing.

Amber finished the last of her Photoshop. She took one of the original photos of Drayton and positioned it in the knot garden. She hadn't seen him since going over to Young's house. Maybe he knew what he was talking about after all. She started to doubt she'd ever seen him.

But the camera didn't lie.

Mors had made it clear that he was living in the barn. The paths were kept clear and the garden clean. And someone was putting up these lights, and it wasn't cold-handed Mors. It was doubtful he'd ever touched a ladder.

It was late but unseasonably warm. A brisk chill raised gooseflesh on her arms. She opened the window. Her chest swelled with creative compulsion. She grabbed her bag and headed for the tree.

Beneath the crape myrtles, the branches tightly wrapped with white lights, strands of lighted icicles dangled among reflective ornaments. The festive lights warmed her from the inside. Down the shortcut, through the bamboo patch... *the live oak!*

Endless strands trailed around the trunk and twined around the heavy branches, the ambient light filling the enclosure with a magical glow. Moss threw shadows across the ground, ferny shadows along the branches.

The bench was hard and cold. She stood on the armrest with her bag over her shoulder, reaching for the lowest limb. Its girth was padded by resurrection ferns. Farther up, the next limb was within reach. She leaned against the trunk and straddled the branch. Her view crossed the garden. The lights went far beyond what she imagined.

Is it really this big?

In the festive glow, she sketched something she'd never done before. She closed her eyes, brought the creative energy to a boil, and began capturing it in broad strokes and bold gestures, letting the energy spill onto the page. It was well past midnight when she looked down at her first ever abstract.

Christmas in the garden.

This place was a village of lights, secret rooms and still waters. And there, somewhere in the middle, perched atop an A-frame ladder, a man was hooking a string of lanterns upon a wire. Carefully, gently, she propped the camera on her knee.

Dialing the lens, she waited for him to reach the top step. With his face next to the lantern, yellow light turned his face the color of pluff mud.

Drayton.

10

"Happy New Year."

Well wishes drifted from a blue cloud that smelled of smoldering cherries, the same smell Amber had experienced when she first visited Young. Someone was seated in a rocking chair with a vape pen around his neck.

"So you must be the one." He leaned forward, hand out. It was dry and slender, the nails shiny. "Dev."

"Amber."

"Well, Ms. Amber, it's damn nice to meet you."

His arm was toned and muscular; a dark T-shirt hung on him like a wire hanger. He was simply dressed and clean-shaven. Despite the short hair, maybe he was a woman, not a man.

"Is Young home?"

"The dark prince is currently away."

Amber stood on the top step and sipped the final dregs of her coffee, watching him send up smoke signals from a boxy vape pen. He crossed his toothpick legs, the beige khakis baggy around his narrow ankles, and surveyed her through another cloud. His shoes were turquoise wingtips, the kind you might see ballroom dancing.

"So... you're the brave one with enough balls to talk with that cranky shit, huh? He scares off the pretty ones. The ugly ones are a little harder to shake."

"I'm sorry?"

"Joking. No one comes around, pretty or ugly."

"Who are you?"

"I'm a little bit of everything—nurse, teacher, babysitter. Overlord."

"You live with him?"

He pointed to the side staircase that led to the second story. "Live up there. Smoke down here."

"Do you know when he'll be back?"

He shrugged and smiled. Something in his expression looked infinitely patient and carefree. That would be a requirement to live here. She liked him already. The lights were on inside the house, but no music. She leaned into the door and shaded her eyes.

"Did you do that?" She pointed at the black and white vortex painting. It was still propped in the corner where she had left it.

"How'd you guess?"

She thought about it then told him the style was different than the rest of the work. "So you're a painter, too?"

"More of a creator," he said.

"Sculptor?"

Stained teeth held the pipe in a smile. "You could say that."

"It's good." She cupped her hands to the window. "I like it."

"He's a dark one." Dev's voice was light but rough on the edges, like a hacky cough was always on the way but never arrived. "The tattoos tell a story, that's all. He's got a space beneath all those quills. Hard to get past them, for most. I don't think you'll have a problem."

"You've known him long?"

"Long enough. Had a sick mother when I met him. Father was dead, so his brother raised him. His legs don't work. He's still a little bitter, you may have noticed."

"Bitter about everything," she muttered. "Surprised he told you that much."

"Get a few drinks in him, he'll tell you everything." The chair protested as he uncrossed and recrossed his legs. "So what brings you here besides the company?"

"He knows a few things."

"That he does."

"And I like his paintings." She peered into the studio again. That much was true. "I'm an artist."

It was the first time she had called herself an artist. She hadn't sold a single work, but that wasn't what defined an artist. People didn't have to like her work, either. That wasn't the definition.

It was the flow.

That was what it felt like. When she was in the garden, she was satisfied, full. She was exactly who she was supposed to be when she was in it and was reminded of something Young had said about vampires. *They don't eat.* When she was in the flow, she was more than what she was. Bigger than life. Fed and full.

I'm a creator, she thought. Perhaps that was what Dev meant, not to be defined by the medium with which she expressed but the energy that flowed. *I create.*

A van slowed in front of the house. The driver threw a ratty ponytail over his shoulder and backed into the driveway. A ramp unfolded from the side door. Samu leaped from the van and waited. Amber started for the steps.

"Don't." Dev nodded with his pipe clenched between thinning lips. "He's like that."

Young wheeled from behind the steering wheel and up to the porch. The golden retriever followed.

"Telling lies, Dev?"

"Just the white ones." Dev gave Samu a good scratch behind the ears.

"That's bad for your health."

"I don't inhale."

"Yeah. You do. And I meant lying."

Young opened the door, let the dog in first and followed. Amber stood to the side, wondering if he somehow didn't see her, somehow forgot she'd emailed him picture number two of the gardener hanging lanterns with a simple message.

His name is Drayton.

She fiddled with an empty cup of coffee. Her inky doodles circled around the Fine Grind Café logo. Dev drew off several puffs.

"You in or out?" he asked.

"I wasn't exactly invited."

"He didn't close the door." The gap was an inch wide. "That's as good as red carpet."

His laughter was phlegmy. She left the gender-neutral person to his vaping and little white ones and went inside. He was definitely lying about inhaling.

Young stared from the hallway, cloaked in shadows. Samu danced behind him then found her way to Amber through the kitchen. She knelt down to pet her.

"Your caretaker seems nice," she said.

Amber looked over her shoulder. Dev was still on the porch, his head in a fresh cloud. No bare spot on the crown to indicate male pattern baldness.

"What is, um, Dev's full name?"

"I don't know."

"You don't know?"

He shook his head. "Points for not saying he or she, though."

She blushed. That was exactly what she was doing, trying to find out the gender without giving herself away. "Well?"

"Does it matter?"

She shook her head. Did the quills ever rest? Dev was likely wrong about her getting past them. She doubted anyone could. Yet there she was.

I love the dark. Can't help myself.

Young went to the back of the house, and Samu followed. The sound of dog food hit a plastic bowl. A refrigerator opened and closed, a few cabinets did the same. A plate slid on a table. She began to doubt Dev's interpretation of red carpet.

New works were on the easels. Wet blobs of acrylics were laid out on boards along with half-squeezed tubes and speckled squeeze bottles. The colors appealed to her, the interplay of texture and motion.

A landscape canvas was propped against the window, a generous array of greens and browns. A sagging line of black was punctuated with bright yellows and whites. There was a face in the middle of it, a hint of gold in the hair, the square slash of a chin. The gesture was calm and peaceful, looking down, unadulterated by desire, completely settled.

The eyes.

Those were the hanging lanterns and the hefty structure of the tree, the splash of foliage, and the spray of a fountain. She'd only sent him the cropped image of Drayton's face, not the surroundings. Not the tree.

The rubber tires squeaked behind her, the tacky grab of errant paint between the floor and wheels.

She pointed. "How did you know?"

He shook his head, looking at it like it was the first time he was seeing it. But he knew what she meant. He'd only seen the cropped image.

"I just pick up the knife," he said, "and let it out."

When she had a pencil, she didn't always know what was coming or why. Even now, she ached to grab a brush, to connect with whatever was inside her, to let it flow.

To let it out.

Young scratched Samu's ear, slipped her a treat, and backed out of the room. A door opened and music thumped. When Amber didn't follow, Samu came back, nudging her hand with a whine.

The hall was dark. Photos were framed on the wall, of horses in pastures and an old plantation house amidst trees draped in Spanish moss. An adrenaline-fueled drumbeat came from the last room, which could be mistaken for a CIA operative's hideout.

The window was blacked out with aluminum foil. Computers were along one side of the room. The other walls were filled with maps of the Lowcountry, notes written in the margins, Xs and Os, and interconnecting lines. Photos were taped and pinned over each other. There were no chairs.

No one had ever seen this room, no need to accommodate.

She looked closely at the photos. Most of them had the grainy feel of surveillance, some in full daylight, but most taken at night. The figures she didn't recognize, the details too fuzzy.

"I was born on a Lowcountry farm. The house was falling apart, but it kept the rain off us, but not the palmetto bugs or heat. Momma worked two jobs most of her life. I was mostly useless."

He patted his legs.

"Daddy left when I was little. Don't remember much of that. They found him on Mount Hood. That's Oregon, 'bout as far from the Lowcountry as you can get. He'd done some fool thing like climbing during a blizzard; found him with his coat stripped open. He wasn't right in the head."

A joyless smile.

"That's when *he* showed up."

Young pulled a photo from the wall. It was framed like the ones in the hallway, an old photo shot early in the morning, ghostly sheets of humidity floating just off the pasture. In the shadows of a tree, someone sat at a wire table with legs crossed and a teacup and saucer.

"He didn't look much older than my brother, just some kid who appeared on the front porch dressed like us. I thought he was lost, needed a ride or work or something. I don't know what was stranger, him just showing up or Momma inviting him inside. She wasn't like that. Everything changed after that."

A dustless square was on the wall. It was probably the first thing he ever hung up in that room.

"He needed a place to stay, that's all he said. And Mama gave him the attic room. I'm telling you, it didn't make a lick of sense. He didn't sleep, either. Or eat, as far as I could tell. Bo said he'd catch him at night standing in the upstairs window, just staring."

Chills swept up Amber's arms. She knew the feeling.

"In the mornings, he'd be out there with his tea. He'd drink a cup and *witness the sun rise*, as he put it. It was like he just stepped into the family and no one seemed to notice. Me included. I couldn't explain it, not then. I mean, he didn't have a change of clothes, didn't ask for nothing, just some stranger who moved in and life went on. Think about that, a kid shows up and my momma—my paranoid, ass-whipping momma—just opens up our door. You tell me if that makes sense."

Amber had that same feeling of that altered reality, how the strange and unexplainable seemed logical until you looked back and realized just how absurd it was. Even now, she realized the garden was changing in ways it shouldn't be. The tree seemed to be growing, and the walls were farther apart, but then once she was back, it just felt… normal.

"Some shit went down with this guy we owed money. Drayton comes out of the barn, and that fat old prick turned white as a feather, drove off the property, and died of a heart attack, the fat fuck."

He hung the photo up.

"And then he was gone, just like that. Left us like he was never there. Not long after that, the inheritance showed up. No one could explain it. Momma didn't have to work anymore. Life went on, and no one remembered what really happened. None of us. We didn't question why the money just showed up all of a sudden or why life was so good. We didn't question where he went because we forgot all about him. It was like a fucking dream. We just accepted what was presented to us."

He rolled back and stared at the photo, pulling back his hair and tying it with a rubber band. Samu licked his hand.

"And then I remembered him."

He was lost in memories. She could walk out of the room and he wouldn't notice. Maybe this was the first time he'd ever said these things out loud.

"I don't know why it happened, but I just remembered. Bo never did. Even though Drayton was out there helping him with chores, he thought I was cracked. Momma did, though. She'd have to think about it a minute, then say she remembered when someone came out to help one time and that was it. I think she was just going along with it so I'd shut up. After a while, she didn't pretend, just said I must be thinking of my daddy or something."

He trailed off, nodding to himself and mumbling. Samu whined a little. He reached down and hiked up his pant leg, exposing the collage of ink work, and slapped the big face staring back at him.

"It's why I did this, thought I'd forget again like them."

She looked around the room, examined the maps, and read the notes while he covered up the tattoo. The articles were about local deaths and occasional sightings of a witness of the same description: almost bald, black and young. Someone would claim to see him at the deceased's side, as if he was helping them. Cause of death was never anything malicious, a heart attack or cancer.

Or stroke.

She wondered if he had been there when her mom died in the flower bed, or her dad when he collapsed near the Battery. Did he comfort them? Try to help?

"Nassfau Rauttu," he said.

"Sorry?"

"That was the name he gave when he first showed up at the house. My momma always insisted on birth names when someone came over. I searched the internet for Nassfau Rauttu. Even found a record of someone by that name from the Civil War who fought on both sides. Pretty weird, right? Not at the time, it wasn't."

He thumbed through a filing cabinet and dropped a folder on the table. There were copies of antique photos, grainy black and whites of men in uniforms with brass buttons and horses and flags. A battlefield littered with bodies, cannons in the distance, carrion roosting. They were all dead except for one man. He'd taken a knee like a priest listening to a dying man's last request, ear turned toward his lips. He handed her a close-up of the kneeling soldier, the details unmistakable. That was the gardener in the Civil War.

"It could be anyone," she said.

"I got photos going back over a hundred years, and that guy right there is always the same, always near someone dying, always listening. Witnessing."

She studied it and couldn't deny the likeness. "You think he's a vampire?"

Young didn't blink or shrug. Just stared.

"He doesn't have fangs." She laughed, this time a little nervous and a lot condescending. "There's got to be an explanation."

"He doesn't suck blood or live in a coffin. He has a reflection, walks around during the day. None of that horseshit has anything to do with this. The evidence is there, Amber."

He shook the folder at her. Samu whined.

"I can't explain how I know, but he was with my daddy when he died, found him on the mountain just before he froze."

"How do you know—"

"I just know."

"That's not evidence."

"It's the only thing that makes sense of why he came to our house. These pictures, he's always listening. Maybe that's what happened on the mountain, that's why he found us, like he had some sort of debt to pay. How does a man live that long? There's no other explanation."

"A vampire?"

"Call it what you want. You know how you felt when you first met him, don't you?"

A sudden urge to weep flooded her chest. She turned away. The photo on the wall, the dark figure beneath the tree with the teacup so delicately balanced. Did her parents whisper something to him? Was that why he was there when Macon climbed over the wall? *To protect me?*

She knew what it had felt like at the garden, what Drayton's presence had been like when Macon was there. That explained this room. Young was tracking him down. He wanted to feel that again, to feel safe. All this effort was illogical, irrational, but the way Drayton's presence felt...

He felt like he mattered.

"Why a second photo?" she asked. "You knew I wasn't lying."

"I needed time to think."

"You're scared?"

He turned his cheek, jewelry clinking on his ear. "He'll know you met me. The second he sees you, he'll know we had a conversation. Probably already does."

"So?"

"Why are you staying there?"

She shrugged. "I'm renting a room on the property."

"The Eilif home." He frowned.

"Yeah."

"Was Drayton already there?"

"No. He got there a few months later."

Young stroked the whiskers on his chin then made a short lap about the room. Tattooed branches interlaced with a patchwork of ink along his forearms. He reached for another folder, this one crisp and thin and sitting next to the computer. There were pictures of the Garden House from the street, screen grabs he'd pulled off the internet, and a satellite shot. Some historical articles of the elderly couple were included, lines he'd highlighted.

"I think you're in danger."

"What?"

"Some things aren't adding up. I don't know. Something's changed. I can't explain it. I need more time."

"Nothing's wrong. Come over, I'll show you. You can meet him."

He moved to the center computer and brought up a story about a recent death. Natural causes, it said. There was a photo of a woman slumped next to a church, sweetgrass baskets all around. *Est. 1825* was carved in the foundation beside her. Young opened an AVI file. The video was low resolution and choppy. The angle was from the opposite side of the church. The woman was barely in view, the scarf tied over her head.

"How'd you get this?" she asked.

The time stamp rolled in the corner. A few minutes passed when two people emerged from the church, a young man guiding an old woman to a waiting car.

"Mrs. Eilif," Amber said. "And Mors."

"Who?"

"The guy she's with, his name is Mors. He's the grandson."

Young jotted a note on the folder. A third person came out of the church. It was Drayton. Young was right, something was different. She couldn't say exactly what, but he was missing a quality that was apparent even in the video's poor quality. He was tense, his hands clenched, shoulders rigid. The way he stepped out of the church, the way he turned his head. It looked wild, savage. A lion in the brush.

He remained on the top step well after the car left. He seemed stuck, lost in thought. Three minutes eclipsed before he urgently left.

Young stopped the video and looked at her. When she didn't say anything, he clicked the player. "Watch again."

As he stood rigid and waiting, Young tapped the monitor where the basketweaver was sitting and suddenly slumped over. She would be found lying next to her wares, dead of natural causes.

"Can you stay somewhere else?" Young said.

11

*a*utumn had turned the allee of crape myrtles bright yellow. The rising sun caught the dew-dripped foliage on the wispy branches. Details didn't often escape him.

This is new.

It was as if space had unfolded inside the garden, and in it was a path and trees, a new niche to explore. It could also just be something he hadn't noticed. That was unlikely but, given the latest gap in memory, not impossible.

The garden was alive.

It pulsed with life that did not exist outside the walls. Was Amber walking among the trees like an insect exploring the glands of a Venus flytrap?

Or is she the pulse?

Everything was so alive when she was there. Foliage shimmered and the ground quaked. She strolled under the crape myrtles, her hair shimmering gold. Her red and yellow bag hung from her shoulder. He often watched early in the morning and paid special attention to that section around the live oak to keep it tranquil and weed-free.

She stayed late this morning.

Normally, when the sun rose, she was on her way to campus. This morning, she stayed. He could feel her current touch the air and the tips of branches. It smelled like fresh rain.

Wheelbarrow loaded with mulch and sedums, he dipped beneath the arching branches of a pyracantha heavy with orange berries and journeyed down a gravel path hemmed in by holly hedges.

Water lapped against the pool. Undulating waves rippled over the infinity edge. Something was carving long strokes in the water. There was a brief silence then a small kick. Drayton searched for a presence, combing the atmosphere for intentions and thoughts. Someone was swimming.

Her mind was blank.

He waited beneath a barren cherry tree. At the far end, the domed pool house was empty. White pillars were wrapped with ivy. Its reflection was shattered in the pool's rippling surface, water heaving over the marble edge.

And then she emerged.

Head thrown back, water coursing over short black hair, rivulets tracked down equally black cheeks and dripped from her chin. Jewelry rang on her ears. She threw her arms over the infinity edge. They were smooth and undulant and toned. Her smile was as gentle as morning fog. Her eyes gray disks contrasting.

"Lovely what you did for her." Her accent was strongly Southern with strange foreign hints. "Sweet girl."

She cast her eyes down. Drayton felt it break away, as if her gaze had released him. With an amused chuckle, she sank below the surface and didn't come up. Several seconds later, a dark form fluttered toward the other end of the pool, legs swaying like reeds in the undertow. She climbed into the cover of the pool house and stripped away the tiny bits of a swimsuit, her nude form shrouded by shadows. She slipped a long T-shirt over her lithe frame.

Drayton, still clenching the handles of the wheelbarrow, watched her approach. The damp shirt clung to her gentle curves that rocked with each step. Nipples erect, her pubic bush was outlined beneath the thin fabric. There was no polish on her nails, no makeup or coloring. It was her.

"Who are you?" she said.

"I am the gardener."

"A gardener? Is that all?"

Her fragrance was raw and earthy, the natural elegance of swaying cordgrass along the edge of a wetland. Beneath it was the intoxicating hint of cinnamon, as if spices grew from the muddy water. She dropped her knees into the soft ground, dug a hole with her hand, and kneaded a flower in place.

"How do you know," she asked, "when your duty is done?"

She looked up, a small mole on her left cheek nudged by a wry smile. She reached for the wheelbarrow. She was as blank as the day he'd felt her on the boardwalk.

"What's your name?" she asked.

"Drayton."

"Drayton, then." Her wry grin spread into both cheeks.

"And yours?"

"A rose is a rose, Drayton. Where do you live, besides the barn, I mean?"

"Right here."

"This very moment? How very wise of you, Drayton. You look quite young for a man of such wisdom."

She planted the second flower then rinsed her hands in the watering can. Her fingers were slender, the nails long and shapely. She flicked excess water at him.

"Perhaps the garden is home, Drayton. This beautiful garden you've helped to cultivate. The Lowcountry, perhaps. Did you miss roaming the wetlands? The pluff mud between your toes and the ships in the harbor? The serenade of cicadas? Is that why you haven't left?"

The small mole was nudged by a grim smile this time.

"Duty, is that it? The thing with gardens is that it's always growing. It captures the very essence of change, of life and death." She tugged a flower from its pot and cupped it in her hands. "All things are born to die. You understand that, don't you, Drayton?"

She placed the plant in Drayton's hands and closed them with her own, holding them with a cold embrace. Her sharp eyes cut across his face.

She turned and walked away, shallow indentions left in the gravel. On the far end of the property, on the third-floor balcony of the Garden House, a young man was watching. The flower lay wilted in Drayton's hands.

All things.

* * *

DRAYTON MOVED DEEPER into the shadows of his room.

Amber emerged with a bag over her coat and a scarf dangling. Pale clouds puffed from rigid lips. She glanced up at the barn. Some nights, he felt her peeking from the guesthouse to catch him at his window, where he remained as solid as the corkscrew topiaries below him with a watchful eye on the night.

It wasn't until she was deep into the garden did he move.

His strides were long and quiet upon the path. Autumn brought an early cold spell that had wilted the hydrangeas. Foliage dangled from swollen twigs, discolored and water soaked. Drayton listened for her. She had taken this shortcut since she'd found it to discover a section of the garden that had previously eluded them both. Its presence defied logic.

Logic a loose rule in the garden.

He had come to realize this place simulated the outside world. It operated on a different set of rules, laws that were moldable and expanding, laws that responded to thoughts and energy, the flow. Yet for all its unexplained absurdity, everything seemed uneventful.

He followed her presence, his mind a bloodhound of thoughts. The narrow gap widened beneath the allee of trees. Below was a path of cut bluestone, all rectangles and squares of grays and faded blues. Thickets of ferns and farfugium crowded each other between muscled wax myrtles, the trees increasing in numbers and girth.

"Mrs. Eilif requests your presence."

Drayton jerked around. The young man who drove Umi's car, the one who had approached him on the front porch to deliver that exact message once before, was standing on the bluestone path. His short-sleeved shirt was pressed and tucked into creased shorts. His hair parted sharply on the side.

He didn't wait for an answer.

Drayton followed him to the Garden House. The gate was open. Umi's car was backed onto the courtyard. The driver stood with the back door open, a grim line between his lips. The attic light was off.

Drayton heard the foliage shudder deep in the garden. He hesitated.

"She'll be fine," the driver said.

Drayton swept through him and picked at the thoughts pasted to the surface of his mind. A façade appeared to hide what was beneath.

"What's your name?" Drayton said.

The line tightened between his lips. His teeth flashed as they pulled back. Slowly, he surrendered.

"Mors."

Drayton contemplated. "The grandson?"

Young Mors chuckled, nodding. Drayton understood that death brought sadness to those left in its wake. Perhaps Young Mors had wished for his grandfather's death rather than lamented it. Or maybe it was the absurdity of death that remained, as if one might console water for transforming into vapor.

He drove in silence.

At this early hour, the streets were empty. The horses were still stabled and the bike taxis parked. The long market where tourists flocked for sweetgrass baskets and prints of multicolored sunrises was shuttered. The car came to a stop in front of a multi-brick-spired building. Crucifixes displayed high atop daggered ornaments. Arching stained-glass windows paired along the four-story steeples. The church sat on a solid foundation of pale concrete blocks.

The year the building was constructed was etched into the corner.

"She's waiting."

Young Mors didn't offer to open the door. He sat with his hand on the wheel, eyes hidden behind the smoky lenses of aviator glasses. The car eased away as soon as Drayton reached the first step of a long and wide staircase.

A basketweaver was unloading sweetgrass.

She was preparing to sell to tourists. The first pang of hunger twisted inside him, a vacuous emptiness that filled his throat and nibbled at his vision. He pulled himself up the metal railing, the black paint scuffed and pitted. Heavy walnut doors awaited him. The onset of hunger had nothing to do with church, despite the myth-building of monsters that were defeated by crucifixes and holy water.

Vampires.

They were predators who were labelled as evildoers feeding on the human race. Drayton understood the interpretation. How could humans see a predator of their own kind as anything else but evil? Birds that see their young swallowed by snakes, fish plucked from the water by eagles, insects digested by a flytrap would all have the same beliefs.

Predators were evil.

Somehow it was accepted that God was opposed to death, that death was somehow the dominion of something heinous and wrong. Ebola was no more evil than a tornado. Perhaps the most egregious misinterpretation was the most obvious.

Humans are good.

The doors swung open easily and silently. Dark pews were aligned in parallel rows. Candlelight flickered on an immaculate altar, shadows dancing along the arching white pillars amongst the pews. The glow of city lights lit the stained glass. The image of a beaten savior was beneath the weight of the cross.

A white hat covered the person near the front, the rim wide and the ribbon yellow. Drayton passed the offering of holy water. The eyes of a crucified man followed him toward the altar. Umi sat forward in the fourth pew, arms resting in front of her. A rosary rattled around her hands. Drayton sat next to her, the seat creaking beneath his weight.

Each bead slowly rolled between finger and thumb.

They sat quietly for some time. Umi's eyes closed, lips silently moving.

"I come for the solitude, Drayton," she stated. "There's something about the atmosphere I find appealing. Gratitude comes easier, I suppose. Maybe it's the candles or the ornamentation. It brings peace."

She sat back with a slight groan and turned toward him, her gray eyes looking from beneath the wide brim of her hat. Specks of candle-light danced in them.

"Hope," he said.

"That's right. Hope there is more after this life. Despite the lack of evidence."

She grimly acknowledged her doubt and turned back toward the ever-watchful man upon the cross. The rosary clattered on her lap.

"This life is all there is. We tread this planet always with one foot in heaven and the other in hell. But this is the holy city, Drayton. Charleston, the land of churches. You cannot go a city block without gazing upon the hope of sky-stabbing steeples that touch the cloak of God, summoning his promise that all will be well when this is over. By virtue, this is the city of hope. Hope that humans have a purpose, that all of this means something. That's important, to mean something, Drayton. That's why Mors and I built this church, to give the people hope."

Drayton sat quietly without a rosary to fuss with. He would agree that the atmosphere was comfortable, what many attribute to the presence of God, as if his presence was somehow more within these walls than in the outside world. He closed his eyes and rested, silently asking for forgiveness, a habit resurrected by his past.

A legitimate request.

She patted his thigh gently, reassuringly. As if she granted him the forgiveness he wished for. A perfume of roses and lavender masked something old and ancient.

Someone entered from a side entrance and lit candles in the decorative alcoves before tending to an elevated pulpit. Umi's eyes followed her across the altar, watching her perform the daily rituals that kept the place of worship tidy and worthy.

"Have you fulfilled my husband's request?"

Drayton could rarely answer such a question any more than an artist knew when his work was done. If his duty was to protect her—whether that be Umi or Amber—then when was it finished? Upon their death?

"There was a young woman on the property a few weeks back." He described her swimming in the pool, her ebony skin and lithe and dangerous body. "She lives in the Garden House?"

"You or I have no need to fear her any more than to fear my driver."

"Mors's grandson?"

She turned a glance his way. "Do you find that curious?"

"That he's a servant?"

"A role, Drayton. You understand that blood and relation cannot get in the way of purpose. I am beholden to what life demands as much as he is. As much as you are, Drayton. It is not my right to show favoritism. When we truly serve life, we serve blindly."

"And the young woman's name?"

"Where I come from, Drayton, names are sacred. One doesn't give it upon a whim, or undeservedly. I'm certain you understand that." She leaned back and grinned. "What could you possibly have to fear from her?"

Many predators lure a victim with false security and comfort. All the way to their final breath. *Is that what she's doing to me?*

Umi spoke of blood and relation, but there was a great disparity in the color of their flesh. Drayton, however, knew skin color could be deceiving. After all, he'd possessed various tones throughout his life. The skin he wore changed not what he was. Or what he did.

"Perhaps I'm concerned with the student," he said.

"You can call her by name, Drayton. Ambrogina is our guest. You know her." She sighed deeply when Drayton stiffened. "A troubled young woman when she arrived. She seems to have adjusted nicely in the garden, I believe. And I see you are protecting her."

Macon.

"She is special, wouldn't you agree? Perhaps my husband foresaw this need before his death? We all need protecting, Drayton. I believe you are very capable."

Drayton looked up at the Christian savior, the eyes compassionate and welcoming. Grace in suffering.

All things are born to die.

"I'm sure you understand that a garden has to grow in order to live," she continued. "It has to die, as well. Flowers senesce to give rise to seed that will germinate to begin the cycle again. Life decays to enrich the soil. The great cycle churns over and over. No one flower, no one tree lives forever, but the essence within continues. God and the devil are rich in these parts, you know. They are benevolent and evil, opposites that give and take. Yet without the reaper coming for life, who would willingly give it? No one wants to die, Drayton."

She patted his leg again.

Drayton attempted to look inside her, to see her thoughts. Like her grandson, there were fleeting thoughts and brief memories, but nothing deep or revealing. A façade for his benefit.

Who are you? he thought.

"I invited you here to join me, Drayton, to celebrate life and death. One foot in each, you understand. It's easy to embrace life, but another to welcome death. What is death, after all?"

"Who is asking that question?"

Her grin widened.

It was an answer he couldn't claim as his own. While he had spent much of his time in monotheistic churches such as this, those that worshipped a one true God, Drayton had dabbled in Buddhism around the turn of the sixteenth century, practicing as a monk in a very remote area of Tibet. There he'd sat meditation and learned to quiet his mind. The teacher had presented the question to temple one morning before the sun rose.

What is death?

In that instant, Drayton had experienced a moment of illumination, what many described as enlightenment. That night, he had crept into the master's bedroom and taken his life. He had been sitting zazen when Drayton appeared at the door, and had not resisted when he'd put his hand on top of the teacher's head.

There is no birth. There is no death.

And now Umi was presenting another koan for him to answer. He would not slip into her room to sip her essence while she sat zazen. Another question was presented. Another game afoot.

Young Mors stopped in the center aisle, Jesus reflected in the aviator sunglasses. Mors offered his hand, and she took it, holding it tightly for a few steps.

"I enjoyed our little chat. The garden is in need. Continue looking after it. And take a moment to stretch your legs before the holy city wakes. It's a grand little walk. I think you'll be delighted to know it still hold secrets."

The grand pipes of the organ came to life on the balcony. An organist conducted a boisterous symphony for her exit. They passed through dull columns of colored light streaming through the windows and pushed open the heavy door to a gray morning.

Drayton followed them out, standing on the top step as the car pulled away. The basketweaver had settled against the foundation of the church, her wares spread on the steps.

A mad twist of hunger clutched his throat.

12

Shrink-wrapped in his own flesh, knobs jutted from Drayton's wrists, knuckles outlined. The hunger hadn't been slaked by the basketweaver. Finding his way across town, avoiding the temptation of nearby essence to wet his tongue, to cool his throat. The rack of hunger pulling him apart... until he reached the garden.

Home.

There was no other way to describe it, the intense pleasure inside the walls, the peace it offered. He was well aware that love was often confused with a pleasurable sensation, those moments when desire was fulfilled. Things that felt good equated to love.

He felt love for the garden.

The hunger came with such ferocity, an undeniable force that drained the basketweaver before he could stop himself. He felt full at the same time as ravenous—an addiction that promised emptiness—but when he stepped into the garden, the hunger seemed to leak from him.

Not leak... pulled. As if someone drew it from me. Is that what my victims feel?

The camellias shimmered. Their late winter blooms seemed to

open wider, the buds swelling. Drayton clasped the rake and closed his eyes, breathing the current. A wintergreen, lively sensation cleansed the old and tired and brought new life to the weary.

Amber.

It had been a month since she'd slept in the guesthouse. She had been staying with her grandmother. Something troubled her but he couldn't see her thoughts clearly, as if a frosted layer of ice obscured her mind. Macon didn't seem to be the problem. Perhaps it was her grandmother's health, or the long tail of homesickness.

Her Jeep was in the courtyard. She returned to visit the tree—*her* tree. The garden rejoiced, as if the sun would rise when she entered the walls. He glimpsed her sneaking down the path. From the vantage point of her tree, whose branches seem to swell with each passing day, she surveyed the garden. Drayton was careful to stay out of view.

The garden sighed when she left, leaving the Jeep parked outside the barn. He spied her crossing the street, backpack over both shoulders. Drayton waited until she was a block away before following.

Hunger greeted him.

It was distant and yearning, but not undeniable; it lacked the strangeness of bloating fullness he had felt after the basketweaver. He passed people on the sidewalk without taking them. He crossed the street, closed his eyes, and felt her footsteps on the cracked pavement.

Protect her.

Her grandmother lived in a brick Tudor with steeply pitched roofs and an arching doorway. Amber slept in the upstairs bedroom, the same bed she'd slept in as a child. The white hair of Grandmother Harper was in a window to the right of the front door.

Drayton moved into a driveway across the street and stood next to a dumpster of a house under renovation. He would remain for a few hours, until Amber left for campus. Sometimes he would follow her to class or watch her at lunch, then return to his post as she slept in that childhood bedroom.

Eyes closed, breathing in his surroundings, sensing the inhabitants of the neighborhood, the daily worries that possessed them, he breathed until he disappeared, no longer a man standing and thinking, no longer a being with purpose. No longer a self, he allowed his hunger to just be hunger until it twisted and knotted and teetered on the verge of taking the essence it craved.

Eventually, it would not be denied.

* * *

MID-AFTERNOON.

Amber's grandmother was making lunch when a woman walked out of their house, pausing beneath the arching brick porch. Drayton held motionless. At no time had he felt her enter the brick Tudor or sense her inside. Her flesh smooth and molded around finely tuned muscles, taut over bare shoulders.

Amber was unharmed; he could feel her upstairs, sensed the focus of her study. Her grandmother was moving about, her thoughts of daily living and not the stranger now leaving through the front door.

Drayton followed.

She moved without purpose, a leisurely stroll through the downtown market, where tourists crowded for local goods, prints of seascapes, T-shirts and sweetgrass baskets. She stopped at a booth selling homemade fragrances, chatted with the vendor, a woman with a hoop through her eyebrow, and greeted strangers with a smile.

Drayton followed from a great distance, sometimes losing her in the crowd, a ghost in a sea of struggle. Temptation wrapped around him. Hunger gnawed his bones. And then she would appear again.

Who are you?

The question drove him forward and further. She wandered with no apparent destination, stopping at the pier to watch ships deliver containers to the port before moving north.

* * *

SHE SLIPPED between the headstones of Magnolia Cemetery as the moon hid behind clouds. She entered an old gate on the far side of the cemetery where Mors Eilif's remains lay. A rusted padlock hung loosely.

The shackle was undone.

Ahead, the alabaster gleam of the crucifix haunted the canopies. The iron bars of the Eilif family crypt were swung wide. Crickets and treefrogs announced his approach and masked the crackle of dry twigs beneath his boots. Drayton stopped on the concrete step. A musty atmosphere oozed from the darkness, a damp presence sliding over his cheeks and around his neck.

Drayton pushed the heavy door, the surface hard and cool. Palmetto bugs skittered in the dark. The moon eased from the cloud cover and seeped inside the crypt, touching a network of spiderwebs. There was a shelf on each side of the little room. No doors to enclose a coffin or bleached bones on display, just the hollow of darkness. Dust filled his nostrils. He reached inside a tangle of silken threads.

Empty. Both of them.

Not just empty, but choked with webbing. Mors's body wasn't there. It never had been. Drayton had witnessed the delivery of a coffin, watched Umi arrive for her final visit.

What was she doing?

"Did you find what you were looking for?"

The voice, her voice, crept out of the trees. Drayton bent at the knees then stepped out of the crypt. She slipped from the darkness as if the night had taken a woman's form, lithe and confident, and spat her out. The white of a smile shined.

"Tsk-tsk. What kind of predator are you, Drayton the taker?" She casually strode toward him. "Who are you protecting? Have you answered that question?"

Her laughter crawled over him, electric teeth that nibbled the back of his neck, a thrill ride that raised stubble on his scalp.

"You feel her, don't you? The girl. Why do you think she shows so bright? Why does she radiate so? I can feel it. The garden does, too. She's not even aware of how bright she shines, so kind and innocent. Aren't those the best ones, the innocent? Essence just slides out of a child so clean and fresh. And you left her all alone."

She stepped closer. Her scent, like her mind, scintillated his senses, humming in his head, spicy traces of muddy surf. His mind swept through her, a net attempting to capture fog.

Who are you?

"Who are *you*, Drayton? Would you like to know?" Muscles writhed along her arms. "You are not this noble highwayman, no. Not a young man who serves the dying as long as they pay your price. As if they could stop you. It must be difficult not knowing who you truly are. Is it? All these years to be a mystery to yourself."

His muscles ached. He was the prey, the deer, the antelope. She was no longer hiding in the weeds.

"There." She sensed his agitation, the coil of attack. "Feel what you are, the roots within you."

All these millennia, he'd never once sensed another like him. Centuries alone. Beautiful and dangerous, movements natural, fluid. *Where have you been?*

"Show me," she said. "Show me the man beneath the dignity. Let your true nature out, let it breathe. Let it eat."

She exploded with brilliance, a headlight plowing through him, shattering his identity, his thoughts scattered and blown apart, spilling the depths of memories from days when he was more beast than man. The smell of earth, the feel of it, the taste. The stink of death on his tongue when his flesh was scarred, his hair long and knotted.

"There."

His joints locked and helpless, flesh sealed in paralysis. In the pit of his belly, a fire roared. Its flame flashed behind his eyes and consumed his thoughts.

"Let it—" *hunger, bottomless* "—feed her."

She struck his neck, the webbing between thumb and finger crushing his windpipe. Head snapped back, breath trapped. Heels catching soil, curled fingers slashing his chest, flesh flayed long and bloodless, meat swelling before his back was to the earth. His soul, his consciousness—who he was—continued falling through time and space, drilling deep into his past, until it found the bottom of his true identity. His true purpose.

Where the animal lived.

Teeth bared, he sprang like gravity had no purchase, his body light and floating, clamping his hands around her throat, tendons springing from wrists. Arms locked, she turned her hips and threw his momentum to the side to keep his teeth—foamy with saliva—from tearing the carotid from her neck. Through the leaves, clashing through trees, they traded blows—slashing and gouging, kicking and twisting. Growls became furious roars, guttural explosions of animal lust.

Alive with carnal desire for the tang, the gush of essence to slake his throat and fill his hunger.

To take.

He lifted her above his head, one hand on her neck, fingers buried beneath her jaw. She clasped his forearms with both hands. He would break her in half, spill her organs. She wanted to loose the animal inside.

Eyes bulging, the color purple swelled on her tongue. Somehow, she squeezed out words that would be the last thing he would hear as the corners of her lips curved upward. Her dangling legs wrapped around his neck. Before the world went into a spin cycle.

"There you are."

PART III

Have good trust in yourself... not in the One that you think you should be, but in the One that you are.
  – Maezumi Roshi

DEAN MIDDLETON

Fucking dog.

The incessant barking bled through the couch cushion on Dean's head. No matter how muffled, how distant, he could still hear it. A commercial for zit cream was blaring ten feet from his head, but it was that fucking dog.

He heaved the cushion in the direction of his roommate's bedroom. Something crashed. A lamp or a photo or glass or something. "Goddamn it!"

He rolled off the couch and pulled the underwear out of his crack. The remote went bouncing on the floor. His Crab Shack T-shirt (*I Got the Crabs!*) crept up his belly. He pulled it down on his way to an open door and looked at an empty bed, the blankets swirled on the floor.

Fucker still wasn't home.

The dog was going nuclear. Bitch was supposed to be in the pen instead of running down imaginary squirrels. Something bit hard into his foot. Dean hopped his way back to the couch and stripped off a hanging sock. A chunk of glass ricocheted off the table. A red dab spread between his toes.

The dog kept going.

Sock in hand, he went to the window and spread the half-fucked blinds with two fingers. The streetlight was out. Dean flipped on the porch light. Boxhead—half pit, half boxer—was knuckled over at the chain-link fence. He tapped the window.

Something was in the ditch.

He slid into a pair of boots and winced. A warm stain leaked from the open gash. Laces dangling, he held the screen door open to get a look. Ordinarily, he wouldn't think twice. People dumped shit on the road all the time, but Boxhead wouldn't be trying to shove her giant head through the fence for a cardboard box.

"Hey."

She turned toward him and went right back to it. Dean stepped onto the porch. It looked like a bag of laundry.

"Holy shit."

He snuck up to the fence, his boots clunking through the dirt. The street was dark. Three more streetlights were out. The one on the corner was flickering a slow death.

The neighborhood was shit. People got smacked, car windows bashed, and drugs were o'plenty. But ain't no one ever died on a fucking doorstep. With the amount of shit in the house—the weed in the closet, Ziplocs of oxy—they didn't need a dead body decorating the front yard. He considered bailing or dragging it up the street.

He flipped his phone on.

Yeah, dead body. Not his roommate, though. This guy was black. *Black-black.* Maybe they got the wrong address.

"Shut up," he hissed at the dog.

She was going to wake up the goddamn neighbors. Dean chased her off. Bitch came back even louder.

"Shit. Shit, shit, shit."

He had to call the cops. No two ways about it. They weren't going to search the house. He could hide the oxys and, fuck it, let them have the weed setup. He didn't kill anyone, didn't do anything, just woke up and found a dead asshole in front of his house. Ask all the questions you want, that was all he knew.

He turned off his phone and looked around. No one was coming out. Dean slipped through the gate without letting the dog escape.

"Hey. You all right?"

He squatted down and, one last time, looked around for a parted curtain or cracked door. Even if they did, it was too dark to see anything. He patted the body's back pockets, reaching inside to see what he had. He reached around and searched the front pockets. The body rolled.

"Holy shit."

Dean fell on his ass. The face was collapsed like he'd just crossed a desert. The lips were pulled back, the gums dry. The eyes were set far too deep. He'd sucked on the long end of an industrial vacuum cleaner that shrink-wrapped his skin.

The shirt was shredded.

Four gouges had been carved out of him, deep tracks that went through the sternum. The insides were white and pulpy, like the flesh of cooked fish. A bear had opened this poor fuck up.

Dean forgot about looking through the last pocket. There was no smell, either. This was starting to look like a goof, some sort of real-doll shit that somebody ditched—some skeevy jerk-off got a little murder-rapey with a mid-twenty, black sex doll and ditched it after they got disgusted with themselves, or traded up for a teenage Asian doll with full O-lips.

The dog stopped.

He didn't see it happen. There was no blur, no sound. Dean felt an arm around his head, the icy hand over his mouth, the burning.

It was piercing at first.

Cool air stung the exposed tissues of his neck, teeth cutting through cartilage, tendons popping, muscle tearing. Air suddenly escaped through a hole in his throat. Something probed into his opened neck, a hot spike searching and finding an artery. His carotid stretched then popped. Then great suction.

The world faded with his eyes open.

13

ron.

It flowed.

His tongue pried the carotid open, spilling the contents. Drayton drank from the font for the first time in a century. It gushed over his tongue, dribbling off his chin. The man known as Dean Middleton rolled to the bottom of the ditch, his T-shirt riding up his torso, underwear wedging between his buttocks.

One boot was missing, a red spot on his sock. *Iron.*

There was no memory of arriving, just the rise of animal lust. Dean reeked of perspiration and the promise of blood. Drayton's instincts filled his belly, bathed in blood essence.

It renewed him.

He sat quietly, feeling for curious eyes. The road was dark. A siren was distant and fading. Calmly, he examined the wound on Dean's neck. Those were human marks. An investigation would conclude it was unlikely that a man or woman could bite through muscles and tendons like that. Still, those were human. That would be a problem.

The dog sat patiently. Panting.

Drayton unlatched the gate. She trotted over, eyes on the tattered shirt and wine-stained front, and sniffed the body, licking fresh specks from his cheek. Drayton pressed a thought into the dog's mind.

She sat. She waited.

Drayton walked to the end of the block. Two minutes later, a car stopped. The driver would not remember picking him up or detouring through Charleston to drop him off. Before he closed the back door, Drayton sent out a thought.

The dog began.

* * *

KOI—GOLD, white and orange—swam through reflections, lazy and fat.

Drayton cupped the water to his chin, rubbing away the stains, sticky and clotted. He stripped off the tattered shirt and dipped it, scrubbing the crimson stain from his chest. A pinkish cloud spread across the surface. The shirt in ruins, he tossed it in a wheelbarrow. His midsection was flawless—smooth flesh rippling over pecs and abs. No scar tissue.

Perfectly healed.

Drayton had experienced severe burns, bullets through the chest, spears in the gut. He'd fallen from cliffs onto jagged shores, floated out to sea. Fingers and toes had regenerated days later. His left arm had disintegrated in cannon fire. That had taken a month to return.

Never had he lost his head, and he wondered if that would end his life. For humans, the brain was the reservoir of thoughts and memories. Clearly, he was something else, but would it regenerate? Would he know what happened if it did, born again with his memories?

Is that why I don't remember the beginning?

She could've done it, could have removed his head if she wanted. She was toying with him, having fun. Pushing him. He was not alone.

What is she doing?

She'd dredged up the animal, triggered something deep within him, released the monster he had been, brought the savagery out. The taste of blood was still under his tongue, coating his throat. It restored his strength, made him new again.

Dean hadn't deserved that.

His moral fiber was questionable, but he was young. In time, he would grow, he would learn and evolve. Drayton had benefitted from thousands of years, his adolescence paved with death. Had he been judged for the folly of his youth, he would find a place in hell.

Perhaps I still may.

She'd infected him with the bloodlust again, and that uncontrollable urge had ended Dean's life. It also healed. Dean's suffering was acute and short-lived, but his sacrifice fed Drayton's need. There would be news of the accident. A neighbor would find his body. It would be assumed he'd bled out when the dog mauled him. No investigation would reveal the obvious.

Why lead me out to the cemetery? Did she want me to see the empty grave?

His instincts to leave the Lowcountry had abandoned him. He was now the prey, the victim, but he didn't know why or by whom. Confusion was a predator's best weapon. Drayton had walked into whatever this was—starting with a death request. Or maybe before that.

On the boardwalk.

Was that why he hadn't left the Lowcountry? Did she plant thoughts in his mind, create motivation that he had mistaken as his own? That was what he did to human prey. How would he know if these were his thoughts or hers?

A predator greater than Drayton flew higher in the sky.

The greatest predators in the universe did not run down their victims, did not struggle or risk their lives to feed. True power seduced. The victim gave himself knowingly, willingly. Embraced his own end.

Is that what I've done?

* * *

LIKE THE REST of the Garden House, the first floor was clean and organized. A series of spears were displayed in parallel arrangement. He swept his mind through the house.

The door was locked.

He took the spiral staircase to the second floor. Crumbs were on a plate, an empty espresso cup on the table. The French doors were slightly ajar. Drayton listened. A grandfather clock swung in the corner. The dining table cleared. The candelabra held candles, wicks still waxen and stiff.

A chill met Drayton as he stepped inside, uninvited. He had intruded upon many houses, had gone room to room to find husband and wife sleeping, children tucked in. It was easy to clip an artery on the wrist, leave the corpses for a family member to find in the morning.

But never was he nervous.

The kitchen was sparse. A teapot was on the stove. Up the grand staircase to the third floor, the bedrooms were empty, the beds without a wrinkle. There were no personal items, no pictures or toiletries, no laundry. The closets were in order. A narrow staircase led to the attic.

Drayton approached in perfect silence, resting his hand on the bannister. The steps protested his ascent, cracking and popping. He could see the pitched ceiling. An early morning sunbeam cut across the room, a square of light over the hardwood.

"You were not invited."

Young Mors turned without expression. Sunglasses reflected Drayton's image, bare feet wide, chest bare. Drayton's mind, renewed and sharpened, swept through him. Beneath the façade there was emptiness.

"Who are you?" Drayton said.

They stood with the room between them. Drayton stalked him. Curiosity piqued. How had he missed the obvious? He had assumed young Mors was a servant, then the grandson.

Did someone plant those assumptions?

Drayton bared his teeth. "Answer me."

He craved another tangle, something to awaken him further, a taste of something sweet and filling. The promise of satisfaction. The promise he knew was false, that should he devour the entire world, he would still crave.

"Who am I?" young Mors said. "Who are you? I don't know if you or I can truly answer that question." He clasped his hands behind his back and lifted his chin, as if offering the carotid. "Do you believe you will be forgiven?"

An eyebrow rose.

"Why are you here?" he continued. "The answer is in your true nature."

Drayton struggled with his words and their meaning. He was part of this game and no longer hiding. That was what coiled inside Drayton like a serpent squeezing his bones—the realization that the answer was right in front of him.

And he still couldn't see it.

Unaccustomed to this role, he fidgeted. His reflection looked back from young Mors's glasses, a dark figure in an empty white room. Fists clenched, emotions trembling.

He knows who I am.

Drayton forced his shoulders to relax, releasing the tension tying him together. His balance shifted. Mors smelled of perfume that could not mask the ancient odor emanating from his pores, an earthy musk mingled with cloves. The smell of Umi, the smell of the mystery woman and the old man Mors. It was obvious who he was.

But let's find out.

A lightning strike to the eyes, Drayton's fingers stiff as a spear aimed to take his sight. Next he would attack the genitalia and the throat—the animalistic instinct commanding his instincts.

Mors turned his head at the last moment. The edge of Drayton's hand grazed his temple. Hands still clasped, he turned his hips to avoid the front kick to the groin, countering with an elbow that sought to snap Drayton's extended arm.

Drayton parried, catching Mors before the blow could shatter his forearm. In the same swift motion, he spun and ducked, aiming a counterstrike for the throat. Mors was ready.

Back and forth, the dance unfolded. It continued with precision, a physical game of chess of high stakes. Mors's back to the window, shoulder blades touching the glass. Drayton pressed the attack, leaning into him. He would survive the fall.

Would Mors?

The fact that the fight had not already ended with Drayton lapping life from an opened throat had already answered his question. Now Drayton pressed with the urgency of animal lust. Mors, however, appeared to enjoy it.

A slight smile curled upward.

Before Drayton could shoot for the man's legs and drive him to the pavers below, Mors struck with an open palm. It drove into Drayton's sternum, the impact vibrating through him like a hammer on cold steel. The wind in his ears.

The wall crushed at his back.

Drayton slumped on the far side of the room. Plaster fell in sheets around him. On his knees, he prepared to pounce—adrenaline humming, heart fluttering beneath a cracked sternum.

Mors crossed the room.

It was a blur. A warning. He was toying with Drayton, moving at a speed that he couldn't match. Mors lifted his hand as if calling for a truce, reaching down to pick up a pair of glasses. One of the reflective lenses was shattered. He tucked the pieces into his pocket.

"Welcome home, Nassfau Rauttu."

The name drained the animalistic adrenaline. Drayton deflated onto his knees. Pectoral muscles attempted to reattach where they'd been blown apart by Mors's open palm.

"You *know* why you're here," Mors said. "You have lived a very long life, but not without purpose. Does that bring you comfort, Nassfau Rauttu? That all the bloodletting you brought to the world has not been meaningless. You are not the lion simply surviving. You are much more than that."

He slapped his hand around Drayton's arm and yanked him onto his feet, his smile as cold as his grip. Outside, a car door slammed. Drayton felt the familiar presence enter the garden. Mors leaned in, lips thin and dry, breath tickling his ear.

"All the essence you take… where does it go?"

Drayton fell against the wall when he let go, sliding to the floor. The indention dropped flakes of plaster.

Mors went downstairs. Drayton gathered himself and made it to his feet. The injuries were extensive. It would take days to heal. He made his way across the room and peered out the window. Amber trotted out of the guesthouse. Mors was there to greet her.

Protect her, he thought. *From who?*

14

The gates opened, slow and hypnotic.

Come, stay a while. Where have you been?

As the front tires touched the pavers, a sensation tugged Amber's belly, a swirl of wanting that drew her in. All was perfect.

The world exactly how it was supposed to be.

The garden was alive and buzzing. Inside her room, the drawings fluttered. She couldn't remember cracking open the window. Perhaps Mors had come up. She'd been gone so much, someone had to notice. She was still paying rent; why wasn't she sleeping here?

Because a very paranoid, very convincing maniac got in my head.

Her phone buzzed.

Speak of the tattoo.

She needed to answer one of his texts. He wasn't exactly timely with his replies, but at least he replied. Now he seemed desperate. The shine was wearing off the vampire conspiracy, and she was starting to see it for what it was. Paranoia was like that.

That's why it works.

She grabbed her book bag, not her art bag, and started down the steps. She would have to force herself to get in the Jeep and drive to

126

study group and not visit her tree just so she could see it, feel its warmth, its buzz, where time warped into minutes then hours.

"Hello." Mors stood outside the door.

Amber fumbled her book bag. Textbooks and notebooks slid out. She squatted down to pick them up.

"I'm sorry to hear about your grandmother."

A brief stall stretched into an uncomfortable silence. His smile didn't falter. Neither did he move to the side or offer to help. There was nothing wrong with her grandmother.

"I'm still paying rent."

"I just wanted to apologize for the last time we spoke. I hope it didn't upset you. We'd like to see you stay a bit longer."

Stay a bit longer? "My grandmother needs me."

"The gardener's gone."

"What?" The window above the barn was empty. Drayton wasn't there, but she still felt him watching. *I'm imagining that.* "He wasn't bothering me."

"Of course not."

"Why did he leave?"

"He has other interests."

"Where?"

He smiled a plastic smile. "I'm so sorry, where are my manners? Can I help?"

He caught a book escaping the crook of her elbow. Another one fell when her phone buzzed. She packed the books into her bag. Mors placed the last one, his icy hand grazing her fingers.

"Well, if there's anything I can do—"

"You've done enough, thanks." She hugged her bag on the way to her vehicle.

Mors stood there watching. A shadow moved away from the attic window in the Garden House. Someone was watching. After all that, it still hurt to leave.

* * *

This time it was a call.

Amber debated answering it long enough for it to end. There was no message. A few seconds later, it buzzed again.

"Hello?"

There was a long pause and clicking of toenails on hardwood floors. "We need to talk."

"I'm busy."

"How about tonight?"

The rabbit hole was deep and dark. Young wasn't going to quit digging in it, ever. This was his life, and hers, at the moment, was school. And she was way behind. Her notes were vandalized by daydreams. Even now she was feeling the ache of withdrawal. She had to focus. And not on hunting monsters under the bed.

"Where are you going now?" he asked.

"Coffee."

"I have coffee here."

"I'm meeting a study group. School is getting intense. You know how it is."

There was a quick sigh, sharp and pointed. She looked at the phone. The call had ended. He was smart and knew what she was saying. It was better if they just ripped off the Band-Aid. He'd been looking for Drayton all of his life, and she wasn't going to help. The least she could do was tell him he wasn't at the garden anymore.

Maybe it was better his dreams of finding him were left undone. A life without purpose wasn't worth living. What would he do when the search ended? Even if she told him Drayton was gone, it wouldn't stop there. If Drayton sat down with him and smoked a bag of weed and philosophized about life and death and proved he was just some wandering, modern-day nomad, it still wouldn't end.

Rip the Band-Aid.

The next time the phone buzzed, she decided not to answer it. It was followed by a text. He'd sent a link.

* * *

"Mucosa."

Perry, the youngest of the group, hummed a tune to remember the nervous system. He had moved from the Northeast and, in a Yankee accent, frequently reminded everyone how cold it was up north, how much he missed the snow and the people and the food. Good ole Southern manners would kindly remind him he could move back.

"I can't wait till this shit is done," he muttered.

"You sure you want to be a doctor?" Mary, a slim blonde from Tennessee, said.

"I'm sure I want to drive a Pagani."

"I don't even know what that is."

Amber was lost in the inky labyrinth on her coffee cup. Sharpie in hand, she was doodling scribbles that led back into a maze. A sharp eye looked out from the middle of it. Brooding, relaxed. Her style had become surreal. But there were always eyes.

Someone watching.

Young was emotionally unstable. A third grader could diagnose him, but it might be worse than that. She had thrown plenty of stones in glass houses, but this was entirely different.

It was human nature to find patterns in nature, to connect dots that made sense out of the world, predict behaviors, find threats, and determine shelter. When that tendency went off the rails, connections were fabricated. Random events began to make sense.

Paranoia fed itself.

His mind was a fiction factory, weaving story lines from events real or imagined. He'd even tattooed a childhood friend on his thigh to make him real. She'd had a friend like that when she was five years old. His name was Saucy, and he had long arms and waddled when he walked. His teeth were sharp. Should anyone come into her room, he would protect her.

She never tattooed Saucy on her leg.

"Amber." Perry snapped his fingers. "Where are your notes?"

"Oh." She put the empty cup down.

"Did you summarize the nervous system?"

"Was I supposed to?"

A quiet passing of glances. "What did you do?"

"Sorry. I think I missed that class."

"Yeah. You did. That's why you were supposed to do the summary."

The study group of six had been strong since day one. The Fine Grind Café was HQ, where everyone volunteered for an assignment, notes exchanged, information quizzed, old exams researched. Team effort would get them all a Pagani, whatever that was.

"I'll be right back." She shook the empty coffee cup.

There was a short line. Jimmy Pop, a skinny white guy with dreads, nodded at her. She held up one finger—a large medium roast. She could feel the study group watching while he filled her a cup. Perry was odds-on favorite to be the first one booted from the group.

Not anymore.

Amber stirred in creamer with a wooden stick, grabbing a moment to herself. If they wanted to send her packing, she would go back to the garden, climb onto a limb, and drop into the flow.

Am I doing this on purpose?

On the far side of the café, someone sat at a cluster of empty tables. A dog was by his side, tail sweeping the floor. The psycho alarm went off in her head.

Code fucking red.

What pheromone did she give off that attracted them? *You emailed him, Amber. Don't act like this is an accident. Get over there and finish it.*

Her hands were shaking. Coffee spilled over her fingers. She put the cup down on the table along with her phone. A tan puddle accumulated on the clean surface. She suppressed the smile she automatically offered to defuse awkward situations.

"How did you know I was here?"

An earbud was in his left ear, the other bleeding music over his shoulder. He appeared incapable of blinking—driving the psycho alarm up a notch—as he reached into a saddlebag to retrieve an empty coffee cup. Her doodles circled the café's logo. She'd left it at his house the last time she was there, and he'd connected the dots. *Real dots.*

"I'm not an ex-boyfriend."

"I didn't say you were."

She looked in the direction of the study group. They seemed to have forgotten her, votes already cast. *Your time here is over.*

The link he had sent was a news story about a man and his pit bull. Neighbors had found him facedown in a ditch, his neck gnawed on like a chicken bone, the meat torn away, the spine a boney attachment that kept the head from rolling off. The dog was asleep in the backyard.

"Tragic," Amber said.

"That's it?"

She knew what he was getting at. "Yeah, that's it, Young. A tragic thing, nothing more."

"He was drained of blood, Amber. Not an ounce left. They said his skin was a bedsheet, like he'd been strung up and bled out."

"That's what happens when a dog rips you open."

His chin moved back and forth, molars grinding. He looked off and pondered, crossing his arms. "I'm psychotic, right? Just another car on the crazy train."

"No, Young, I just—"

"You think you're the first one to analyze me? I'm delusional; I'm schizophrenic. It's nothing new, I get it. Look at me. I ain't normal, but I can see, Amber. I know what happened. You do, too."

"What happened, Young? Say it out loud, tell me what happened."

"A dog doesn't just gnaw open a throat then take a nap." He threw himself forward, almost coming out of his wheelchair. "He doesn't suck out blood, and the body doesn't bleed out, not entirely. You know that, Amber."

His voice dropped to a gruff whisper. "The dog was just a cover."

"A cover?" Amber shook her head. Now she looked away, biting her lower lip. It bothered her that she had connected those same dots when she first saw the story, had convinced herself while she doodled on the cup that his delusion was infecting her, that he was priming her to see things that weren't there.

"Smoke doesn't always come from a gun," she muttered.

"Remember, you came to me." He held up two fingers. "That's why I wanted another photo. I wanted you to think about what you were doing; I had to know you were seeing this. You are, Amber. You know it, and now you're scared. Just because you don't look under the bed doesn't mean monsters aren't there."

"Monsters aren't under the bed, Young!" She said it louder than expected. Even the study group looked up. "Drayton's not there anymore. They fired him. He moved on."

"You went back to the garden?"

"I live there."

"You're supposed to be at your grandmother's."

"It's just a garden, Young. The house is empty half of the time anyway." She was a child making an excuse, an alcoholic explaining why she needed a drink, that she could quit whenever she wanted. Maybe he was right, she was scared.

Scared I won't see the garden again.

"If he comes back, I'll let you know."

"You're moving back?"

"I'm falling behind, Young. I need my own space. I'm still paying for the room; I can't keep wasting money."

"Why are you behind?"

She'd missed more than one class. How many times did she climb into the tree and not come out until it was night, her stomach empty, dizzy with dehydration?

One drink is too many.

"Why are you so obsessed with him?" she said. "You ever ask yourself that?"

"There's something happening, and no one knows about it."

"Ever think it gives you purpose? That this treasure hunt gives your life meaning? When I told you about him, I invited you to the garden, and you refused. You didn't want to come see him. Why?"

"You came to me." He jabbed a finger at her. "Don't turn this around."

"You have a fucking tattoo on your leg, Young. Don't act like you're not advertising your…"

"Psychosis? That what you want to say? I've wasted my whole life, I'm too afraid to admit it? Because if I'm wrong about this, what else am I going to do with my life? I can't walk, can't get a job with these tattoos, what good am I? This is all just a waste of time, is that it?"

"*Delusion* is a waste of time."

"Why do you want to be a doctor? Was that your decision? Or is that just Mommy and Daddy whispering for you to make them proud?"

"I want to help real people with real problems. Do you see the difference?"

He held up his phone. The image of a man facedown in a ditch, stained shirt on display. "Like him?"

"A dog turns on its owner doesn't mean a man you're trying to remember from childhood is a vampire, Young. Two separate events, one is real and the other is not. You can't connect them."

"*Trying* to remember?" He pushed his hair back, earrings singing.

"You had a traumatic childhood. Memories can be skewed."

"A memory that looks like your gardener with the same name. That's a coincidence?"

It all made more sense before she started talking to him—his delusion was like a fucking virus. She wanted to tell him about Saucy, but the quicksand was getting deep. *Don't engage.* She'd suffered through her own family trauma and might be just as fucked up as he was.

But she wasn't hunting Saucy.

"I got to get back."

"A month." He held up one finger then nudged Samu. The golden retriever wiggled forward, tongue out and tail wagging. "Don't go back for one month. I just need a little more time. Stay at your grandma's for one month, that's all I'm asking. After that you can go back and have a nice life. I'll never bother you again."

Samu licked her hand. She had already decided on going back, and now he was asking her to wait. Fangs of withdrawal sank deep and venomous. She dropped her head.

It's a month.

He held out his hand. The palms of his gloves were ratty and frayed, the leather worn through the pads. She shook his hand and nodded. He popped the dangling earbud in and pushed out of the café.

Amber watched the door of his van open and the ramp unfold. His copilot climbed into the passenger seat.

A month. Have a nice life.

She didn't know what was more unattainable, waiting an entire month or having a nice life.

The study group didn't seem to notice she'd returned. Her coffee and phone were back where Young had been sitting. A queer sensation grabbed the back of her neck when she went back for them. The table had been empty when she put them down, she was sure of it.

Now an empty espresso cup was next to them.

DOUG AND ALLISON FREEMAN

Doug Freeman stood in a gutted kitchen.

Allison started the shower in the room directly above him. Exposed copper pipes rattled between wall studs. Water trickled down the drain.

An array of magazine clippings was spread on the floor, each a different vision of countertops. They had decided as a team what they were going to do, both agreeing the speckled granite would match the copper backsplash that had already been installed. This was their third flip. The first two took a year to complete and a toll on their marriage.

Never work with your spouse.

The window over the sink had been widened to provide a generous view into the backyard. Birds flitted around feeders. Allison didn't mind letting the squirrels have their share of birdseed, but she drew the line at cats carting off innocent birds.

Through the bones of the excavated wall, he could see straight through the front room. A horse trotted down the road with a carriage full of tourists. One of those gawkers would see the For Sale sign in the front yard. Their marriage was on life support, but their finances were nearly comatose. They needed to finish this flip before the debt collectors started making dinner dates.

And more fucking clippings weren't going to make that happen.

The shower turned off. The last of the water gurgled down the drain. A beer sounded off. As he flipped the cap into the trash, the realization that stress was a metal jacket became very apparent. If he put that fucker on, he could very well take it off.

It's really that easy.

Stress was a thought. And he didn't have to think about their finances or their marriage. If things worked out, great. If they didn't, great. The planet would still crash into the sun one of these days whether he was happy or sad. It didn't really matter. Life was life, and stop sweating it. He took a long tug of beer and felt the stress fall on the floor, actually heard it pile around his feet in heavy metal links.

Allison was watching.

She stood on the other side of the blank wall, a towel around her. Water dripped from her elbows. Drywall dust caked between her toes.

"You know what I'm thinking?" she said.

Doug nodded. Because he did know what she was thinking. She'd dropped the stress too. The stress lines, a permanent fixture on her forehead, had been erased. And they were both suddenly thinking the same thing. And it was fucking brilliant. Why were they slaving away with these houses?

"Greece."

"Greece," she said.

She opened the towel. Her skin was supple and warm. They made love on the floor, finishing loud and exhausted. They showered again, packed their luggage, and headed for the airport, taking all their money and leaving the flip half-finished. Let the bank worry.

They didn't notice the man in the driveway.

15

Drayton stood in the unfinished kitchen.

The back door was open. Near dusk, mosquitoes would move in in search of a blood meal and find none. From deep in the house, he could see the Tudor across the street. His mind empty, thoughts settled on a sandy bottom. Breath leaked through his nostrils as easily as the tides.

In the mornings, the Tudor would open. Amber would leave for class and return at dark. Sometimes he would follow. Mostly he waited in calm—almost comatose—repose. Careful not to wake the hunger that slumbered on the sandy bottom.

Her thoughts would bleed into his awareness as she returned home, drifting across the street, the space folding between them until they nestled in his awareness—her recent memories, her desire to return to the garden, her struggle to keep up with school. How her hand ached, her heart swelled to create. Counting down the days to when she would return, the days she'd promised Young she would stay.

Young.

Once upon a time, Drayton had sought refuge in the Northwest states, on the snowy peak of Mount Hood. It was there he'd met a delusional man seeking suicide. Young's father had had enough. He'd climbed the mountain with no intention of returning, stripping his coat off and inviting the cold to come and stay a while. Drayton had not stopped him. Before his final breath, the man had seen Drayton at his side and offered a request to help his family. It had been that request that had brought Drayton to the Lowcountry.

And Young still remembers.

Most men and women quickly forgot Drayton, as if he were nothing more than an inconsequential detail, a mundane event that vanished in a lifetime of routine. But Young was different. He remembered. He was searching. He'd warned Amber she was in danger, that things had changed. That maybe Drayton had too.

I have.

After Dean Middleton's death, Drayton's senses had sharpened. The noose of his desire tightened. Blood was a rich source of essence that beckoned.

Essence.

When she was in the garden, Amber's essence was a sea of endless promise. But outside the walls it paled, a faint glimmer of what shined when she sat in the tree. What magic had she tapped into? Some universal truth spilled through her, as if she were the wellpoint that pierced an impenetrable foundation and unleashed an aquifer of creativity. Space seemed to unfold when she was present. Paths emerged; trees appeared. Things grew. She gave to the garden, and the garden gave back, a loop that fed itself.

Drayton had become less certain. Reality was no longer a solid boardwalk for him to explore. He felt lost, a victim in a game he now realized he was forced to play.

He craved the garden, too. Craved that vitality, imagined the endless flow of essence filling him forever and ever. Never to be hungry again.

Protect her.

* * *

MIDNIGHT.

Throat constricted. Skin contracted.

Hunger wrapped around him like a veil of thorns, the second hand of time turning the winch.

He slung a thought into the night. Moments later, the back door creaked. The soft pads of a cat entered the kitchen. Arching her back, she rubbed against his leg.

Drayton reached down.

* * *

AMBER'S MIND stirred from slumber. She had coffee with her grandmother, their conversation trite. Shortly after, she left for class. The sun was up and the birds were at the feeders. Drayton remained in meditative repose until dusk. Casting his mind out to gather thoughts would only awaken the hunger. Following her would require too much energy to stay anonymous, putting him in crowds, where a scratch could awaken the savage.

That he could not risk.

Yellow-gray light colored the dusty windows. She would be returning for dinner soon.

A tiny bell rang.

His pulse quickened. An odor filled the house, an ancient mix of dust and earth, a pine box buried in the ground. It coiled around his throat, the smell slick and constricting.

A thin collar with a bell thudded at his feet.

"I release you from self-imposed moral bondage," she said, "and you eat the fucking cats?"

Beauty writhing in midnight flesh strode across the room. Deadly eyes resting, hips sliding. She approached with dangerous calm, bare feet crossing one in front of the other. Her mind as clear as mountain air, not a single misplaced thought. Pure presence, pure emptiness, her mind slithered around him with scaly finality. A cold breath breathing his bones until he was catatonic.

His body a coffin.

A moonbeam reflected off a bare shoulder as she passed through it. A slight curl of a smile dented her cheek. Nostrils flared as she slowed, rising onto her toes as she sniffed, inhaling him with animal curiosity, capturing every bit of odor that was him. A thin strap fell from her shoulder, exposing the top half of a petite breast. She paced around him, fingers trailing over his chest and down his arm, goose-flesh rising in their wake.

His flesh tingled, coolly.

Amber was across the street, her grandmother's head turning in the window. Slender fingers rode over his shoulders and caressed his arms, over his abdomen and groin. Liquid fire pumped through him.

Laughter softly danced.

The cemetery was a joke. The battle only meant to awaken blood-lust. He was incapacitated, completely helpless as her full lips, wet and warm, tasted his neck. Teeth nibbled his ear as her tongue probed inside. His desire roared into his midsection and swelled in his throat —savage desire he hadn't felt in centuries, the days when he would fuck women and men alike while he feasted on a wrist or neck, plunging deep inside to incite fear, tainting their blood with a sweet tang of horror.

She pressed her cheek against his arm—every touch driving spikes of wanting deeper—and stared at the Tudor. His mind a static whiteout suddenly opened like a window to allow Amber's presence into his awareness. She was looking at a text.

Macon was back at it.

"You know who I am," she whispered. "I am who I want to be."

On her toes, breath—sweet as basil—on his lips. Her small breasts against his chest, hardened nipples driving through his shirt. His erection swelled against her. Her lips travelled down his neck with small suctions, coming to rest in the hollow of his collarbone. She clasped his shoulders.

"You lost your way, Nassfau Rauttu." She cupped his swollen member and smiled. "Now you are found."

His shallow breath stopped. If his heart followed, he would gladly expire in the throes of this passion. His flesh, always winter cold, now baked like brick on a summer afternoon. She stepped back, one bare foot behind the other, a moonbeam capturing her vixen smile.

"Come now. Let's have some fun."

Paralysis thawing, hunger collapsing. He simmered in the throes of unrequited passion. If she was going across the street, there was nothing he could do to stop her. Maybe he wasn't a pawn in this game after all.

Merely a toy.

She was waiting beneath a streetlamp. Eyes closed, the moon full upon her, dark skin flawless and glowing. She inhaled deeply.

"I have been all over the world, Nassfau Rauttu, many times over. I always return to the Lowcountry."

She breathed the night air—a mixture of the nearby harbor and recent rain—then began walking down the middle of the narrow street. Sporadic traffic weaved around them without a glance or a word, completely unaware they were avoiding someone.

He followed behind her until she linked her arm around his, leaning her head on his shoulder like innocent youth, a deceptive young couple no one paid much attention to.

"It made me sad to see what you'd become. You are beautiful, Nassfau Rauttu, when you are insatiable. You're meant to enjoy them. Not to serve."

Never had he considered himself a servant of the human race but that of life. There was joy in that. Their essence wasn't theirs to give. It was something more fundamental. Drayton had come to believe he was undeserving of it. The least he could do was serve.

They approached the market where the sidewalks smelled sour, cigarette butts washed against the curb. Cars honked in swelling traffic. She stepped into the intersection without a care, and no one complained. Traffic narrowly missed them as a stream would flow around a boulder. She threw her head back and arms out, joy as bright as a full moon.

"You are the eagle that soars above the rest, Nassfau Rauttu, the predator that takes at will. You are essential to life. Accept it, be it. That is how you serve it."

"And who are you?"

She turned her smile on him. "There is always someone who flies higher."

Yes. She was the predator that flew above him, one who could feed on him if she chose. No one organism lived on top of the food chain. A microorganism could take down a bear as easily as the bear took a fawn.

Someone always flies higher.

The market was mostly tourists at the tables of local artists, looking at jewelry and T-shirts, carvings and prints. She moved without resistance, the crowd unknowingly giving way like the keel of a ship quietly splitting the ocean, Drayton following in her wake.

Speaking perfect Gullah, she stopped at a table displaying fragrances, the vendor a local who grew up on St. Helena Island, young and slender. She smiled back, as if she couldn't stop herself, and uncorked a bottle for her. She waved it under her nose then held it up for him to try.

Jasmine.

The fragrance unearthed a memory, pulling it to the surface and unpacking it. It was spring. Confederate jasmine was in bloom among the trees. A Confederate infantryman stumbled ahead of him, gray coat half buttoned, left arm dangling like a loose sock. Shoulder shattered, cheek blood-caked. Hand clutching a crumpled piece of paper.

The private had stopped sweating shortly after crossing the South Carolina border into Georgia, where he dropped his weapon. He had no use for it anymore, not for the war or his Southern brothers. There was only one thing he cared about.

The putrid smell of infection trailed him.

At the end of a rutted sandy drive, he fell for the last time. The stately house with white columns and a generous porch was within sight. He began to crawl, the left arm dragging in the dirt. He collapsed with a grimace and a sob. The piece of paper long since dropped.

Private Nassfau Rauttu of the 2nd Louisiana Regiment knelt next to him.

His hunger satisfied a hundred times over, he had followed the soldier off the battlefield. He didn't know why. Perhaps it was curiosity. No longer blinded by hunger's greed, he accompanied the soldier on the long journey home. Now only a few hundred yards from the front door, Nassfau Rauttu picked him up.

He carried him up the stairs to a bedroom that overlooked a sprawling plantation of last year's crops still in the field, withered and fallen. There a young woman lay with a swollen belly. A wet nurse applied a cloth to her forehead. Her parents looked up from the bedside as Nassfau Rauttu laid her husband next to her.

Drayton Pickett.

Under normal circumstances, there would be panic at the sight, revulsion at the smell that entered. Nassfau Rauttu eased their minds, wiped their thoughts and froze their emotions. They watched with a distant sense of alarm as he stood back and watched the soldier turn his head, a breath puffed through cracked lips.

She took his hand.

Neither she nor the child would survive. Drayton Pickett was in the presence of his family, next to his wife and unborn child. Nassfau Rauttu experienced the sweet release of essence pass from them. Without the tang of blood, it was cool and light. That was the day he no longer wanted to be Nassfau Rauttu.

The day he took a different name.

Drayton snapped out of the memory, returned to the market and watched her tuck the bottle into her pocket and give the Gullah woman a fold of cash.

"*T'engky*," the Gullah woman said. *Thank you.*

"Compassionate, Nassfau Rauttu? Is that what you think you've become?" She reentered the pedestrian flow. "Fear is their birthright. It drives them. It is the fence that corrals them. We are above that."

A young couple was pushing a carriage. She reached inside to retrieve the infant. The parents did not protest. They simply watched as if a family member was doting on their precious. A toothless smile appeared as the child playfully swung his arms.

"You believe the lion feels guilt"—she put the infant back and pinched his nose—"for eating the antelope's newborn?"

Drayton followed as a child would trail his mother, standing aside as she joked with a basketweaver, sharing a laugh before buying the woman's most expensive piece then, twenty steps later, giving it to a homeless veteran to sell.

Has she been watching me all this time?

"You can't save them, Nassfau Rauttu."

"They ask forgiveness."

"In their final moments, you hear desperation. Wasted lives wishing it would have been different. You offer absolution when you have none to give. We are part of this world, but we are not of it. They are the prey, Nassfau Rauttu. No shame in that. That is balance."

They crossed the street. She leaned against the wall. A group of girls marched up the steps toward Market Street Saloon, a bachelorette party with glowing rings around their necks. The bride-to-be was wearing a veil that had fallen to the ground a few times.

"Who are you?" Drayton asked.

"Is that such a mystery?"

She looked out of the corners of her eyes. A little mole on her cheek jabbed by a sly smile.

All this time, he thought, *you were out there.*

"I already had company." She shrugged his thoughts away. "We may be immortal, but that doesn't mean we don't need to be entertained. You've spent all these centuries in some lofty pursuit of karmic balance when you know the scales don't exist. There is no life after this, Nassfau Rauttu. There is only this moment, as it exists now. Everything else is a thought. You know this."

She took his hands and turned them over.

"Honestly, Nassfau Rauttu, I felt sorry for you. Denying yourself your birthright. You know how it feels to be in touch with your true nature, the taste of it. Your charade was amusing but tiresome. I couldn't simply sit back and watch anymore."

The doors at Market Street Saloon opened. Music heaved out on a cloud of perspiration. A small group of college students fell onto the sidewalk.

"The cemetery?" Drayton said. "Where is Mors's body?"

"Yes." She smiled. "Like I said, we need entertainment. It was fun, wouldn't you agree? The mystery woman in the pool, following me and challenging. Don't you find it interesting to not know everything?"

She raised her eyebrows.

"I mean, all these centuries you read these fools, you know their thoughts and motivations, you control their desires with nothing to fear. And now there's something you don't know. A little treat, Nassfau Rauttu, as I reintroduce you to your roots. You can thank me later."

"This is the game you're playing? You and Umi and Mors. You've brought Amber into this for entertainment?"

"Oh, it's more than that. And Amber is not innocent. In fact, she's the reason you're here."

She leaned onto the sidewalk. Three young men had just stumbled out. Hair mussed, clothes wrinkled.

"Pardon me," she said. "Do you have a light?"

There was a moment of indecision; then they all reached for a lighter. She waved, and two of them kept walking. The third one cupped a flame. Drayton recognized the curly hair and flip-flops. A dirty bandage frayed from the big toe.

"And a cigarette?" she said.

"You just want it all?" Macon said.

"Why, yes. I do."

His entourage lost interest, had already forgotten about the barefoot woman with the sheer summer dress and feisty hips. He found a bent cigarette and lit it for her.

She looked back at Drayton. "Want to play?"

MACON LEARY

Freak.

She found a gospel channel and turned up Jesus till the speakers were bleeding. But when she started singing and clapping and that strap fell off her shoulder, that little titty popped out and almost knocked Macon off the road. He yanked the wheel, and she looked sideways at him and, swear to God, his cock moved like it was on a leash.

She was fucking radiant. Not a dash of makeup, as far as he could tell; had those eyes with bottomless pupils, big and round and wired.

"You like to party?" she said.

A wink and a smile and he was almost on the curb again. He leaned over and opened the glove box, drifting into the wrong lane as he dug deep. She pulled his arm out and retrieved a bag of weed then laughed hysterically.

"Fuck's so funny?"

A coal of anger fired up his belly. The way she unrolled his stash sounded like she was laughing at a small dick. He wasn't a fucking comedian, not down there. She was about to find out he was no laughing matter. Not down there.

Macon checked the rearview.

A gut check told him to keep an eye behind him, like someone might jump out of the backseat. *This could be a setup,* he thought.

Then the thought went away.

She laid her head on his shoulder, fingers dragging across his chest then crawling to his lips. She put two fingers in his mouth. They were musty and damp like a dead twig or dirty root, the taste hitting his brain like a gasoline trail.

He wanted more.

"Take the bridge."

The tip of her tongue was in his ear. His balls tingled like nine-volt batteries. She cupped his package then went back to praising the Lord. Images of plowing her in the backseat while the church choir raised him higher flitted through his head. His jaws clenched. If his prayers were answered, then indeed he would give credit to the Lord and savior.

The rearview mirror was still clear.

While her groove rolled on, Macon dug his phone out. With one hand on the wheel, he snapped a shot of her bouncing, head down and shaking and a whole lot of mumbo jumbo coming out of her mouth. If she started speaking in tongues while he was six inches deep, he wasn't going to last long. A dose of GBH might cool her down and put them both in the right head space, make this night last and last.

The Lord works in mysterious ways.

The tires galloped over the line as he thumbed a text. He had to send a pic of this crazy bitch to his boys. They had to know. Maybe he'd set up the phone and film a backseat party. His resumé had a long list of white chicks and one Hispanic.

First black.

He wrote that then deleted it. *Imma smash,* he thumbed. The tires rode the lane reflectors again with a steady rhythm before he hit send. He got the car straight—

Something isn't right.

He was staring at the Arthur Ravenel Bridge—the enormous

diamond-shaped concrete towers that supported the cable-stay bridge crossing the Cooper River. There were two of them. He was staring at one of them. He couldn't remember if he'd sent the text. His phone wasn't in his hand. The car was parked.

The radio was off.

They were in the middle of the bridge. Cars whipped past at fifty miles an hour, the vehicle shuddering in their wake. He turned his head in slow motion. Details starting and stopping, jittering.

"Let's get high."

She was in the passenger seat. Her hair cut so short, her skin so dark. Eyes so big. A painful erection pulsed against his leg. The scene flickered, and she skipped in space like a strobe light. She was there then not, the passenger door open.

A car honked.

Macon jumped back. He was high as fuck and parked on the bridge. Someone would call the police in minutes. This bitch was crazy for real.

And then he got out.

It happened like that. All the worry and concern just—*poof*—gone. Like putting down a bag of bricks. Rules and laws were manmade, man. She was more than that. She was real life.

He followed her like a wolf on a wounded animal. The trail led to the tower, where a door was open. He'd gone in that door before; it had been a field trip in grade school. They'd ridden to the top of the diamond and looked over the city. It had been cold that day and windy.

She was waiting inside.

He wondered why it was open or how she got it to work, but those legit concerns played like sirens in the distance that had nothing to do with him. He wanted to fuck.

She was in the corner, bare foot hiked on the wall as the doors closed. He leaned into her, her scent drawing him like a shark in tainted waters—an earthy tide filled with sweet and endless promises. Her lips tasted spicy.

The rise of the elevator gushed into his groin. His legs weakened as she tore his shirt off. He ripped the thin straps off her shoulders and put a dime-sized nipple in his mouth. Her small-dick laughter stabbed but didn't stop him.

His insides were roaring.

She bit his lip. A coppery taste flowed into his mouth. She shoved him into the corner. For her size, she was strong. Clenched and smiling, he stared unblinking from hooded brows. He snatched her up, hand around her throat.

Slammed her on the wall.

She smiled back and hooked her heel around his waist. He sucked her tongue out of her mouth and bit down until he tasted her juices then flipped her around and shoved her face into the corner. She didn't scream.

She fucking moaned.

He folded the back of her dress over the curve of her ass— perfectly round, flawlessly smooth. Kicking off his flip-flops, he peeled off his jeans. His cock sprang out throbbing. Wet and warm, he slid it between her heart-shaped buttocks and shoved every inch inside her.

Eyes fluttering, he shuddered. Hands on her hips, one long stroke and he reached for her neck, wanted to choke her as he came—

"The fuck!"

For a second, someone was in the elevator, some black motherfucker next to them. And the bitch wasn't bent over and his cock wasn't inside her. He was completely nude with a full hard-on and humping the air like a dog. And she laughed. She laughed that small-dick laugh.

I am tripping fucking balls.

A sheen of sweat suddenly drenched him, turning frigid as nighttime huffed into the elevator. Fear trickled into his noodling legs, but desire still fueled his penis. Images of forcing himself inside her as vivid as the concrete wall. Black mamba danced, tight hips rocking.

"You like to play." She gestured with both hands.

He was prepared to fall on his knees and beg. He practically whimpered. His skin shrank and dimpled, the frigid air momentarily stealing his breath. She leaned against the wall. Something fluttered over the railing. It was his clothes.

"Dance for me."

Automatically, his knees wobbled back and forth; then his hips began to gyrate and thrust. His erection bouncing, scrotum shriveling like wet leather, he heard her laugh.

He wanted to stop.

The fire that warmed him was doused, a cool dunk of water killing whatever desire that, seconds before, had been consuming him. He was naked and out of control, the stars above and the wind inside him, watching the crazy bitch climb onto the railing, bare feet balanced on the ledge.

Arms out.

A bubble of snot popped in one of his nostrils, eyes blurring with tears. He quivered as he danced, convulsed as he jumped up and down. Sobs clogged his throat as he moved closer to the wall, jittering as he tried to stop. Her dress snapped around her knees.

He climbed next to her.

The water black and ominous, moonlight rippling five hundred feet below. A salty stream of snot quivered off his chin. He couldn't feel his legs.

"P-p-please..."

She slid one hand on his cheek. The wind was frosty; her palm numbed the side of his face. Her expression was dead, eyes deep and black like ancient tombs.

Something sharp nicked his neck.

A warm slick pooled next to his collarbone. It came in spurts. Someone was with them, standing on the ledge. It was a man as dark as she was. A man with hunger in his eyes. A vague and distant thought occurred to Macon as he heard an animal feed on raw meat.

I've seen him before.

Macon felt the popping on tendons and a wet suction. A sharp tongue. The wind picked up and began to howl in his ears. The stars spinning. Her hands clutched his face, eyes boring into his while the man greedily nestled on his neck.

He realized they were falling.

16

An early breeze swept through the cordgrass, muddy flats exposed in low tide. Tiny crustaceans raced near the water's edge. A hazy odor hung in the crawling current.

Sunlight glinted off a side-view mirror.

A long cable was attached to an overturned truck and stretched to the nearest shore. A group of men and women stood near a tow truck. An ambulance was ready, but they wouldn't find a body. Macon Leary would float to shore later that day, half-eaten by the ocean, nearly unrecognizable. Nude and puckered, bits and pieces soggy or missing.

A pale empty sack.

They'd identify him, connect him to the truck that had been run off the bridge, and assume he'd washed through the windshield. The accident had occurred sometime in the small hours. A kayaker reported it at dawn. A Ziploc of Xanax was in the glove box along with several ounces of marijuana.

His friends would be in shock, but not surprised. Macon Leary was a wild one. No one, though, would ever know how he'd danced nude on the diamond tower, snotting down his chin. How he'd shriveled in the cold, warm crimson rivulets trickling down his arm.

A blue heron glided over a long dock, came to rest on a sea-green post, and folded its wings with an eye on Drayton. His boots toed the edge, water lapping beneath the boards. Guilt did not weigh on him; there was no remorse for taking blood that spilled freely. His instincts had seized control when she'd nicked his throat with a thumbnail.

Footsteps echoed on the boardwalk, the dock shifting. Barefoot, she watched the tow truck pull the cable taut, her dress stuck to her legs.

"Humans are born and die. They are the turn of the wheel." The truck turned over as the tow truck's whine echoed off the bridge. "We are not evil or good, just or unjust. We are, Nassfau Rauttu."

"Or are we parasites?"

She tugged the bottom of his shirt, the front stained from the gush of Macon's last moments. He let her peel it over his head. A new shirt was large for his torso, a collared shirt with thin horizontal stripes. His jeans were heavy and wet with streaks of mud.

Her dress was damp but clean, clinging to the curve of her hip, the shape of her breasts. She was a perfect form of a woman—power and danger disguised as frailty. Lust did not stir within him, did not take control, although he was certain she could light that torch if she wished it to burn. Her power over him had been clearly demonstrated. Over them.

Unparalleled.

Perhaps she indulged in the fleshly pleasures from time to time, taking on a strong young man before nipping an artery as he achieved orgasm, dripping his life into her open mouth as she drove him deeper inside. Drayton had done much the same, but he'd evolved beyond animalistic pleasure, something beyond intellectual stimulation or spiritual awe. Why would she play with such base emotions?

"What are you hiding?" he said.

She brushed the wrinkles from his shirt. "Am I the one hiding, Nassfau Rauttu?"

His past was hidden, even from himself. *Maybe I don't want to remember.*

"I don't trust you," he said.

With a quick smirk, she stood on her toes and kissed his chin. "Should you?"

The truck was lodged in the muck. The emergency response team was considering other ways to pull it out. It would be hours before they cleared the scene, eventually connecting a body testing positive for drugs and alcohol to the truck. No investigation would follow.

An elderly man was waiting for them in the carport of a sprawling vacation home. A textiles industry CEO, he would run mundane errands—a half-gallon of milk and a carton of yogurt ten miles from home. He wouldn't have a good reason for driving so far. He also wouldn't remember the young man and woman in the backseat.

There was nothing he could do about it.

17

———

There was a delicate thumping on the window.

A fly crawled along the sill, momentarily cleaning its wings before throwing itself against the glass again. It would do that until it starved. Freedom a fraction of an inch away, the promise of another world it could see but never reach.

Amber had been staring at her notes for an hour. The diagrams and photos, the complex formulas and symbols meant nothing. They were meaningless. She had filled the margins with intricate doodles that circled the page and leaked between the lines.

Was this her parents' dream?

She wanted to help other people, but everything felt so empty now. The pencil had become merely a stick of wood. The paper just paper. Sitting in her grandma's house, the stagecoach was just a pumpkin.

I can't even help myself.

Her dad had had a sunfish sailboat. When life got heavy, he'd shoved into the water to find a lonely spot off the coast to camp. He'd return toasted from the sun and with batteries fully charged to find Mom somewhere in the garden with a pile of weeds. They'd both had jobs to pay the bills.

But passion pumped their blood.

Amber wanted to draw, but not here. Not banging her head against a cold window. Her passion was waiting for her somewhere else. Did bills need to be paid if the blood wasn't pumping?

She dumped her notes and went downstairs.

Grandma was sitting in her chair. The news was on the television. Amber sat on the couch. She'd tell her about moving back to the apartment after dinner. Red lights were on the news. Police waded through the low tide toward an overturned accident.

She recognized the truck.

* * *

It was hot for April.

The sun was bearing down on a blue canvas tent. Immediate family was gathered beneath its shade. The overflow gathered around it. From inside, the preacher's voice beseeched the heavens to look upon them all with love and comfort, to hold them in their moment of grief. Amber could hear the sniffling from her distant perch far outside the tent.

She really didn't want to talk to anyone.

Macon was a piece of shit; that was a fact. She wasn't there to pay her respects. This was someone who'd once come home without his underwear and called her a whore. A tiny bit of her hoped he'd suffered before he died. For that, she felt guilty. But she wasn't there to be absolved of guilt or out of some misguided cycle of abuse.

She came for inspiration.

This was a reminder that it could all end with a reckless night, one misjudged turn or passing out behind the wheel. She wondered if he had been awake to feel the truck hit the water, whether he'd heard the glass break or felt the ocean nibbling at his face. She hoped he at least had been awake long enough to regret his life. Death was easy. Amber was here to remind herself of that.

She wanted to live.

Is that what Macon was doing, squeezing the juice out of life? Did he play hard because he loved to live or because he was afraid to live?

She wanted more than simple pleasures, wanted to connect. She couldn't feel the trees or the earth anymore, not like she did in the garden. Birdsong didn't flutter in her chest; dew didn't comfort her heart. She wasn't going to plod through life to get it over with. If she was going to do that, then might as well pack up and make a sharp left turn between the bridge towers. She wasn't going to let life be meaningless.

Someone else was watching from a distance, standing under a willow oak. Hands in his pockets, he stared through mirrored glasses as the preacher finished his prayers.

Mors walked off.

He meandered between the tombstones, occasionally stopping to read a faded inscription. No car was waiting for him. He crossed the road on a long walk home. She wondered if he knew the family. She knew he didn't.

The congregation began to shuffle. Macon's family stood at the head of the casket. Uncles and aunts, cousins and nephews were among them. Frat brothers meandered outside the tent. Family would return to the house. Friends would gather on the beach and pour drinks on the sand. Later, they'd go to a bar. They'd drink all night and drive home.

For Macon.

A van was parked behind the waiting cavalcade. The window was down. A tattooed arm hung out, inky vines and muscled branches winding around.

Jesus, she thought. *The flies can't stay away.*

Macon was dead, Mors was lurking, and Young was stalking. She was a beacon for the weird and the brooding. A hard line of percussion grew louder as she approached the van. A dog was in the passenger seat, tongue out.

"Why are you here?" she said.

"Why are you ignoring me?"

Cars pulled around the van. The family was still back at the tent. She sighed deeply.

"Let me guess. You think Drayton did it." She pointed at the tent.

"Let's say he did. Let's say all of this is true, that a vampire is loose in the Lowcountry. Can you stop him?"

"That's not the point."

"That is the point, Young. Your obsession is the point, face it. Pack and leave fantasyland before you end up like Macon."

"Is that what you're doing, facing reality?"

"I'm willing to change."

He watched the family retreat toward waiting cars. "Do you know how a slaughterhouse works?"

Amber crossed her arms and looked away. This was the last time they were doing this.

"Cattle are raised on a farm until they're ready for harvest," he continued. "That's when they're funneled toward a building. One by one, single file, they willingly walk through the door on four legs and come out in packages because they don't know any better. If they're lucky, they don't feel the bolt between their eyes."

He nodded at the tent.

"Drayton can do that. He can plant a thought in you, Amber. He can make you walk through the door or drive off a bridge and make you think it was your idea."

"Macon was a fucking idiot, Young. He played chicken and lost, and no one over there is surprised, trust me. He didn't need a vampire to make him do it."

Some heads turned down the road. Maybe they heard; maybe it was just the volume or the tattooed creep with a dog that caused them to stare. She didn't care.

"They said the neck was torn open."

"That happens to floaters, Young. Every poor bastard that drowns feeds sharks, not vampires."

He looked across the cemetery. Mors's distant figure had reached the gates. It took her a moment to realize he was watching Mors. Young reached between the seats and held a jump drive between two fingers.

"The facts, Amber."

"That's what these are, facts? Are you going to send them to the newspaper? Post them on a blog or social media with all the other airtight theories on aliens and government mind control, only this one is about vampire aliens that seeded the world with humans to farm them? *No, really. This is true. Crazy but true.*"

"You're afraid."

"Even if it's true"—she rolled her eyes—"what are we going to do, Young? Not one steer has escaped the slaughterhouse. They all get the bolt. If what you say is true, then we're going through the door no matter what. And you didn't answer my question. Why do you care so much about Drayton?"

His eyes were empty, maybe tired. This was why he didn't tell anyone what he was doing, why he'd spent years on this journey alone. The world would belittle him just like she was doing.

"He's real," he deadpanned. "You saw what he did to Macon at the Garden House. And he's not the only one who can do that."

He shoved the jump drive in her hand.

"They're hiding in the open. Once you see it, you'll realize they're not really hiding at all. And no one cares, Amber. Everyone stays in line and follows the person in front of them."

The jump drive felt hot and sweaty. The plastic creaked in her palm. She wanted to throw it into the sea of granite headstones.

"You ever thought about why you still remember Drayton?" she said. "All the people he must've met, the ones you said he helped, and no one remembers him. Only you, Young. Why do you think that is?"

He cast his gaze through the windshield again. "I could make some shit up, call it an accident. Maybe I'm special. Truth is I don't know. I'm only telling you what I do know. I'm not going to the slaughterhouse quietly."

The music suddenly thudded from the van. She felt it in her chest. He pulled away, hands on the steering wheel controls. Samu watched her recede behind them. Amber stood there until they were down the road.

She went for a walk around the cemetery. By the time she got back to her car, the tent was down. Workers were packing up.

The jump drive was still in her pocket.

18

"Shit."

Grandma let go of another one. It was something she did when no one was around, if something spilled or broke. *Shit-shit-shit.*

Amber fell on her bed. This wasn't how she wanted it to go. She was set to dance her way back to the garden, and now a jump drive was in her pocket with the weight of a ship's anchor.

Her phone had been silent. The study group was dead to her. She'd been pruned out. They'd moved on and so did she. But moving on suggested there was somewhere to go. Self-doubt was a childhood friend that never seemed to go away.

Why aren't I packing?

She made the mistake of looking up more details about Macon's accident. There were reports of his truck sitting on the bridge with the doors open. But no one saw it actually drive off the bridge, and there were some inconsistencies about how his body was flung from the truck and how it got so far away. Not really a deal breaker as far as the police were concerned, given the level of booze and dope in his system. And his history.

Throat torn open, one source claimed. But ocean life could do that. *Because there were no passengers, and there are no vampires.*

She dug the jump drive out of her pocket and plugged it into the laptop. There was only one file. If it was more nonsense, she could empty her pockets of guilt and return to the garden without inviting self-doubt to come along. A Word document was dated and written as someone would write an old-fashioned letter to a pen pal.

Dear Amber,

You're reading this. I knew you would. You want the truth. That's why you came to me the first time. Somewhere inside you, you know something is wrong. You knew it when Drayton handled your boyfriend. It didn't make sense then. It still doesn't.

That first day she went to the garden, she'd felt something special. It was the view from the room and peaceful environment. But then there was the way she felt when she began drawing, the way time stopped, the way she was transported by her imagination, the liveliness of the ground beneath her. It didn't make sense, but she didn't want to lose that.

Nothing is an accident, Amber. I have a tattoo on my leg. You saw it before you ever went to the garden. You came looking for me, and here we are. Your parents died when they were relatively young. So did mine. You ever think about that? Maybe Drayton was there when they died, too. Maybe that's the connection between us, between you, me and him.

Or maybe you're right.

I'm just some tattooed kook, and all this is purely chance. I'm a little unhinged, I can't argue that. But we all connect imaginary dots, Amber. You too. You're making up all sorts of reasons to go back to the garden and skipping over all the ones telling you not to. I get it.

Our senses are all we got to translate the universe. Ever think of that? All we can do is see, hear, taste, touch and smell. That's all we got. All that input goes into our brain, we make sense out of it, they become memories, we use those memories to see patterns, and voila.

Here we are again.

I can't convince you Drayton is who I say he is. You can use your memories to come to a different conclusion, one that fits your needs. We all do it, but it doesn't make me wrong. I can show you all the evidence, all the times he stood in the corner of operating rooms dressed in plain clothes or observed someone drawing their last breath on ICU. No one else seems to see him but me.

I can't explain that, either.

Maybe I'm certifiable and making all of this up, or maybe he's something else. Either way, there's a history of him with dying people. He was around during the Civil War, and maybe before that. I don't know if he was always like this, or if he still is. I don't care if you believe in him or not.

But the garden, Amber. The garden is different.

Amber got up to pace. She had been clenching the chair as she read. Her arms ached, her neck stiff. Tears were building on her lower lids that refused to blink. She was afraid this would happen. He was right about one thing: she didn't care about Drayton anymore. He was gone. Her parents had died of natural causes. There were no bite marks, no missing throats. If he wanted to suck the city dry, it wouldn't affect her.

But the garden.

Standing behind the chair, she read from a distance.

The Garden House is the largest residential property in Charleston. You probably already knew that. The walls enclose just over two acres. It was one of the first houses built in 1670, when Charles Town was born. A wall was built around the property, bricks stacked high enough that no one could see inside. Even then, there were rumors of the lush garden despite no evidence of slave labor.

Text was hyperlinked to historical documents—universities, the Charleston Historical Society, Wikipedia pages. She clicked and scrolled.

Hard to believe the first house built was so large and extravagant. Some historians have said the same thing, I'm not the only one. Charles Town was under frequent attacks from land and sea. It was the French and the Spanish and pirates and general marauders that invaded the area. The Garden House is only one of three buildings still standing from that time—the Powder Magazine, the Pink House, and the Garden House. The first two are not even close in size and preservation. And only the Garden House is thought to be haunted.

Even back then.

The Gullah decided this was the center of haints. It was said that very few people went inside the garden. But late at night, every now and again, someone would just get up and leave their house. They would go through the gate as if it was unlocked for them. They would never be seen again.

A link took her to a Gullah website with dozens of urban legends. Gullah had started on the islands outside Charleston, a rich culture that existed before Charles Town. A haint was a ghost and for some reason didn't like the color blue. And that was why Charleston houses had haint-blue ceilings on their porches and sometimes doors and around the windows. In the country, you could see blue bottles on branches.

To keep the haints away.

Then there was the landing of the famous pirate Edward Teach. Blackbeard. This was 1718. He took hostages, demanded ransom, and then let them go before sailing up the coast, but not before leaving behind his flagship, Queen Anne's Revenge. It was mysteriously shipwrecked and abandoned with all its treasure aboard. It was reported that the crew had all died rather suddenly, found scattered upon the deck. It didn't say they were bloodless, but it was described as if the reaper's scythe had impaled them with the tip of the palest blade. As if the full moon had bleached the life from their flesh.

All of this is history, and I know history is a record of a man's wits. There's no evidence otherwise. Like I said, the senses can be fooled and memories duped. So maybe I'm still connecting imaginary dots. There's nothing here to convince you not to go back to the garden. But in 1861, a portion of the city was burned. Very few buildings in that part of town survived.

The Garden House did.

She clicked a link. The website described the fire that torched one hundred and sixty-four acres of Charles Town. It took some scrolling to find what he was referring to. The townsfolk fled the fire, but many of them abandoned their homes and families to protect the Garden House from the flames. Some speculated the fire would have been much less damaging if so many of them hadn't been obsessed with protecting that one house.

Abandoned their homes and families, she thought.

In 1865, William Tecumseh Sherman led Union soldiers through the South. He ravaged Atlanta and burned Columbia to the ground. But he spared Charleston. No one knows why. Historians guess he had a fondness for the city, having lived there once upon a time. After the war, he returned for a visit and was heartbroken to see what the war had done to it. It didn't say if he went to the Garden House. I don't know what that would mean if he did. But there is this.

Another link.

This one she hesitated to click. So far, it read like a history lesson with Young's interpretation. Maybe he'd omitted the facts that didn't fit his fairy tale and molded the ones that did. For some reason, this link felt like the pin that would hold it all together.

When she clicked, she heard it fall into place.

It was a website that displayed photos from the Civil War. Restored with amazing clarity, the repository showed everything from portraits to artillery to infantry. Young's link, however, went directly to a photo of Charleston. This part of town had been laid to waste—piles of rubble and portions of brick columns stood like broken teeth. Charred beams. The semblance of a street. Amongst it all, a single house stood, the brick wall around the property still intact. On the second-story porch, a man and a woman sat like spectators. It was too far away to see the details, but she didn't need to see them.

Mr. and Mrs. Letum Eilifuer built the Garden House in 1640. Letum is the version of another name. That name is Mors. And Eilifuer, as I'm sure you already have guessed, was shortened.

There's no telling if it's the same Mors and Umi Eilif that live there today, so I'm back to connecting imaginary dots. All those haint-blue porches that surround the Garden House and the Gullah folklore is just my own imagination.

But this isn't.

The letter didn't end with a sincerely yours or a plea for her to reconsider. No PS, either. It was three links.

One was labelled Mors, the second Umi, and the other Eilif. She hovered over them and saw they led to Wikipedia pages. Her palm stuck to the mouse. The back of her hand ached with tension. She leaned forward to click them and read only the first section of each link.

The definitions of their names were spooky and, if someone besides her read them, circumstantial. They proved nothing. But the words crawled into her brain, nonetheless, and locked her into the chair. She slammed the laptop closed.

As if that might trap the haints inside.

Grandma called from the steps. Supper was ready. Amber ran downstairs like she was five years old and had heard a strange noise under the bed. Grandma was waiting at the dinner table with her tea, waiting for Amber to sit down. Amber dipped her head like she was praying. Perhaps a little prayer was in order. What did the Gullah say to ward off the haints?

But the old man died, she was thinking. *Mr. Eilif is dead.*

"You should get some rest tonight," Grandma said. "Stop studying for once. I hear you pacing all night."

When dinner was over and they'd cleared the table, Amber went to the sink, a warm and soapy foam filling the basin. Her reflection looked back from the window black with night.

Mors meant *death.* Umi, *life.*

Those were unusual, the two sides of a coin, the black and white of yin and yang. But the last name was the one she couldn't forget.

"Are you still thinking of moving back to your apartment?" She asked it flippantly, like it suddenly popped into memory.

Eilif means immortal.

"No."

19

Drayton's feet were buried in a dusting of topsoil, a levee of fallen leaves around his legs. Crabgrass, the harbinger of summer, had reached a four-leaf growth stage. By June, they would be sending out multi-fingered seed heads.

Eyes forward, hands at his sides, the garden felt limp. Between clumps of fading annual bluegrass, pansies wilted with disease and broccoli had gone to seed. The garden was silent. Not even the buzz of mosquitoes or scamper of anoles.

It had been weeks since the gates had opened.

There was no use in contemplating the mystery of Umi and young Mors and the young woman or where the old man's body was; his thoughts on the matter would only swirl like dust around him, making as much sense as leaves blown from a path and twirling at random. In this endless moment, he let his thoughts settle and waited for clarity. He remained this way.

Day into night. Night into day.

* * *

FOOTSTEPS BRUSHED THE PATH.

Umi wasn't slouched like a woman of her age. A scarf was bunched around her neck, and earrings dangled from long and sagging lobes. She stopped in front of him, eyes kind and clear, hands over her stomach. A smile wedged a dimple into her cheek, the sound of private laughter in her throat.

She looked around at the disarray—the polluted gravel paths and dying flowers—without saying anything. He was not the gardener anymore.

They both knew as much.

She brushed the leaves from the deep crevice of an Adirondack lounger that rested beneath Chinese elms. Before falling into it, she cleaned the chair next to it. Between them was a circular pond, small, only five feet in diameter and six feet deep. Three yellow koi gracefully hovered near the surface.

Umi tossed pellets into the water. She did not groan when she did so, did not move with the aches of tiresome knees or a failing back. She flicked her hand as a child would toss a Frisbee.

Young Mors approached with a tray. For once, he wore trousers that went to his ankles and leather sandals. Drayton watched the spectacle as a spectator would observe a private moment from a distance, how he bent carefully to slide the tray onto the pond's bluestone coping.

"Thank you, darling."

It was a tone different than she had taken with him before. One of affection, gratitude. She took one of the teacups. He took the other. Together, they sipped, legs crossed, watching dusk fall into the garden along with the sound of crickets. It had been far too long since Drayton had taken such a moment.

"A garden needs attention to grow." Umi looked at Drayton. "It requires planning and detail, the soil turned over, compost added. Seed is sown, water given, and sunlight provided. But what does a garden need most?"

She sipped while young Mors looked on.

"Time."

She contemplated her words, letting them hover in the quietude.

The lamps hanging over them threw warm shadows over their figures. As they lifted their cups, Drayton did not move.

"We've always been watching you; I think you know that now. We have seen you evolve into this selfless being that took but not without repaying. Once a savage, what did it take for you to become this? It took time."

The blood was back on his tongue. He was becoming what he once was, as if he never had control of whom he wanted to be.

"You never lost the taste for it." She chuckled kindly. "I think if you're being honest, you would admit that much."

Honesty was not an option, not for him. She could see into him, his thoughts and motivations merely objects floating inside a glass figurine for her to observe. She was the one hiding.

"What do you want from me?" The words crawled out of his throat, deep and husky.

"We have a garden, Nassfau Rauttu. A very special one. And she needs you."

Drayton turned his head. She was speaking of the garden, but he played his confusion a bit dishonestly, hopeful he was mistaken about whom she was addressing.

Amber.

"Yes. *Ambrogina.* Even she is unaware. We're admirers." She balanced the teacup on her knee. "Collectors."

"Not her."

"Oh, don't be shallow. How is she any different than all the others? Why is she deserving of your pity any more than the boy you put in the ditch, or the one you ran from the bridge?"

He had been there for both of Amber's parents' deaths, had taken their essence upon their last breaths, had seen the trouble their absence had brought her. He hadn't caused their deaths. He hadn't saved them, either. How was she different?

Protect her.

"I won't harm her."

Her laughter was lighthearted, yet cynical. He would harm her if she asked him to do so. They both knew it. "We didn't bring you here to harm her, Nassfau Rauttu. Quite the opposite, actually."

She leisurely drank, sighing deeply. Young Mors stared ahead.

An odd wave of relief broke over him. He didn't want to cause her harm, would refuse to no avail if told to do so. The thought of sacrificing himself was preferable. Or perhaps an end to a long, remorseful life would be liberating. The hunger finally quenched.

"We ask you simply give her what she needs," Umi said.

"Ask?"

A kind smile followed a nod. She wouldn't ask.

"Why?" It was all he could say.

Why all the deception? The mystery woman, Mors's missing body, Umi pretending to hire me, the reawakening of bloodlust? Why the game?

The ease with which the nameless woman had overpowered him in the cemetery clearly demonstrated his helplessness. Instead, confusion was their weapon. They could have forced him into the garden. Instead, they baited him.

We fly higher than you, Drayton.

"The desire to grow needs to be cultivated in a garden. The apple tree must *want* to produce. As you can see, our garden is wilting. How do we make the garden *want* to grow again?"

"Not her."

"Your guilt is senseless," she snapped. "Ambrogina is what she is, Nassfau Rauttu. Don't have feelings about it, you're not human. You're above that. You're here to feed her, Nassfau Rauttu. I would think you would find it curious that you do not know what she is to become. None of us do." She leaned forward. "None of us do."

The boredom of immortality was combatted with the search for the unknown. Very few things surprised Drayton. Even fewer, he suspected, surprised Umi. How could they challenge themselves if they knew everything and could manipulate reality?

The unknown flies highest of them all.

She looked at young Mors, patting his hand. He had yet to even drink his tea.

"The Buddha once said that this present moment is all that exists," she said. "Hearing him say it is quite another thing from reading it. But he was still human and is quite dead. Life is indeed suffering, and we are the purveyors of suffering, Nassfau Rauttu, a natural phenomenon of life with beginnings as mysterious as the universe. It's our duty to cull the human herd, to discover new potential. You were one of our discoveries."

Discovery?

Umi touched young Mors's arm. He fetched another cup of tea. While they waited, she sat with a pleasant smile, one patient and composed. The predator that flies higher than all the rest has little fear. Her teeth were slightly crooked, not pointed.

Young Mors returned with a teacup. Ritually, she rested the bone-white cup—different than the others—in the saucer. It was empty. She turned pensive and stood up.

The gate opened on the far side of the garden.

"All these millennia," she pondered, "you've questioned your existence, wondered why a God would inflict such a punishing being such as yourself upon the world."

A man came around the hedges. Old clothes hung on him, loose and frayed, the kind dug from a bin of donations. His beard was spotty, hair knotted in nappy cords. He sat at Umi's feet, a puppy folding legs beneath him. His tongue jutted out to caress sores on his lips.

She leaned forward to stroke his neck, tangling her fingers in his hair. Jewelry danced, the bracelet sliding on her sun-spotted hand. The flesh, thin and speckled, grew darker. The spots began to spread —first tan then chocolate.

They coalesced and consumed her papery flesh. Her fingers seemed to elongate, thinning and stretching as they darkened. Her clothing sagged on her shoulders.

Young Mors stood at her side. Gray streaked through his jet-black hair as it began to coarsen. Always vigilant and upright, his shoulders slumped and his head pushed forward, folds of flesh sagging from his chin.

Drayton moved for the first time in weeks.

Umi, the old woman who lived in the Garden House, the old woman once married to Mors, the old woman who invited him into the garden, was no longer in front of him. It was her, the young woman in the cemetery, the one who'd reignited Drayton's bloodlust.

You know who I am, she had whispered to him. *I am who I want to be.*

Umi—once old and white, now young and black—caressed the kneeling man's neck. Once a young man, now old and familiar, he stood by her side. Mors's body wasn't missing from the crypt. It was never there.

He never died.

"We hide in the open," she said. "Ageless. Raceless. We are who we want to be."

She slid slender fingers over the man's shoulder, down his arm to lift his hand. Fingertips upon his pulse, stroking, loving. The fingernail she'd once used to open Macon Leary now teased the blue veins along his wrist. She pulled it through his soft flesh. It opened like a gaping mouth, whitish tissue peeking out. The man never flinched.

"We created you, Nassfau Rauttu."

Mors knelt with the bone-white teacup. A crimson stream trickled from the knob on the man's wrist. It pattered on the bottom of the cup, minute sprays dotting the white china. The salty tang lit Drayton's nostrils, saliva pooling beneath his tongue.

When the cup was half full, the droplets plunking with deep thunder, Umi dipped her finger and painted her lower lip. Mors held the cup beneath his nose, inhaling deeply before placing it on the pond's edge. The koi swam at the surface.

"Ambrogina will join us," Umi said, the voice now coming from the young and thick lips, sexuality dripping from them. "You will help her become what she is meant to be."

She took Mors's hand.

The old man and young woman left him staring as the man bled out. The Garden House was dark when they climbed the spiral staircase, their bodies merely vehicles for the power lurking within.

We do not hide from them.

* * *

A TAN SHIRT at his feet, dark stains on the collar, the fabric in crusty patches. A fetid stench hung in the stagnant alcove, thick and steamy.

Drayton turned to the sky.

A steely tang slid down his throat. The stars looked without judgment at the bodies stacked like logs, their limbs flopped at odd angles. Flies leapt from cloudy eye to cloudy eye, crawling over swollen lips and bulging tongues.

Drayton was full. Saturated.

Every night, the gate would open. Someone would wander in, serenaded by treefrogs and crickets, cicadas inviting them to find him as still as an oak. Some nights it was a man, others a woman. Always, they were men and women sleeping in abandoned houses or ragged tents. They would rise without warning and wander across the city, answering a call to find him.

Tonight it was a woman.

Her hair had been cut with a dull knife, the same one she used to carve words, some long scarred over, others still pink. *Bitch. Fuck. Chaos.*

She dragged her feet, long laces dancing around her. Like all the rest, she dropped on her knees. From the balcony, Umi and Mors watched. Sometimes they presented themselves as a young power couple; other times they took on various tones of flesh—pink or white or tan or black.

Tonight Mr. and Mrs. Eilif.

Drayton remained resolute, arms at his sides. He drew long, slow breaths and emptied his mind. But as all the ones before her, he grew stiffer with each breath. His hands clenched. Each breath was pulled through thicker layers of resistance. Oxygen had become wool scratching his lungs. The hunger swelled in his stomach, clawing into his throat.

It lay beneath his tongue.

The young woman looked up. "Please."

Janie was her name. He wished he didn't know that, wished he wasn't presented with the tragedy of her life. Janie wasn't there anymore, her will subsumed by the pair watching from the balcony. Was her life any worse now?

Will this be compassionate?

She began to writhe, her body set in fluid motion. Back arched, head thrown back, neck exposed. White bubbles formed in the corners of her mouth. Drayton resisted the seduction. He knew how this would end, how it progressed each time, how the bodies piled up.

He would resist until she lifted her hand.

Her teeth blackened by abuse, she bit down on her wrist and moaned as if penetrated by Adonis himself. A dark stream mixed with saliva escaped. When the first drop splashed at his feet, it happened.

His resistance audibly snapped.

She groaned with pleasure as he opened her up, her moans gurgling as her life spilled. Drayton's hunger opened the gates. She joined the rest of them, the last hint of her frenzied delight fading into a lifeless stare. He just dragged the body across the ground. Another log on the pile.

Satisfied, he resumed his place in the garden, grateful Amber had not been the one who had walked through the gate, that the gods on the balcony did not feed her to him.

I will feed her.

20

"Where you going?"

Dev spoke through swirls of blue-gray vapor. Young slid sunglasses over his eyes. Shirtless, his torso an inked mural. A massive tree was the anchor across his back. The limbs extended across his shoulders, the roots down the back of his legs. It was the first tattoo he'd ever gotten. Drayton was the second.

The rest were decoration.

"On a walk," Young said.

"Lucky bastard."

"Why you down here?"

Dev hit his vape pen. "Thought you might need help redecorating."

The black and white vortex painting was on the porch, leaning against the wall. That was the only painting Dev had ever done. The rest of the paintings were scattered on the studio floor. Tubes, brushes and tubs of water spilled over split canvases and broken easels. There was no memory of doing it. It was like a gang of critics had broken into the house and critiqued Young's work with tennis rackets.

"It was a party of one," Young said.

"It always is."

"Aren't you supposed to be teaching or something?"

Dev smirked. "It's Sunday."

Young looked at his phone. It was Sunday. *Fuck.*

The slender caretaker had an adjunct position at the Citadel, teaching ancient history. He didn't need the money, as far as Young could tell. The guy ate like a bird and wore the same T-shirt and jeans every day. His entire wardrobe could be bought at a garage sale for a dollar, and that included underwear. He taught just so he could talk history with a captive audience.

Meanwhile, Young had thrown a three-day pity party. No wonder the house smelled like a urinal.

Young dug through his saddlebag and found a Ziploc. A metal pipe weighed down the plastic corner. He attempted to pull it open and fumbled it onto the porch. Dev fished out the pipe with chopstick fingers.

"You could've just started with this." He packed a bowl. "Would've saved you a few days and all those paintings."

"That wasn't the point."

"Ah. A brain-cell massacre, was it?"

"Something had to die."

"They are *your* brain cells, you know." Dev pulled a drag before passing it.

"Not anymore."

A thick column of smoke exhaled toward the ceiling. Young tapped out the ashes. The lighter sparked up round two, and another white cloud floated up. A wave of sweet relief filled his head. Dev was right, he should've gotten high instead of blackout drunk. Then again, obliterating thoughts and memories had been the goal.

Mission accomplished.

"Must be nice as a cripple." Dev crossed his legs, bouncing his slim, turquoise shoe. "All the medical marijuana you can toke."

"Oh, it's great. The parking, the handouts. Fucking outstanding."

"I'm assuming that was about the girl." Dev nodded at the room.

"You know what they say about assuming."

"Something about assholes."

Young was rising toward the ceiling. Another hit and he'd go over the wall and land in the world of paranoia and predatory thoughts. He'd spent enough time there already. The office was proof—the map with red lines, scribbled notes on Post-its, and reminders in the margins. Five years of work linking unsolved crimes and unusual behavior that led back to Drayton was on the floor. Looking down the hall, it looked like the office had vomited up the remains of a conspiracy.

Amber was right.

All those thumbtacks were imaginary dots. His life wouldn't have meaning if he second-guessed what he was doing. And once he started that, it was like tipping over the first domino that even the almighty Jack Daniel's couldn't stop.

"She was into you, man," Dev said with a mouthful of vapor. "She must be damaged."

"You're high."

A smile dimpled Dev's cheek. He was a fifty-something who looked more like twenty and maybe never shaved a day in his life. Young went to the edge of the porch. Vague memories of punching out paintings were beginning to surface. The office was fucked, he remembered that. That was where he'd started.

"You need to get back to it. Do something," Dev said. "Besides sit there."

"How do you know what I'm doing?"

"You have a secret office. I'll bet it's not for hiding porn."

"You been inside my office?" Young was suddenly sliding off a mellow cloud.

"Everyone has secrets, Young."

It was something he said from time to time, usually after they were deep into politics and completely stoned. Yeah, they did. Maybe he was transgender, or on the run, or he shot porn upstairs late at night. He was a fifty-year-old virgin renting a room and changing piss bags.

Everyone has secrets.

"You know what I'm doing back there?"

"I can read smoke signals." Dev blew an O-ring.

Young wondered how much he knew. He was careful to never

leave the office unlocked, but Dev had picked him off the floor drunk plenty of times. How many nights had he found him in the office with the door wide open?

"Did you find what you're looking for?" Dev asked.

"Yeah." Young's eyes were wide with sarcasm.

"Did you?"

"Did I what, Dev?"

"Find what you were looking for?"

Dev fixed him with a lazy gaze. The smile dropped off and Young looked away. Did he find what he was looking for? Yeah, he'd found what he was looking for. He'd found Drayton.

What he didn't find was still on the farm, back when Drayton had first arrived. He didn't find that feeling of protection when he had been staying in the house, or the way Mom had looked before she died, before his brother had been T-boned by a drunk.

Before it all went to shit.

"Yeah, Dev." Young grabbed his hair with both hands. "I found it."

"Doesn't look like it."

"What do you want me to say? Life is shit, roll on, I learned my lesson. I was chasing a dream, my eyes were closed, however you want to say it, man. You're right. Okay. You're right. Happy?"

"Life is shit. Paraphrasing Siddhartha, that's good."

"Whatever."

"Where I come from, there are no mistakes."

"Well, you're in the South. Go back if you don't like it."

Young snatched the pipe and pulled another hit. The house smelled like a gas station toilet bowl, and he had nowhere else to go and nothing more to do. Besides, he was going to hate himself more for dumping on Dev.

Thank God for Dev.

Young was alone in this world without him. That was why he had bought this place. The second floor was a suitable apartment. Young had only been up there once, the day he bought the place. The realtor had left two peppermints on the table, one stacked on top of the other.

A month later, Young had opened the office on the first floor and called a tattoo artist.

"Sorry," Young said. "It's just been… never mind."

He could explain his world had nose-dived in the last several months, that everything was a lie. *I've been looking for a vampire who made me feels safe, Dev. He's been running loose in the Lowcountry. Turns out I'm crazy. Welcome to reality.*

Dev lifted a glass of sweet tea, condensation sweating down the sides, and drank most of it in three swallows. The ice cubes rattled when he put it down.

They sat in silence.

Samu was curled up next to the black and white vortex painting, the colors swirling toward the center. Young felt the porch begin to tilt if he stared too long at the center. He grabbed the rubber wheels before he started rolling toward it.

One toke too many.

"Can I tell you a story?" Dev asked. "It's ancient folklore. I think you might like it."

Young nodded absently. He was back on the tracks, rising on a cloud of smoke. The vortex swirling black and white.

"It's about the last wagwam." Dev crossed his legs and sat back.

"All right."

"So there were these mythical creatures called wagwams that lived in a world where it was always daylight. The sun would cross the sky then back again, horizon to horizon, back and forth. And the wagwams had a habit, no one knew why, of always following their shadows. They always kept the sun at their back. At noon, they stood still."

Young sank deeper into his chair.

"So one morning, when the sun touched the opposite horizon, this wagwam woke up and the world was completely different. He had no way of knowing how long he'd been asleep, just that the world was green and lush when he did, and now it was a desert sand."

Dev waved his hand at the horizon.

"There were no other wagwams around him, no footprints to tell him which direction to go. Just fucking sand, right? He thought maybe he was dreaming, but it turned out he was definitely awake. So there was nothing else he could do but start walking.

"He kept the sun at his back and walked in one direction, stopped at noon, then went the other way. Back and forth he went, each time seeing his footprints from the last time. He didn't know why he followed his shadow; it's just what wagwams do. There's a whole world out there, and he's going back and forth. So he went sideways."

Dev held up a finger.

"Now he went in another direction, and guess what he found? More sand. Turned out the whole world was a desert in all directions."

Young's face had grown heavy. He felt a smile somewhere under the mask, but nothing moved. He pictured the wagwam as a furry bear with purple and black rugby stripes and big spade-shaped teeth. Probably something he'd seen in a bedtime story.

"The next morning he woke up to see something on a distant dune. Ignoring his shadow, he raced on all fours for the entire day. The tree was much farther than he thought because it was a titan that touched the sky, with branches lying on the ground. Trees were sacred to wagwams. They were the first to capture the sunlight and perpetually cast a shadow for them to walk in. The wagwam got to the tree and immediately began to cry.

"The world was once full of trees, and now he'd finally found one, but the branches were barren. His last hope was shattered. He no longer wanted to walk anymore. His journey was over. He was going to stay there and wail until he no longer woke. That was when something hit him in the head. Three acorns bounced between his furry ears and rolled across the ground.

"There was hope after all. He could plant the acorns and bring the world back. So that was exactly what he did. He dug a hole and placed an acorn on the damp and sandy bottom. After burying it, he curled up like a striped mother bear to keep it warm and went to sleep.

"That sleep, he heard a voice. Wagwams didn't dream, so this was shocking. He heard a tiny voice whisper, 'Deeper.' The wagwam woke immediately and looked around. No one was there, but just to be sure, he dug up the acorn and found that it had shriveled up like a raisin. So he dug a deeper hole for the second acorn.

"This hole was so deep that a shadow fell across the bottom when he finished. He had to climb up the wall to escape and bury it with an entire sand dune. Again, he curled up to sleep and, once again, a tiny voice whispered, 'Deeper still.' The wagwam woke in a panic and dug up the second acorn, finding it shriveled and dead. There was only one acorn left. He could not let it die, so he swallowed it to protect it from harm and began to dig.

"Wagwams dig not with their hands but with oversized pointed teeth. He ate the ground a bite at a time, going deeper until he was in the shade. Going deeper until the walls were moist. Going deeper until the sky was a blue dot. He dug until he no longer saw light. Deeper until he no longer heard the grinding of earth, until he no longer smelled its richness, until he no longer tasted its grit. Deeper until he no longer felt his body."

Young had closed his eyes. He was floating in a dreamy vision that was black and spacious; tides of breath ebbed and flowed, and Dev's voice guided him.

"He had given himself completely. The wagwam had devoured the world until there was only space. No sun or earth, no limits. He was completely free. There was space for everything to exist."

The sound of water roared in Young's ears, beads of moisture on his cheeks. It reminded him of the time they'd visited Niagara Falls. Mom and Bo and Young had worn rain suits as they toured the bottom of the falls. The water had been deafening, a force that couldn't be stopped. Young had imagined what it must be like to get caught in that unstoppable current.

"In that limitless space, the wagwam spoke for the acorn that was safe inside his belly," Dev continued. "'I am the dark,' he said. 'I need the light.'"

Bright strands of color burst from the dark, rushing into Young with overpowering force. The light was as limitless as the eternal space, the flow filling him until the acorn wiggled in his belly and branches sprang from his nostrils and ears, roots dangled from his mouth. The universe roared.

I am the dark / you are the light / one and the other / can never be apart.

I am dark / you are light / one without the other / leads asunder.

Young was staring at the painting, the black and white vortex swallowing strands of color. Tears wet his cheeks. He thought he'd closed his eyes and begun dreaming, but his eyes were open and dry. He rubbed feeling back into his cheeks.

Birds were singing, crickets chirping. Clouds hung in the sky. Dev and Samu were watching him in a surreal moment of stillness.

The hell did we smoke?

Young didn't feel high. He felt something he'd never felt before. It was clarity. It was like the power of Niagara Falls had swept away the clutter and wiped the slate clean. Dev had told weird stories before.

"What the hell happened?" Young stared at his hands.

"There's wisdom in dreams. The hard part is figuring out what is the dream and what is not." Dev lifted his sweet tea for a sip. "Turns out it's all a dream."

When he put the glass down, it was still full.

PART IV

Let go over a cliff, die completely, and then come back to life—after that you cannot be deceived.
    – Zen Proverb

HARPER SINCLAIR

Harper was old.

She was also old-fashioned. The twisting cord of her phone was knotted worse than a wisteria vine. Her television was deep and heavy. It got five channels from an antenna bolted to the side of her brick Tudor, a metal structure her late husband, Mr. Sinclair, had purchased shortly after they were wed. No need for the internet or email, she saw the world through the nightly newscast she had trusted all her life.

No dishwasher, either.

The soapy bubbles dried the backs of her hands from time to time, but there weren't many dishes to wash these days. Since Amber had moved in, there was an additional plate or two. She rather enjoyed washing them. When she was alone—and it had been some time now —it seemed wasteful to fill the sink to wash a teacup.

It had been just as long since she'd heard footsteps in the house. When they had children, all those years ago, she'd spent many nights over a sink of bubbles, wishing for peaceful nights alone. Now she would give anything to have a little noise.

Amber had made this old woman's wish come true.

A pot of noodles bubbled on the stove. A few more minutes and she'd strain out the water and prepare dinner. The backyard was washed in afternoon light. Just past noon, the sun shined through a gap in the trees. It wasn't always like that. When the children were born, the water oaks and magnolia had barely screened the neighbors. Now hardly a sprig of turf grew beneath them.

Where does the time go?

A serrated tooth bit her middle finger. She yanked her hand from the sudsy water. A film of pink water seeped from a gaping slit. Somewhere below the bubbles, a steak knife hid its fang. She resisted sucking the sting from her finger. Instead, she wrapped a paper towel around it and squeezed until her joints ached. A red spot soaked through it. She dabbed at the broken skin.

Someone was watching.

A shadow was playing tricks. For a moment, she saw someone near the fence, but it must have been the stony-faced sun. And then she got an idea. Wouldn't it be nice to relax in the backyard while her finger was clotting?

Yes. Yes, it would.

She put on tall rubber boots, the red ones she wore out to the garden. A chair was waiting for her behind the garage. It was next to the forgotten compost bin. A jagged circle of sunlight fell on the chair. Harper sat down with the paper towel. It had been quite a long time since she'd been back there. It felt good to rest and listen to the birds. Perhaps a butterfly would visit.

The sunlight moved on. Her bottom was sore from the thin cushion. She was also wrapped in a blanket she didn't remember bringing out. A late chill was nipping at her nose. It was almost dark.

Where does the time go?

21

The past saturated this old house, memories sunk deep into the paneled walls and hardwood floors. Little footsteps had thundered down the stairs Christmas morning to find everything from the Sears catalog bright and shiny beneath tree branches heavy with ornaments. There was the time Harper's children had spilled the gravy boat on Thanksgiving, a stain that remained until they were in college and the carpet removed for hardwood floors. The birthday party that had accidentally poisoned three guests with spoiled potato salad. One of the children had vomited in the backyard.

Umi took the noodles off the stove.

The iron smell of blood was rich. The gentle, lonely grandmother was resting behind the garage. There was no reason to take the old woman's life. She would not resist had Umi requested it. Harper, though, was tired. She'd outlived most of her family, her purpose fulfilled. What else was there to do but wash dishes?

Still, Umi let her live.

It was much easier to do so. This was a tenuous moment. It was better to swaddle the grandmother in a blanket until it passed.

Umi was born to embody life, to embrace it and sometimes take it. She no longer required the essence each human possessed. Nassfau

Rauttu would evolve past this need as well if he lived as long as Umi. Drayton, as he now called himself (she couldn't bring herself to go along), would eventually become like her. But that was not his purpose. He was like the grandmother.

His purpose was nearing an end.

Excitement tensed beneath her ribs, a stirring she hadn't experienced in ages. She and Mors had been preparing for this moment for centuries. So much time laying the groundwork, and now the sudden bloom was at hand. Their flower upstairs, the bud swelling. This angel, this saint, this rarest of beauties—the true soul of an artist, the wellspring of creative truth, the unfettered heart that would create something out of the garden.

Ambrogina. A Greek name, the nectar of the gods.

This was the excitement.

Umi and Mors possessed the gift of time. They spent their lives among humans, watched the collapse of civilization and the rebuilding of hope while they tended this Southern garden, waiting for the right seed to blow in and find root.

Nassfau Rauttu was once that seed, a migrant soul living in the wild land before Greece was born. Nassfau Rauttu, his birth name, was born with the unrealized gift that the rare human possessed, one that Umi brought to fruition, igniting him with her own thoughts, fulfilling him with immortality and an insatiable hunger set loose upon the world. They watched him from a distance, how he'd once terrorized the land before evolving into a compassionate taker.

This, she surmised, was the natural order of evolution.

An immortal would not continue on a chaotic path. Given the virtue of limitless reflection, he would eventually give up his carnal ways and seek a higher path. Like Umi had done. She'd lured Drayton back to the Lowcountry.

Then brought back Nassfau Rauttu.

She was a master of the long game, unending patience on an endless wheel of time. She had to avoid Nassfau Rauttu's exceptional senses, had seduced him into service: Mors's death and request to *protect her.* It had to be his desire to do so, for that was the only way to grow a garden.

The apple tree wants to produce apples.

Nassfau Rauttu wasn't the only human she had converted into her own likeness, but he was the most effective. So many of them had changed the world and left lasting marks. But none were like Nassfau Rauttu. He was the taker.

What will Ambrogina become?

Umi read humans as if their thoughts were written across their foreheads. She saw the rise and collapse of civilizations, an endless cycle of greed that eroded the pillars upon which it was built. She knew the human condition, knew it was imperfect and limited. That it was merely food for the gods.

Us.

Ambrogina possessed something extraordinary that was beyond her own awareness, a mystery even to Umi's penetrating mind. And this was the cause of Umi's excitement. The unknowing of what Ambrogina would become, given the right conditions and a sufficient amount of essence. Nassfau Rauttu would feed her.

That was his purpose.

A cell phone rang. Umi silenced it and read the name. She went to the front room while drying her hands with a towel. A van was at the curb. A young man was in the driver's seat, a tattooed arm resting on the door, phone to his ear. This one was interesting.

Mors had warned her about him.

She could see into the young man, knew him like any human within her range, but something disturbed her. She hadn't sensed him sitting outside the house watching her. That wasn't something that slipped past her awareness. Mors had reported the same experience.

The young man felt elusive, although he seemed transparent enough when she focused on him. Even now, he had gone unnoticed until the phone rang. But that wasn't what bothered her most.

It was the connection to Nassfau Rauttu.

It wasn't impossible, the odds not long enough for her to be concerned. But she had noticed. Why did Young remember so much?

Nassfau Rauttu was always a shadow that disappeared when the light of attention shined upon him. Very few people remembered him, the memories fading like snow in turbulent water.

Young remembered with great clarity.

With Ambrogina ready to bloom, Umi couldn't be distracted now. She would return to investigate the paraplegic, perhaps lure him into the garden to test his own potential.

Perhaps tempt him to walk.

She swiped the phone and erased the call. The van remained idling at the curb. Seconds later, it pulled away.

"Amber, hon? Can you come down?"

Umi stood near the bottom step. Her voice hadn't changed. A slender black woman was still in the front room, toned and fit and attractive, a form she preferred when outside the garden. What Ambrogina heard, what she saw, was something quite different.

Humans were filters. Their awareness was the recipient of information through the senses. They had no ability to absorb reality, to become it, to be one with it and know it directly. Umi simply altered what Ambrogina was seeing and hearing.

It was that simple.

Footsteps neared the top, the old boards protesting. Amber slid her hand down the bannister, her bare feet falling on each step. Umi took a step back. She resisted shielding her eyes.

The brilliance was blinding.

A babe of innocence, completely unaware of her potential. Humans everywhere knew so little. They were victims of their own biological clocks, their lifespans lasting but a century, not nearly enough time to evolve, to know true nature.

To become it.

This child contained a seed of potential like no other. Even Nassfau Rauttu paled in the presence of her radiance. All she needed was fertile ground and an ample supply of essence. Umi had waited for someone such as her for a very long time. She needed her to want to come back.

Umi was there to guide her.

* * *

"Everything all right?" Amber asked.

Grandmother stood stiffly in the front room, mouth slightly agape. At first, Amber thought she'd received bad news, that perhaps someone had died suddenly—a car crash or something. But then there was no one in the family left to crash a car.

Something was burning.

A pot of soggy noodles was on the stove. The water had nearly evaporated. A spot of blood was on the kitchen counter.

"Did you cut yourself?" Amber called.

"I'm fine, hon."

"Why is there blood?"

"We need to talk."

They stood a few feet apart. Grandmother wrung her hands, Amber clutching the bloody paper towel. A stranger might guess they were negotiating the price of something. The silence stretched out as her grandmother seemed lost again.

"You need to leave," she finally said.

"What?"

"I've enjoyed your company, hon. I really have. But you don't need to be living with your grandmother. Your heart belongs somewhere else."

She took her hands with a jolt of static electricity. There was no carpet in the house, but the shock was long and strangely pleasant. It was the kind of jolt that dissolved barriers, the experience she'd once had after Macon had dosed her drink with a tab of LSD.

An oceanic experience.

Her body melted away. There was no more separation between her and the universe, between her and her grandmother, or the chair or walls or the pot of noodles. For a moment, two people were holding Amber's hands. One person was her grandmother. The other one she didn't know. And then it was just her grandmother again.

"Leave tonight," she said.

She didn't say why. She didn't say she had to. It was just permission. Why was she still staying?

There are monsters out there.

It wasn't the monsters Young was talking about that kept her from leaving. Amber was afraid to face the monsters every kid fears, the ones under the bed and in the closet, the ones in her head that sprinkled seeds of doubt. The ones that told her she wasn't good enough. It was better to hide her head under the pillow than look around. Monsters like Macon were out there.

And Macon is dead.

Amber went upstairs and packed one bag. She wouldn't need much. That evening, she left the Jeep in the garage and started walking. She never looked in the backyard.

Where an old woman was sitting in a chair.

* * *

THE CITY WAS QUIET.

A welcome breeze carried the briny scent of the harbor down the street. She walked with her eyes closed, feeling the jagged cracks of the root-split sidewalk beneath her feet.

Home.

She stood beneath a buzzing streetlight. The gate opener was still in the Jeep. The Garden House windows were black. Darkness hung over the walls like a curtain. Life outside the garden was a heavy suit of skin—her flagging medical career, the broken relationships, the heartache. The absence of purpose. A walk back to retrieve the gate opener felt long and burdensome. She wished it would just open.

The gate began to hum.

A lump was huddled on the pavers. She stood on the sidewalk, adjusting to the darkness. When she recognized what was waiting, she stepped inside and felt the gate close behind her.

Her art bag was waiting.

The perfumy scent of new gardenia blooms greeted her with the song of crickets and cicadas, the occasional blat of treefrogs. Branches rustled and foliage unfurled in a rogue breeze. The breath of the garden—sweet and warm—said hello. It carried something green and promising and something empty and dying. Plants grew and died and decomposed to feed seedlings struggling in the soil.

The circle of life and death.

Amber found her tree wanting. Clumps of Spanish moss hung from its branches, strands of miniature lights glowing silver-gray. Its massive trunk had split at the base. A cavity had opened between gnarled root flares. The lateral branches were as large as tree trunks, reaching out into the surroundings, their girth resting on the ground.

Amber slipped off her shoes and walked onto an outstretched branch, the coarse bark gripping the soles of her feet. Before nestling against the trunk, she looked over the garden. Yellow lanterns swung on long strands. Tiny sparks drifted like fireflies.

The itch that crawled beneath her skin had vanished. Her outer self, the false self, the one left yearning and lost, was outside the walls. Droplets splashed through the canopy, falling on her cheeks, her arms. A patter steady and warm as it wept from the sky.

She took a pad of paper from the bag. The pencil resting between her fingers, she swiped across the rough surface. Each cutting line seemed to bleed from the page, every stroke pulling air through her fingers. It tingled inside her, exhilarating tissue and bone and muscle. It swept through her pores and lit her from within.

Page after page ripped from the binding. A rattling thunder cascaded in the canopy, each creation blending into the one before it until there was just one continuous line after another. The tree held her tightly, the crevices deepening and biting into her thighs, snatching at her back. Sweat on her cheeks. Breeze on her face.

The flow beckoned her.

She was still fully conscious of the pencil between her fingers and the branches beneath her legs. The drawings drilled deeper into the well where creativity was limitless, the eternal potential to be anything and anywhere was possible. Each slash another surge into the earth, another step into the flow. By morning, the ground was covered in paper. The walls so much farther away.

Deeper, she went.

It was an early morning when she surfaced. There was no sense of time passing and vague memories that the sun had risen more than once since she'd arrived. An avalanche of abstract images covered the ground—shapes and textures, faces hidden within dark forms. Each a man as pitch as coal, still and standing, a silky stream flowing from him. It felt clean, exhilarating. Filling her.

Sweat-soaked and aching, fingers cramped and clawed. Clothing clung like wet sheets. All that drawing and still there was more to discover. The depths of the flow had not been reached. A behemoth lurked in the deepest part, as if buried in the center of the earth, waiting to be tapped. To be born.

She stripped off her clothes. Wadded and damp, they fell with a heavy thud. The ripeness of her flesh was a tangy aroma. The ridged bark clung to her. Somewhere, the sun was rising. The air was steamy in the dense foliage, occluding her view. There were strands of lanterns when she had arrived. Now there were vines as thick as sewer pipes and swards of moss.

Her breath rattled the foliage.

Still unsatisfied, her skin felt like a suit too small to contain her. She needed to shed her old life, needed space to become more.

Become everything.

The bag was empty. The pencil, a nub. Unwilling to leave, she swung her hand like a composer, fingers curled and puffy. Paper and lead were just crutches. Her mind was the instrument. The drawings were a side effect. She didn't need tools, didn't need to draw. She wanted to sculpt.

To create.

She imagined abstract colors and shapes, felt them mingle and merge. The tree undulated on the backs of her arms, the heels of her feet. Eyes closed, colors spilled from the darkness. She danced on the balls of her feet, wrapping her arms against the girthy trunk, hips gyrating, pelvis grinding.

The energy swirled through her groin; fireworks exploded in her chest. She achieved orgasm loudly, tears flowing. Climbing a ladder of ecstasy and never returning, the flow pushing her higher and higher.

She could feel the garden now. It wasn't contained by the fig-covered walls. Space wasn't finite. There were dimensions hidden within it, waiting to be discovered and released.

Set free.

She conducted the symphony, dancing and swinging, spinning and leaping. The world swooped up to meet her with a blinding clash.

The mossy ground cushioned her fall.

She had crashed awkwardly, her foot twisted completely around. The bones in her ankle rolled like marbles. Numbness squeezed her leg. There was a sharp bend in her chin, the bone pushing against the flesh. Agony melted with the ecstasy, a hot kettle of emotions that moaned and cried, laughed and sang.

Paper crinkled beneath her.

Too high to care. Too awake to panic. The absurdity of it all and these feelings were just sensations, these emotions just thoughts. None of it mattered any more than anything else.

I am the light.

She dragged herself between the root flares. A cavity had opened on the trunk, a vaginal slit that welcomed her inside. The smell of earth was in her nostrils. A drawing lay in front of it. The figures were pale, the features recognizable, like an infant knowing the smell of her mother's milk.

Mom. Dad.

There was no memory of drawing them, but there they were. She'd left her grandmother's home, but her parents were the final piece keeping her from complete release, the last fragment of her personality unwilling to let them go.

The tree's cavity exhaled warmly.

It was dark and musty. Amber dragged herself on scuffed elbows, pulling her dead leg behind her, her foot flopping uselessly about, and climbed inside.

The garden quaked.

She clutched the page with her mom and dad, balled it up and breathed it in, absorbing the last of their memory. And then let it go. Somewhere in that dark cavity, it tumbled out of sight.

The final wall had fallen.

She broke through the last mantle of earth's crust and plunged into the endless aquifer of flow. Her flesh dissolved, her thoughts purged, and her nervous system branched out like roots. Stripped away, she became her true self. She became the light. She merged with the universe and discovered lifetimes of memories waiting for her.

Memories that didn't belong to her.

22

No one came to sit at his feet this time.

They did not beg to give themselves, did not squirm in the throes of pleasure when he took them. This time the lanterns swayed. The trees shook. The stench of empty carcasses was away. A sensation raced through him.

Amber was in her tree.

A late spring shower drifted out of the dark sky. Droplets floated like crystals, landing softly on the ground, melting into the soil. He felt the first stroke of her imagination.

Thin filaments penetrated the soles of his feet, netted tendrils stitching him to the earth. Fear shivered through him—not for his death, that would be welcome. Fear that the garden was pulling essence from him.

He began feeding her.

* * *

THE SUN ROSE and fell seven times since she arrived.

Umi and Mors watched from the balcony, as if mesmerized by the event long awaited. Whether their gaze settled upon him or the tree in which Amber rested, he was unsure. Their thoughts, once invisible, were apparent.

The garden had become an interconnected jungle. Drayton was no longer separate from it. He sensed their thoughts probing him like flesh-eating insects. Each day that passed, the emptier he became. The world was dimming. The light was being drawn from him.

He was powerless to stop it.

Memories trickled through his awareness as they were pulled from him, memories from his victims throughout the ages. Thousands of years he'd walked the world and had always assumed he was digesting this essence, or had it pass through him like a breeze through a windmill?

I'm a vessel.

Amber's presence swept beneath his feet, soaking up memories as they escaped. The stack of sacrificial bodies, the young man in the ditch, the sweetgrass basketweaver at the church. *We built this church,* Umi had told him. A church established in 1825, a fact he had somehow missed.

Or had she clouded my mind?

There were the countless souls he had recently taken in the hospitals, the ones dying of old age and accidents, heart complications and rare diseases, their lives an endless string of pearls. He was once the taker; now he was the giver.

My purpose.

The air was dewy and thick. Condensation clung to his forehead like perspiration. Wrapped tighter in shrinking flesh, he witnessed the essence of every victim drain from him, yet two of the most recent ones he held tightly, instinctually clinging to them like a religious man clutching holy beads.

Brenda and James.

A massive stroke had taken James; his death Drayton had foreseen. A death he'd revealed to allow James to process his mortality, to mend things broken. Brenda had passed away in a bed of flowers, her back to the soil, her eyes in the clouds. She'd welcomed him as a friend.

Perhaps she'd sensed James within him, had even seen him as Drayton approached.

He would not let these memories slip into the stream and find their way back to the tree. He would hold onto them and continue breathing, push away death until it was time. Empty and alone, he looked back upon his own life now and the memories that were once drowning in a river of his sins and the suffering he set up on the world. Now those memories of his beginning gushed up like a field of the most precious oil to greet him.

To remember his roots.

* * *

A PRAIRIE.

Rolling and uninterrupted by scrubby tree or errant boulder, grass the color of honey before the harvest. A haunting wind rode long waves through seed heads brushing Nassfau Rauttu's bare chest. It wasn't exceptionally tall.

He was young.

The hair on his arms was fair, but hung in clumping knots around his ears and over his eyes. In his thick and scarred hand, he held a miniature totem, one he'd carved before arriving, one he must present to the elders upon his return.

Thirty suns must pass.

A crude knife was fastened to his bare hip by a taut string of hide. Nothing covered his boyhood. The faint whisper of manhood had begun to grow around his genitalia. His skin was reddish-brown. Despite his lack of development, he was of age. Thirty days would pass. He left a boy.

Would return a man.

Abandoned in the wild, he would find food to survive. There was a stream nearby. He'd gathered wood from the scrubby brush to keep warm at night. Fear ached in his joints when morning dawned. Sleep haunted his vision and skewed his hearing. He had seen the other boys return from their quests, hollowed and wide-eyed. Some were crying. Nassfau Rauttu would not cry.

He broke that promise on the morning of the third sun.

When the twentieth sun woke him, he had decided that he would not become a man. He had failed to capture a fish or trap an animal to cook over his feeble fires. Already slight and stunted, his ribs now pressed his flesh like protruding twigs. When the sun fell that night, his fire snuffed out long before the moon took its place. He lay shivering without kindling to restart it.

That was the night he was stalked.

He had seen the four-legged beast two days prior to that night. It kept its distance, lurking in the weeds. The fire kept it away, but now it was dark. The grass had begun to crack in the distance. Nassfau Rauttu would not become a man.

But he did not want to die.

It was not fear of pain or the ending of life, but the unwillingness to give it to another. It was his life to keep. Another could not have it, four-legged god or not. He lay still, locked with tension. Fear in his throat. Senses engaged, a prayer came to his lips, and he squeezed the totem. He opened his mind to receive the blessings of all the gods, that they allow him the strength to see beyond what could be seen.

His eyes burned.

The sky seemed to catch fire and roar across the prairie. The grass rustled wildly. In it, the four-legged beast crouched lower to the ground. Nassfau Rauttu felt the predator as if a lump had settled on the skin of his mind, as if the grass blades growing in the earth had become tentacles he could control like fingers or toes. He could feel its hunger as if it were his own. Saliva pooled beneath the beast's tongue, satisfaction near. Its breath came in short gulps, stabbing in and out. Muscles bunched on its shoulder blades.

Nassfau Rauttu felt it all. He let it all in, even the fear that was in the beast's own heart. Fear that tasted of metal. The prairie bent to his will, every blade of grass, every insect and spore. Death nestled beside him.

He welcomed that too.

There was no separation between Nassfau Rauttu and the beast, no beginning or end. There was his body, but that didn't define him. The beast rose, eyes just above the withering prairie. Nassfau Rauttu revealed himself.

At first, the beast crouched out of sight, but hunger stilled it from bolting away. But it did not bound forward, either. It found itself locked in place, as if the will to attack or flee had left it immobile.

Nassfau Rauttu approached, hands brushing the bobbing heads of seed. A strand of saliva slowly oozed from the beast's black lip and vibrated like a windblown strand of silk webbing. Nassfau Rauttu reached out and touched its nose, sliding his fingers between its eyes. A cool patch of something was between the beast's ears, an icy pool just below the hide.

Nassfau Rauttu inhaled between pursed lips.

It rode through his fingers. It tingled beneath the cage of his ribs. The beast rested as if tired.

His hunger vanished.

When the sun arose on the twenty-second day, he was sleeping against the beast's belly. Bloodstained fur was near Nassfau Rauttu's ear, his crude knife inserted between the ribs. He had no memory of ending the beast's life. Clutching his totem, he awoke to see the elders staring down. They were not supposed to come for him. He was to return to the village on his own on the day of the thirtieth sun. But it wasn't the elders that looked upon him.

It was a woman and a man.

They were unlike anyone he had ever met, lacking tribal markings and wearing strange clothing that was loose and clean. No weapons in their hands or at their hips. A woman with burnt flesh and eyes as gray as a rainy morning. A man a few steps behind her, as if waiting or following.

They studied Nassfau Rauttu. He could feel their gaze warm his bones and crawl beneath his flesh, a strange sensation that scattered his thoughts. Uncomfortable, displeasing, he was unable to escape, lying still as their gray eyes bored into him, the edges of the totem biting his palm.

"Are you gods?"

If they were gods, they would not say so. But if they were gods, they would know that Nassfau Rauttu prayed to them, that this quest was in the service of their names. The woman reached down and dipped her fingers into the beast's wound, a gaping slit pried open between ribs. Fingertips wet, she painted Nassfau Rauttu's lips, and a salty tang of iron seeped into his mouth.

Nassfau Rauttu, he heard. The words were not spoken but rang in the hollows of his mind.

He began to shake. A deep and vicious possession thundered his bones. Teeth clenched, eyes pried wide, he watched her stand over him.

They are for you.

She pursed her lips and drew a breath that sounded like the winds of a storm. The buzz of insects and song of birds that filled the prairie suddenly went still. When she finished, the world was silent. Gray eyes upon him, she knelt once again and put her bloodied fingers on his chest.

He never saw the world the same again.

Flesh peeling, bones cracking, a cool and silky storm tore through him, a river running wild through his heart, filling his stomach and expanding his mind—his mind so spacious that no echo of thought returned.

Take them all.

The sun was above him when he opened his eyes. The shadow of the gods was not upon him. The prairie was silent. Only the wind carried life. All else was empty. The essence stolen from the smallest of creatures.

Colors leaped from the golden stalks, the sky shivering with vivid depth. He looked down at the hands of a stranger, paler of color. His arms were not the scrawny limbs of a child. They writhed with muscle. He rose upon legs of effortless strength. Every boy returned to the village a man but still in a boy's body.

Not Nassfau Rauttu.

He heard the distant crack of a twig, could feel the patter of young antelope's pulse, could taste the grass between its teeth. His nostrils flared. He could smell its desperation. It filled him with desire.

Take them all.

Nassfau Rauttu returned to the village on the day of the twenty-second sun. He began his eternal journey by taking his brothers and sisters, the elders of the tribe, attempting to fill the endless hunger that powered the engine of greed. A journey that would not prove eternal after all. It would end at the garden.

All the essence he'd collected over the centuries delivered.

Drayton lay on the ground, breath leaking from him. He clung to the last of the essence and the memories it contained, protecting the final traces of Brenda and James from the garden's greed, hiding them from the tree that searched for more. It was all he had left.

And she wanted more.

2 3

Umi had witnessed miracles.

Stonehenge. The great pyramids. The birth of islands spilling from oceanic faults, the wonder and splendor that enveloped this rare planet teaming with life—single-celled and wonderfully complex. She was there to witness it all.

Yet it paled.

The garden unfolded in ways this world had never known. Once a modest plot of land, the Garden House was now buried in a sprawling jungle. Space, it seemed, bubbled from a mysterious fountain like an artesian well.

Something created from nothing.

Umi guided humanity, manipulating nations into war but preventing complete annihilation. Tragedy was necessary to growth. A human mind would not appreciate such guidance. Without her, they would still be bashing each other with clubs.

Was she evil?

Her callous position on death would be regarded as such. She allowed men such as Hitler and Stalin to cause such suffering. The Christian God did too, yet he was regarded as good. She doubted historians, if they knew of her existence, would see her as such, but they couldn't understand what she had done, what would have happened to this world without her. Yet even with all her prescience, she did not anticipate this.

Ambrogina.

The balcony doors opened. Mors carried two teacups. Hunched at the shoulders and slightly shuffling, the old man placed them on the table. None of the aches and pains accompanied their aged figures. Time had no grip on them.

They had shared a drink for most of their existence, usually in the morning. The flavor they consumed depended on what the culture embraced. They were quite proficient at blending in.

He leaned upon the railing and grunted.

Rarely did they speak out loud. Their companionship had transformed into a shared consciousness. They knew what the other was thinking. At least, that was his experience. The best way to keep a secret was to fool another into believing in complete transparency.

Trust was as much a weapon as it was a tool.

Did she know Ambrogina was extraordinary? Of course she did. The child was a rare human who possessed latent creativity. The power it carried was underestimated by humanity. The ability to create with the mind was the cornerstone of the universe.

Still, Umi had not expected this.

Space was expanding, the wall distant features. The tree a living skyscraper. *The true power of creativity.*

"Extraordinary," Mors muttered.

Umi's smile was slight. His boyishness entertained her. After all these centuries, he still found joy in such a childish manner.

"So much more than Nassfau Rauttu," he said.

Ambrogina was unlike Nassfau Rauttu in so many ways. She was already beyond any semblance of humanity. Nassfau Rauttu, their dear progeny, was feeding her.

"Do you remember when we found him?" she said.

Mors turned. It wasn't often she initiated conversation. Sometimes it was fun to play human, and she was feeling quite spirited. He sat next to her, not having touched his drink.

"We stumbled upon him," she said, "in the field, wielding that rare talent without the knowledge he ever possessed it. Think of all the glorious mistakes that slipped through our hands, Mors. The ones that popped up and we were not there to catch, shooting stars burning up before they could be captured and nurtured."

She snapped her old and spotted fingers, unveiling an empty hand. So many opportunities missed.

"We caught her."

There was a clearing in the dense overgrowth where vines circled and branches wept. It was the only ground visible. Upon it lay a shirt-less form. Breath trickling from him, the last drops of essence keeping him alive. All that he had collected now fed swaying branches.

"What did we do with Nassfau Rauttu?" she asked. "We did not set him free for the sake of freedom. We gave him a purpose and freedom to fulfill it. Purpose is the only way something grows. Every being desires their true nature." She lifted a crooked finger. "Nassfau Rauttu was no different."

She had not anticipated his evolution into such a subservient crea-ture. Possessing the unstoppable powers of mind and body, he'd voluntarily eschewed his savage ways to serve humanity. This was beneath him and did not serve her needs whatsoever. He'd required some manipulation to reignite his bloodlust—a move that clouded his vision and hid Umi and Mors's true identities. It also tightened the snare.

Luring a victim with their own will was more effective than the tip of a spear.

His purpose was to take, not to serve. He did so without knowl-edge of his fate, for to know his destiny would change his desire. He reaped essence from the human population to feed another greater than himself. Umi didn't know who that would be until she had discovered Ambrogina.

The tree was still growing. Ambrogina had become the garden, converting essence into creative brilliance. Branches stretched toward the sky, and vines strangled each other like twining snakes. Flowers released perfumed scents clouding the air. A light beamed from somewhere in the thicket, streaming with the intensity of a star.

Vines reached the balcony. Drayton had been sacrificed on an altar of dirt, his essence spilled like the blood of a lamb. Mors watched with stupid reverence, the light caught in the watery puddles of his eyes.

Umi resisted the same expression, although awe was rising inside her. This answered the most fundamental question of all creation, a question steeped inside every sentient being, a question even immortals asked.

We exist to grow. That is our purpose. Everything is born to grow, to create, to give. It's an innate instinct in every living thing. Humans give birth to children and ideas. Ambrogina will give birth to a new dimension of reality.

Umi was the one who had discovered Ambrogina. Without her, she would be wasting away in an apartment somewhere, scrambling with one failed relationship after another. It was Umi who had brought her to the garden, Umi who had allowed her to fulfill this purpose. Without Umi, Ambrogina was nothing more than a seed.

Withered and wasted.

* * *

QUIET FELL OVER THE GARDEN.

The haze settled. Light from the tree faded to a dull glow. The garden had stopped growing. Nassfau Rauttu was nearly empty. He held a trace of essence, but it would not be enough. Death might seem like a reward for him, but the preciousness of life was never clearer than when death was near.

Live, Nassfau Rauttu, Umi thought. *You earned that much.*

She hid a secret smile behind her raised teacup. It was a thought, an idea—something she hadn't considered until now. Loyalty was a weapon employed by the powerful to subdue the weak.

"Perhaps we should slow down," Mors blurted.

For a moment, Umi thought he might have glimpsed the secret she was hiding, his tone slightly desperate.

"Why, darling?"

His bushy eyebrows pinched like wooly caterpillars, casting shadows over his gray eyes. It was not suspicion that knitted his brow. It was concern.

"Are you afraid?"

"No, love." He paced the railing and spread his arms. "You gave Nassfau Rauttu immortality, but this I do not understand. And neither do you. Let's not rush into the unknown."

"Now is not the time to be fearful, Mors. A daylily blooms for but a day. Turn our heads and we miss its beauty. The garden is in bloom, love. It is why we have grown such things. Now is not the time to be timid."

The separation between them was palpable. It had been quite some time since they had spoken so many words. She was hiding intentions from him, and he would soon feel it.

"It's not fear from which I speak, I assure you," he said. "Space is unfolding, Umi! A new dimension of… of what? What will come from it? It could swallow all that we know. We must understand it."

"Are you afraid someone greater than us will emerge?"

"It is more than that, love. This is… we don't know what this is."

"Precisely the point, Mors. Ambrogina is not meant to walk the planet, not someone for us to observe. It is not up to us to decide her true nature."

"You decided Nassfau Rauttu's true nature. You made him what he is."

"No. I did not change him, only fulfilled his true nature. He roamed the planet for this, love. For this. To grow this garden, for it to become something beyond our comprehension. This is pure creation, Mors. If we stop this now, it could wither."

"And what *is* this?" he whispered.

The railing creaked in his hands. A green tendril had wrapped its way through the baluster and reached for his leg. She waved off the greedy thing. Ambrogina was beginning to starve.

I will feed you, she thought.

Umi pushed away from the table and took his hand. They appeared old and feeble, a helpless couple at the end of a very long life. What would life be without someone to witness it with her?

"Let's find out," she answered.

PART V

We shape clay into a pot, but it is the emptiness inside that holds whatever we want.
— Lao Tzu

* * *

When you do something, you should burn yourself up completely, like a good bonfire, leaving no trace of yourself.
– Shunryu Suzuki

NORMAN HOLBRECK

Norman Holbreck was a chef. Past tense.

Three collapsed disks and two surgeries later, he was a professional pill-popper. Instead of a kitchen to run, he fed Ms. Doody in the morning and scooped her poop at night. Norman's prime objective was to avoid pain. Every day, he came close to achieving this goal, some days closer than others. But every day he failed.

This day was no different.

He was on the couch with pillows strategically positioned between his knees and under his armpit. The pills were starting to take effect just in time for an infomercial. The fog of nerve-deadeners covered him with a warm purring blanket. He entered the joy zone when he thought the cutlery that cut aluminum cans as easily as steak sounded cool.

Ms. Doody leaped onto the arm of the couch and pawed her way onto his hip. Normally, he shoved her off. Extra weight wasn't part of the equation. This time, he let her stay because he didn't care. The cloud-ride to titty town was full steam ahead.

An old war movie was on. He couldn't remember what happened to the infomercial, distantly hoping he didn't order the entire set. A bridge had just blown up. Ms. Doody was still on his hip, and the pain was gone. As in mission accomplished. Not since college could he remember life without it. The mystery deepened. He was two hours past his last dose of oxy. A miracle was in the works, and he hadn't prayed to Jesus in over a year.

An idea came to him.

Ms. Doody jumped down and gave a sour meow. He threw his feet on the floor. Norman turned off the television and filled the cat bowl to the rim. It was enough food to keep her alive for at least a week. The neighbors were bound to find her in time.

The goldfish was fucked.

Norman walked outside in his bare feet. It was a perfect summer day. The trees were fully flushed. He swung his arms like windmills, remembering what it was like to climb trees, how aches and pains were temporary and blind courage led the way. Now he walked bare-foot despite broken bottles on the curb.

A few blocks down the street, he stopped.

The Garden House stood dark and empty. The air around it simmered like a summer afternoon. The fig vine quivered on the brick walls as if a fan were blowing from the inside. He'd lived down the street from this historic house for over ten years and never saw the gardens. It was off-limits, and the owners never participated in tours.

Today was his lucky day.

Just to the right of the house, a green gate was cracked open. Norman put his hand on the latch and felt it shudder. The same vibra-tions went through the soles of his feet. He expected to see neatly trimmed boxwoods and expensive fountains.

It wasn't that.

The property was only two acres, but the greenery went on as far as he could see. In the middle of it all was a building-sized live oak that hid in the clouds. The branches groaned like leviathans. Vines and Spanish moss fluttered over its muscled bark. The weird thing was he hadn't seen it from the street.

But, strangely, nothing seemed weird anymore. Just as long as the pain was gone.

He didn't notice the vines, or the path narrowing with budding branches. All he saw was the light. Somehow, he was making that happen. Willingly, lovingly, he wanted to feed the flagging tree.

To make it burn brighter.

He didn't feel the ground as he fell, or his flesh shrivel and deflate. The last experience Norman Holbreck felt was something he would describe as a trickle.

24

*Y*oung was officially a stalker.

It was the fifth time he'd parked across from the brick Tudor. To his credit, he usually only stayed for a few minutes. First he'd call Amber's phone and then watch the upstairs window. He never left a message.

The voicemail was full.

Afterwards, he'd stare at the steps. There were only two of them leading up to the front door. They might as well be stepladders. Occasionally, he'd stay long enough to see her grandmother; she'd sit near the window with a newspaper, harsh light from the television flickering off the walls. He didn't do this because he was a creep. He did it because he cared.

That's what creeps say.

She wasn't acting like herself. Sometimes a good intervention was needed to get a friend back on track. Dev had somehow done that with his surreal story about a wagwam and a bag full of sticky. That was what friends were for. Amber wasn't really a friend, but he told himself she was.

Stalkers said that, too.

But there was something else. It had to do with the first time he'd parked outside the house, the time he'd seen her grandmother standing at the window. She was staring at him. Something funny about her, he couldn't put his finger on it. It was her posture or the way her arms were locked over her chest. It didn't look like her.

She never stared like that again, never even looked out the window. Every day, the old woman sat in that chair and read a newspaper. Sometimes she fell asleep.

Amber wasn't answering her phone, and no one was going to build him a ramp. This time he wasn't going to let that stop him. He turned the van off and activated the side door. The ramp unfolded into the street. Young quickly backed out from the steering wheel and up the driveway.

Tying stray hair off his face, he cruised up to the house. Amber's grandmother was asleep, her head rocked back in the chair, mouth open. A few pebbles on the window would wake her, but then what? A tattooed long-hair didn't calm someone from her generation, wheelchair or not.

The driveway was two paved paths with groundcover in between. The side door was close to ground level. He could knock on that but with only slightly better results than throwing pebbles. No one knocked on a side door. He went around back. The patio was ground level with a sliding glass door. He clutched the rubber wheels and teetered.

The garage door was slightly ajar. A black vehicle was inside. A Jeep was parked in the middle of a two-car space. He hadn't seen another car in the driveway. Maybe there wasn't one. The Jeep was curiously parked in the middle.

Young looked at the house before pushing inside the garage. It smelled normal—dusty and moldy. The shelves were neatly arranged with storage bins. Young pushed up on the armrests of his chair and peeked inside the Jeep. There was luggage behind the backseat and bags in the front. She'd been living here for months but never unpacked?

Or maybe she just packed.

A melodic tone sounded off when he opened the door. It wasn't the alarm type that warned of intruders, but the kind that reminded the driver the lights were on. Or the key was in the ignition. There were two garage openers in the door's cubbyhole, different makes and models. He considered snatching one.

He closed the door quietly, leaving the garage door exactly the way he found it. His tires sank slightly in the lawn as he ventured into the backyard. The garden was weedy, and a ceramic birdbath was decorated with seedy white blobs. He spun around and noticed something behind the garage. It was nothing unusual, just a little out of place.

It was a chair.

It had a hard back and narrow legs that were sunk in the soft ground. A blanket was thrown across the seat. A creepy chill wrapped its arms around Young's neck. Something wasn't adding up. He'd told himself that a lot over his lifetime, and Amber had made him realize he could be making that up. Stare at numbers long enough and they just become funny lines.

"What are you doing?"

Young pushed across the lawn. The glass door snapped closed when he reached the concrete patio. He glided to a stop. The lock clicked in place.

"Is Amber here?"

"I'll ask you to leave my property," she hollered through the glass. "You are trespassing."

"I need to talk with her."

"There's no one here. You need to leave."

"That's her Jeep in the garage."

Eyes glassy with sleep flicked to the garage. She blinked several times before her jaw set, but confusion remained. Maybe he had it all wrong. Amber wasn't hiding. Her grandmother had dementia. Amber just didn't want to talk to him.

But all her stuff is packed.

He swiped his phone and redialed. A muted ringtone sounded off. The old woman looked around then went toward the kitchen. She came back with a smartphone wrapped in a striped furry cover. She held it with two hands then stabbed at the glowing screen, holding her finger down a second too long, not quite grasping the subtleties of touchscreen technology. His call rolled over to a full voicemail.

"That's her phone," Young shouted.

A look of angry surprise dug into her forehead. She reached for the wall and brought back a corded touchtone phone.

Young sped down the driveway. The van door was sliding open. He stopped on the curb. Maybe the cops would be a good thing. Amber would have to come to the door then. She would have to talk to him.

That was quick. The police were already a few blocks away.

The strobes weren't flashing. They were talking with a few people on the sidewalk. Grandmother wasn't at the window. Maybe she was watching from farther back. Amber wasn't coming out of the house. And if Young talked to a police officer, nothing was going to change. *I need to warn her about vampires, Officer.*

Young drove past the police cars, slowing almost to a stop as he neared the conversation on the sidewalk. A woman was shaking her head. The front door of the house was open. It looked like more cops were inside.

A few more blocks and he passed the Garden House.

This time he stopped in the middle of the road. The gates were closed. Trees hung over the walls. There was nothing odd, although he could swear the atmosphere behind the house shimmered like a bonfire was blazing.

* * *

SOMETHING PINGED in the rear of the house.

The house was still a wreck—torn canvases and shattered frames, broken brushes and tubes of paint spattered like roadkill. Drayton's eyes stared from shreds of canvas. The office was open. He hadn't bothered locking it. The Lowcountry maps were strewn across the doorway, thumbtacks sprinkled on the floor.

A green light glowed on one of the computers.

The monitors were black, some of the computers trashed. Some of the backup drives were in pieces, dents in the drywall where they had shattered. He had outdone himself.

Another ping went off.

Cables were tossed around like dead snakes. It took some effort to clear a path and plug one in. Color flickered across a dead monitor. One of his alerts was pinging, a police-chaser app that followed 911 calls.

Earlier in the week, a former downtown chef had gone missing. He lived down the street from Amber's grandmother. The door had been left open. The neighbors had found the cat roaming around and a goldfish floating in a tank.

Police had responded to another missing persons report.

This time it was an elderly couple who did not come to church. Edwin and Margaret Platt hadn't missed a service in over twenty years. When they didn't answer their phone, someone from the congregation went to their house and found the front door open.

Young searched the address and found a Street View shot of the blue house. It was across the street from the Garden House.

He didn't sleep that night.

Make-believe or not, the connections were making a hell of a lot of sense. Sleep came near dawn. It was only a few hours, but during that brief interlude, his dreams were vivid. He thought about the wagwam and the tree. The story had invaded his dreams and taken root. Every night he felt the endless, cool space. And the hole he was digging. The hole too deep to climb out, even if he wanted to.

I am the dark.

Samu followed him to the kitchen. Instead of two scoops, Young poured six. He slid it on the floor.

"Celebrate."

This was it. Whether he was psychotic or the world was plagued with vampires, he was going to keep digging until there was nothing left.

Dev wasn't on the porch. The ashtrays were empty. There was no coffee cup or folded newspaper that suggested he'd come down at all that morning. Young taped a note to the door.

Take care of Samu.

* * *

HE SHOULD HAVE WAITED until dark.

There would be less of a chance someone would see him. They were likely to call the police if they did. Rolling into the garage during the day was risky, but he wasn't going to steal anything.

Just borrow.

Amber's grandmother's white hair, all properly done up, was in the window. The electric light of a television was on the newspaper. Her back to the street. Young glided confidently up the driveway, not too fast, not too slow.

The garage door was still ajar, just like he'd left it. He didn't waste time looking back. The Jeep was still there. He opened the driver's door. The vehicle melodiously told him the keys were in the ignition.

Both door openers were still there.

The light on the box bolted to the ceiling was off. A chain drooped to the garage door. Decko was written on the side of it. Young looked at both controllers. One of them was a Decko. The other one said LiftMaster. He tucked the second one in his saddlebag and threw the Decko back in the Jeep.

He darted down the driveway. A neighbor was walking her dog. The chocolate Lab pulled toward him, but the woman didn't seem to notice. Her eyes were cast farther down the street.

The chef who had gone missing lived two blocks down the street. A cluster of cars were gathered maybe a block past that. Young let the woman pass. She yanked the Labrador when he looked back.

The white hair was still in the window. The newspaper turned silently.

Young crossed the street and quickly navigated the buckled sidewalk. He hadn't noticed all the cars in the street. Maybe there had been just a few of them when he arrived. Now there were vans with telescopic satellite dishes and a crowd across the street. There were five police cars and another one on the way.

Young stopped on the fringe of the loosely gathered neighbors. Quiet murmurs passed between them, some with their hands to their lips, their eyes wider than normal.

There was a man wearing slippers and a *Clemson Dad* sweatshirt. The loop of a coffee mug was hooked on his finger. His eyes were sleepy, but a hint of concern pulled at his face. Young was about to ask, but Clemson Dad volunteered an update.

"Whole family," he said. "Charles saw them walking single file down the sidewalk."

"Missing?"

"He come home late, about midnight or so." He pointed the mug. "Sat in the driveway for a minute when he said the door opened and out they marched out like Canada geese. George and Marlene were in the front, and the little ones followed. Like they were going on a midnight stroll."

The concern had reached his eyes.

"Sixth one this week," he said.

"Sixth?"

There was the chef and the old couple in the blue house, but that was it. Clemson Dad finally looked at Young. His concerned eyes walked up his tattooed arms and, for a moment, rested on the line of gold hoops in his ear. He barely stifled a chuckle.

"Paul." The coffee cup pointed in no particular direction. "Gail said he hadn't been home in days. They don't get along so well, but he's never gone away for this long. Then there was Ansley Meredith and her daughter, I don't remember her name. Yesterday it was Gabe Mosley. His dog was on the front lawn, the door open."

"You said six."

"Doug and Allison." He pointed the mug up the street. "They were the first ones, actually. They were working on a house and just left. Maybe they'll be back. Maybe they'll all be back."

Young followed the general wave of the coffee mug. There was a dumpster in a driveway. Tension coiled around him and squeezed. It was across the street from a brick Tudor.

"You include all the missing pets," Clemson Dad said, "and it's a lot more than six."

"Pets?"

"Mostly cats. Happened about a month ago. Figured someone started trapping them, but this..." Coffee mug wave. "Something isn't right."

Cats.

Even if someone had reported it, it never would've triggered an alert. And if it did, he would've ignored it. Drayton didn't do animals.

Maybe someone else does.

Clopping hooves had arrived with a load of tourists. One of the cops came out to direct traffic. A news van was moved to make room. Sunburned and flip-flopped, the vacation-goers stared at the gawkers, and the gawkers stared back. Before the horse pulled them through the bottleneck, they looked at the house. A few cameras aimed at the open door. The rest of them pointed phones. In a few minutes, a dozen photos would be uploaded to social media. All those ghost stories the tour guides told them were true.

Yes. Yes, they are.

Clemson Dad stared down. "You live around here?"

He suddenly seemed more concerned about the tattooed long-hair than a missing person. Young worked his way through the crowd with an occasional excuse me and a few bumps on the leg. Clemson Dad watched him from across the street, coffee mug hooked in place.

Before long, he was hitting speedbumps in the sidewalk. The carriage had stopped at the corner. This was where the tour guide would tell them about the Garden House. The tourists, though, were still looking back at the missing family's house.

What does missing cats mean? It could be a rogue bobcat in the neighborhood or some dipshit with a .22. But all the cats?

But there was a time gap. Clemson Dad said the cats stopped going missing. It would've been good to get an exact date and a count of how many were missing. Six houses had been emptied and the doors left open. One of them across the street from Amber's grandmother. And Amber wasn't answering the phone. If Grandma wasn't sitting in the window, Young would drag a cop down there and start banging.

The family, according to Clemson Dad, walked out on their own. They did it in a single file, like marching orders had been given. Young didn't ask which way they went.

The Garden House was around the corner. The tourists were still turned around, wide-brimmed hats and black sunglasses aimed at the crime scene. Two children, bored out of their skulls, watched the tattooed headbanger push his way to the corner. Young paused for traffic and then stopped.

Something was off. The trees around the Garden House were twisted, and the air was thick and marbled. The brick wall that surrounded the garden was quivering. The horse began dancing, hooves stamping the brick road. The tour guide offered soothing words, but the horse grew agitated.

A news truck barely slowed down at the corner. It threaded the narrow gap between the carriage and the curb. They were heading toward a story the entire Lowcountry would soon be following, what social media would later dub the Lowcountry Apocalypse.

A teenager was half-running down the sidewalk, a Nikon strapped around his neck. Armed with a phone in one hand, something he could upload immediately, he held the camera against his chest to keep it from bouncing. As he approached the Garden House, wisps of mortar puffed through the vines. He made it to the checkered sidewalk that paved the front of the dual curving steps.

He went down like a sock puppet tossed on the pavement. His face met one of the white marble squares. The camera cracked beneath him, and the phone skidded into the street. A white nugget came to rest on one of the black checkers. It was a tooth.

Strands of hair blew off Young's face.

The breeze was cold and densely humid, almost wet on his cheeks. A ghoulish hand seemed to flow right through him. Still staring at the broken tooth, he didn't notice that, despite the billowing gust that seemed to breathe from a deep freezer, none of the foliage stirred. The trees and shrubs were motionless in a stagnant early morning.

He started across the street to help the kid with the missing tooth when a heavy dull thump landed on the street with the ring of buckles.

The horse had collapsed.

Its legs were bent at odd angles and the head was twisted. The tour guide tumbled off his perch, falling backwards like a scuba diver dropping in. His head hit the horse's hindquarters and came to rest next to the poo bag.

Then came the tourists.

They fell like synchronized narcoleptics. The ones on the outside did headers into the street. Their skulls met the pavement with hollow ripe thuds. Floppy hats and sunglasses scattered between them.

Farther up the street, glass broke.

The news van that had passed the carriage earlier barreled into the back of one of the police cruisers. The wheels jumped the curb. Beyond, the crowd of onlookers lay like sacks of grain dumped from the side of a trailer. Clemson Dad's bright orange sweater was one of them. Young cringed as the news vans hit them like speed bumps.

Then came the birds.

The first was a cardinal. It hit one of the overhead wires and tumbled in a shower of feathers. The others thudded out of sight like a plane had dumped a shipment of fist-sized cargo. They banged off roofs and shot through foliage. This was joined by smaller projectiles.

Insects rained down like gravel.

Black beetles and cicadas and dragonflies pitter-pattered the streets and sidewalks and lawns. Young covered his head and ducked. The noise reached a crescendo then tailed off like the last few kernels to pop.

Silence fell at last.

The chilling breeze had evaporated. The trees stood still. Feathered clumps littered the sidewalk among a layer of dead bugs. Young was still cold. Whatever had happened left an icy brittleness in his bones. He had to get away, had to get back home and warn Dev. Whatever had happened inside the garden was coming out. But something stopped him from turning around. Everything as far as he could see was lying on the ground.

Everything except him.

She was in there, he just knew it. She was in the garden. And whatever had happened in the streets had started in there. He reached into the saddlebag and pulled out the gate opener. She'd left two openers. One was for the garage. He wheeled down the street, exoskeletons crunching beneath his wheels, and aimed the opener. The gate began the slow crawl.

It was not what he expected.

25

*V*alleys had formed. Crevices deep in the earth exposed coppery boulders and knobby roots. At its deepest, multiple rivulets fed a cold stream.

The street couldn't be seen from the Garden House anymore, but Umi could feel the cars passing, felt the locals walking their dogs, the gathering of neighbors down the street. An approaching carriage. The land inside the walls appeared to stretch over rolling hills and wild frontier sprung from Ambrogina's imagination, a dream molded into reality.

A veritable universe was being born, the girl's mind sculpting the essence of life, warping the physics of time and space of this world.

And she's still hungry.

The family of four was the last to feed her, their bodies already hidden beneath the sprawling bramble, thorny stems pulling at their ashen skin. When their lives were released, the tree had grown brighter and taller, but it was like feeding a whale goldfish. Nassfau Rauttu had brought eons of harvest, and still it wasn't enough.

Ambrogina needed guidance. She needed to be fed, to be nurtured. She needed a mother to help her fulfill her true potential, a mother to line up the entire Lowcountry and march them in one by one.

She needs me.

Umi stretched her mind, concentrating on life just outside the Garden House, and locked onto the essence that flowed inside them all—men and women and every living thing that flew through the air or crawled in the dirt: insects and birds, rodents, cats, and dogs, even earthworms and fungi and bacteria. She latched onto the very soul that flowed through their cells.

And inhaled.

A current drew to her like metal shavings to an electromagnet, first escaping a young man running down the sidewalk, then farther out to the horse and carriage and beyond to the crowd down the street. Her mind thrust outward, ethereal spokes plunging through each living organism. She held one of the thick vines that had curled around the bannister. She would not be the recipient of such treasure.

Only the conduit.

The foliage quaked and tremored in the undergrowth. The ground swelled. A hollow crack resounded deep within the earth. In the distance, the tree swayed. A smile lit upon Umi as she reached farther in the Lowcountry—

"What have you done?"

Mors stood in the doorway. His mouth hung thickly open, a ghastly expression prying his eyes wide.

A ticklish sensation danced along Umi as she felt him cast his mind out and assess what she'd done. Never before had she so frivolously swept away such a large swath of life. Sipping from humans here and there was their way to remain unseen, never greedy. There were many instances where she drank from lower forms of life—the insects and micro-organisms and fowl overhead, even the callous consumption from an open neck—but never on this scale.

But this wasn't for her.

"What have you done, love?"

Perhaps he sensed the thoughts she was hiding from him that caused a slight wave of panic to ripple through him. Or maybe it was simply what she had done without sharing her intentions with him. Rarely did they act alone.

But a new universe was dawning.

"Look around you, dear." The warped landscape groaned. "This world is meant to feed what Ambrogina will become. She needs us."

"You don't know what she's becoming, you said so yourself." He swept a hand at branches reaching deep into the sky. "You emptied… this is not a missing person. You created a phenomenon. It won't take long for them to discover we are at the epicenter. They will come for us, love. There are limits to what we can do to stop them."

Her mind had scoured a square mile. It would look like a bomb, the perimeter roughly circular. An investigation would drop a pin in the center.

"Let them come," she said.

"This isn't the fifteenth century. These aren't villagers with pitchforks; we can't wave them off like flies. They'll come knocking on our front door. They'll have sophisticated technology that will overwhelm us. We cannot manipulate them all, love. What then?"

He sounded like a child with his hand in the cookie jar. *What then? I'll take them, too. They'll line up at the gates and march in like the others, little ducklings throwing themselves to the fox.*

"No, they won't submit," he said, reading her grin correctly, her thoughts now readily displayed for him to see. "This story will cross the world. They'll come to investigate, they'll learn what we are, that we have our limits, that we can't reach our minds around the world. They'll stay outside those limits, love. They'll bring twenty-first-century weapons. They'll follow the crumb trail we've been leaving for the last thousand years and smell the wrongness. They'll destroy us, love."

Her lover lacked imagination. If she willed it, she could leave the Lowcountry without a trace, part the crowd that waited for them. She was the fish that could swim through the net, unscathed and unnoticed. But she didn't need to escape. The world that Mors thought was coming for them was about to change.

"Destroy *us?*" she said.

"The garden." He waved his hands. "All of this."

She hid her thoughts. If he caught a whiff of her true intentions, he would resist her. Or perhaps not. Resisting Umi was futile, he knew that. Ambrogina needed her.

Feed me, Mother. I need more, she cried.

Long before Nassfau Rauttu, she had turned Mors into an immortal, reaching deep into his soul to change the code in his human DNA. He had no memory of his immortal birth; neither did Nassfau Rauttu. Or Umi. She had come to the conclusion that she was an evolutionary mistake, a branch of the human species that never died. It was nice to have a companion, and Mors had served that purpose well. But perhaps her subconscious had made him immortal for another reason. Perhaps her subconscious was prescient.

Mors has a purpose other than dispelling my loneliness.

Umi held out her arm. "Let's go see her."

* * *

THE JUNGLE WAS IMPENETRABLE, a tangle of toothy vines and twisted stems without cricket song or jungle rodent. Only the sound of snapping twigs unfurling bright green. Sensing royalty, they opened, an earthy path red with iron beneath their feet.

Umi curled her hand on the crook of Mors's elbow.

A clearing appeared clear of weed and root. Half-buried, the body of Nassfau Rauttu awaited their approach. Ebony flesh that was once newborn and flawless was now faded and drought-stricken. Deep cracks dug across his forehead and the corners of his eyes.

Umi knelt next to him and brushed the dust from his scalp where veins throbbed. He clutched the ground like the sheets of a hospice bed. White threads had risen from the earth and sunk into the valleys between his ribs, stitching him to the ground.

"He's alive." A tone of suspicion laced Mors's words.

She stroked his brow, dry and tight. "The last moments are the most precious."

He was clinging to memories of Ambrogina's parents. Perhaps there was some wisdom in this, holding back memories that might remind her of who she was. Nassfau Rauttu was embracing his true purpose.

She is not Ambrogina anymore.

There was another memory tucked in his awareness. Umi could root it out but decided to let him have it. Memories were jewels to remind him of the life now behind him, the last drops indeed priceless. She bent over and kissed his scalp and delivered the reply Nassfau Rauttu always gave his victims as their essence released. Essence now feeding her garden.

"Thank you," she whispered.

Mors held out his hand and helped her stand. She moved like an old woman. Although lacking the aches that afflicted aging joints, she preferred the slow pace of wisdom. Their journey had been a long one. There was no need to rush.

There never is.

They walked the newly born path—vines unwinding, branches twining overhead. White flowers bloomed upon sight, petals splashing the ground with a delicate touch, a snowy layer that refused to melt. The tree's shade fell on them gradually, gently, the temperature dropping until their breath huffed in thin clouds. Fierce light bled through fissures in the ground.

And still it was a great distance to the tree.

The botanical mammoth creaked and moaned as they approached, crevices in the bark deep enough to swallow a man's arm. Warped bubbles floated out like heavy ornaments. Otherworldly colors swam within their depths—spectrums of light Umi could not describe, spectrums not of this universe.

The orbs hovered around them, space bending near their undulating surfaces. Seeds germinated in their wake, quickly growing, flowering and dying in the moments it took for them to pass over the ground.

Space and time were malleable.

The tree pulsed, each beat roaring inside their heads, as if they stood at the beginning of the universe, random blasts blowing back their hair, filling them with a sensation that vibrated at levels unknown to this world, a sensation that brought them to the brink of tears.

Mors's lips fluttered in search of words or thoughts to grasp what he was feeling and seeing, but this was beyond that. This was the center of a new universe, the birth of a new reality. There was no logical understanding. It was pure and virgin.

The moments before a Big Bang.

He was sobbing when Umi guided him through the hovering bubbles floating out of the trunk's crevices. They stared into the tree's cavity—a cauldron of space folding and unfolding upon itself. To look directly at it was to lose their grip on space and time. Look too long and perhaps sanity would be warped as well.

Inside, a form was curled up, naked and alone.

Vines crept up behind them, their tips slithering over knobby roots. Umi maintained her sense of self in the presence of such grandiosity and the promise of selflessness, to become one with the garden, to sacrifice herself, to give the essence she had collected over her lifetime like Nassfau Rauttu had done. The garden needed to be fed, but Umi wasn't going to sacrifice herself.

I am Life.

She projected that thought toward the tree. The vines turned away from her. Face slack, eyes burning with pools of joy, face wet with adulation and rapture, Mors didn't feel them twine around his ankles.

"Do you remember?" She squeezed his hand.

He nodded stupidly. Her question was vague, but he knew what she was asking, what she wanted him to recall. The tapestry of his life was beginning to unwind.

Do you remember the beginning?

The memory was buried deep in his subconscious, rising to the surface and floating over his awareness. The memory of a time he was sitting at the fire and holding a girl.

His daughter.

His mate had been dead many years, having died giving birth. The shaman had pulled his daughter from the womb, her brow slick and pungent, the grass stained beneath her. He wept as he held his daughter. She would be all that he had and would reach the age of childbearing, but now she would never have a mate, never give him grandchildren. Her hair spilled over his arm.

The fire's light flickered in her eyes.

Bodies were strewn in the clearing, weapons in hand. No wounds to suggest how they died. More bodies were in the darkness. A neighboring tribe had snuck up on them, intent on taking their women and slaughtering their men. Very few of them died at the tip of a spear. It was when he heard his daughter scream that they fell in clouds of dust.

Mors wished them dead.

Umi felt the disturbance. It rippled through what she had come to call the mindfield, where thoughts bloomed like fruit she was free to pluck. Humanity was in its infancy nearly forty thousand years ago. None had affected the mindfield other than Umi.

Until this moment.

She walked out of the darkness and sat across the fire, watching him rock his child like he did on nights when the gods threw tantrums. His daughter had screamed in terror. Mors had wished the invaders' death. The burst of his mind shredded everything around him, absorbing the life force from the men that wished them harm. But he was unable to discriminate from whom he took. Everyone fell, including his tribe.

Including his daughter.

She did not die from the thrust of aggression, but from the love of her father.

Umi had walked alone for centuries before that, unaware of her own beginnings but growing weary and bored. She was life. Here was her mate, her companion. The one who would bring her balance.

Here was death.

Unperturbed by her presence, he laid his daughter down and looked across the fire. Energy hummed between them, one chord resonating with the other.

There is birth. There is death. But life is eternal.

The essence that beat the heart was palpable. She had tasted it many times, knew it to be a silky flavor that filled her. Bodies decomposed to feed the worms, trees fell to give back to the ground. The cycle continued. The wheel turned.

Life and death.

Forty thousand years ago, they stood by the fire and began to dance. She passed along the wisdom of death, his true purpose. His daughter was not there to grieve but to celebrate. Hand in hand, they turned in slow circles, eyes lost in each other, locked together to spend eternity walking the planet.

And now, beneath the tree, they danced again.

Hand in hand they would bring an end to this universe. This garden would consume this reality and bring forth a new one. This was how a universe was born, how a universe died.

Because nothing ever really died.

This was her life's purpose. Not a march to find pleasure; not the fulfillment of desire or conquests of challenge. Her purpose was in front of her. Life itself.

Creation.

The garden was creation in its purest sense, the present moment undefiled. The glory of something coming from nothing. The secret of the universe revealed.

This is why I exist. This is why I am immortal, to bring a new existence into being. The Christians are right. There is a god. I will be that god to this new universe, hearing their prayers, watching their lives.

She put her hands on his cheeks, wet with tears, and smiled. Gray eyes surrendering. His life unraveling. He was death. The essence he'd collected over their lives together began spilling into the ground.

The light in the tree grew brighter.

This was the thought she'd hidden from him. She dropped the veil that concealed her secrets and exposed the intentions she had been hiding, let him see his true purpose.

"Goodbye, love," she said.

2 6

Filaments.

They pierced him, wormed inside him, and proliferated. Branching and rooting through organs, behind his eyes, and puncturing his ears.

A film glossed over his gaze. Umi was a lump, nothing more. But he recognized her presence, felt her probing through him, her earthy fragrance in his head. Mors was somewhere behind her, his words warbling through an ocean. She answered, invisible fingers scratching at his brain. She knew he was clinging to a last few memories.

The last droplets of life hid inside him like stubborn dew that refused to drip, reminded him that his purpose was to feast on the world, to bring his collected treasure back, to give it to the one who set this curse upon him.

The sins I have collected.

The memories of James and Brenda Gallagher refused to budge. Did Amber not want them? Did she forget who she was?

Does she still exist?

There was another memory he held onto, one that Umi did not see. It was a death he had witnessed not long after arriving in the

Lowcountry. Her essence was sweet and comforting, the kind associated with a loving family, a dedicated mother.

Umi left him to decompose in the leaf litter.

A vine fell near him, its terminal bud stirring in the dirt. Its foliage expanded, the tip inching toward his chin. Drayton's fate stood on him with all the weight of this universe. Thin air wheezed through him. Dust clotted on his lips. The moments melted on his tongue, sweet and sour.

Excruciatingly wondrous.

And still, he wanted to live. Wanted to taste whatever life had to offer, no matter the moment. To be experience.

To live.

He sank into the ground, deflating in peace, the end unstoppable. The vine tickled his cheek, pressing upon his sagging lips. Perhaps he smiled. No one was there to witness. No one would absorb the essence that would escape him or hear his last wish.

Do I have essence to give? My own?

Death came as a bright light and a thundering gallop. Debris showered the foliage. Suddenly, there was growth. The clearing that held his body shrank with thickening stems. The vine parted his lips and rested on his tongue. A shadow passed over him. The tree blotted out the sky.

Such beauty, her limbs branched out, new foliage unfurling. Beyond recognition, her roots below him, freed from her mortal coil. She had become the garden. She was becoming something else. Something never before in this world. Not of this world.

She will devour it.

The knowledge was clear and present. She was becoming something larger than the womb, a parasite that would consume this universe. And he was feeding her.

And someone else.

Drayton sensed another presence enter the garden. He came through the gate, staring up in wonder and fear. Drayton couldn't help him, couldn't stop Amber. He was helpless. But there was something more. A secret had entered the garden along with Young and revealed itself to Drayton and only Drayton. A secret unknown to Umi. She wasn't a god, after all. Merely a player. There was someone else playing this game. Someone Umi was unaware of.

Someone who flew higher than her.

Like raindrops hitting dry earth, Drayton gave his final memories to a wanting garden.

Death came to him, quiet and warm. His final breath contained the words he'd uttered so often. Among the clamor of an awakening garden, he whispered.

"Thank you."

2 7

The guesthouse was gone.

Vines swarmed in its place like maggots, a scene ripped from another universe. This was where the famous historic garden was on two acres.

Not anymore.

It was a mess of multicolored blooms and sinewy branches and ropey vines. Above it all, a monstrosity presided, a tree that reached into the upper troposphere. Not a giant redwood from the west coast pointing at heaven like a church spire. This was a titan oak with branches like railroad cars that swayed with great creaking groans, vibrations sinking deep in the ground.

A brilliant white light and thunderous explosion left dark spots in his vision. Shockwaves rattled the untamed garden. The ground undulated like the fabric of a trampoline. Something heavy sank into the earth. His wheelchair nearly tipped over. The saddlebag contents spilled out.

The gate remote settled near a widening fracture.

The foliage quivered, tendrils unfurling like giant tongues. Woody stems swelled and flexed, turning toward him like the heads of serpents. They began to slither.

The fracture widened. The gate remote teetered on the edge. Tremors rattled. He leaned over, quivering. The vines scratched the dirt. As his fingertips brushed the button, sweat leaked into his eyes. The wheelchair tipped as he lunged. His finger sank on the button. It gave a satisfying click.

Nothing happened.

The gate had become a fuckfest of vines. The wheelchair was tipping, the fracture wide enough to swallow him now. Tendrils had wrapped around the rubber tread. He held on, contemplating whether he should throw himself forward and crawl. The nightmare welled up like a tidal wave.

A shadow fell over him.

It was cool and dark, blotting out the sky. The tree sounded like twisting metal. Bark popped off expanding limbs and fluttered in corky bits, the atmosphere turning thick and grainy. Debris glowed like fireflies, a dusting of tiny red-hot coals showering the ground.

A strange sensation filled him.

It moved into his stomach, bled into his chest and across his scalp. A radioactive microwave cooking him from the inside, some nuclear fallout that turned the garden inside out was now boiling his organs. The wheelchair was almost icy to the touch.

Someone coughed.

He spun around expecting to see something disfigured and unexplainable pulling itself from the fracture, a herd of zombies crawling out of middle earth. He swallowed hard.

It was a bed.

"Mom?" The word slipped from his mouth, almost as if he'd rehearsed it. As if he'd said it before and couldn't stop it.

The covers pulled tight against her chest, arms resting on top. Metal bars along the sides. She was bald, her face sinking into her skull, a tube taped beneath her nose.

"It's almost time." A middle-aged nurse walked out of the vines, her hair vivid red. She checked an empty pouch on a metal stand. The nurse didn't have to say it. Everyone in the room could hear the wet rattle.

"Come on, let's go." Someone tugged Young's elbow. "You don't need to stay."

Young pulled his arm away and looked up, his throat swelling. The scene grew blurry.

Bo.

It was his brother; he was reaching for him. His older brother, the one who'd tended the farm since Young was born, had cared for him when he wasn't doing chores. The brother who'd cared for him after Mom had died.

The brother who'd died too soon.

They all did. But Bo...

He wanted to say, "You're alive. Bo, you're alive." He wanted to wipe his eyes and grab him and tell him maybe they could save Mom if they just didn't stop the treatment, that he shouldn't get in the car the day that truck ran through a light, that he didn't give a shit if this was a dream. He opened his mouth to beg the nurse to stay, and something else came out.

"Go, then. Get out; leave if you want."

Because those were the words he spoke that day.

And then his arm involuntarily yanked away from his brother because he'd done that too. This wasn't a dream. It was a memory. And it played out on stage rather than the small dark room in his mind.

A featured act.

Her hand was dry and brittle. If he squeezed, it might crumble. And then he was crying. That was what he had done the day it happened. He was doing it now. This memory had been locked away, now fresh out with all the rage and misery and longing, the delicate feel of her hand and smell of her skin. He cried again, just like before. If he could reach back and take Bo's hand too, he'd probably never stop.

Don't go.

The nurse dabbed her lips with a damp cloth. Her tongue darted out and fell back. Even that was too much. Another pause between breaths and Young squeezed.

"It's okay," he said. "Go on, Momma."

Those were the only words he could get out. She wasn't leaving without a fight, never did. Didn't want to leave him. He had to tell her it was okay.

Her eyes fluttered open.

Young remembered looking up to see her staring at the ceiling after the last breath, chest eerily still. Her other arm was out like someone was coming for her, like maybe the angels were coming through the ceiling and a golden staircase was descending. He liked to think that was where she went.

He didn't remember her smile, though.

The sagging corner of her mouth tugged upward just enough. Maybe it was a tick. She was looking across the bed. The nurse had left the room, and it was just Bo and him now. But she wasn't looking at them.

Someone else was there.

Smooth, muscled arms extended from an ordinary shirt, a damp washcloth in his hand. He leaned over and tipped his head to the side. She tried to say something, but only a puff of air escaped.

He came back.

Young didn't remember seeing her smile or Drayton in the room. He had buried his head in his hands just before she died. Bo was behind him. He'd never said anything about Drayton coming into the room, either.

Because we didn't see him.

Heat flooded Young's cheeks. His ribs squeezed and ached. Each sob struck like a hammer. Sparks shot holes through his stomach and rifled down his legs. He fought the pain and stiffened, wiped his face and pounded his fists against the armrests, his legs. His scream was muffled in the closing vines.

He shouted until his throat burned, his lungs ached. Shouted until he was empty. Not caring about the absurd nightmare, the hallucination, the memory he was transported back to relive, how any of this could even be possible. Emotions coursing through him, a lava flow scorching and cleansing his thoughts and ideas, who he was and what he believed. Carving new tracks, opening new avenues for the feelings to pour through, leaving a sense of spaciousness as endless and open as the heavens, a void that accepted his pain without judgment. That everything was exactly as it was supposed to be. Everything was right here. It was this; it was now. A thought, pure and simple, floated out.

I am the dark.

The foliage crackled around him; twigs snapped underfoot. The wind was on his face, the earth at his back. From the slurry of green, a face appeared. Dark and empty, it floated into focus. Eyes relaxed and unblinking. Complexion ashen and slack.

Drayton stared.

This was not the memory he was looking at. The man he'd sought was close enough to touch. But the world was strangely on its side, the earth pressed against his cheek. Drayton's as well.

He had fallen.

Lying in the dirt, the wheelchair gone, they were face-to-face. White filaments penetrated Drayton's pores and rooted into the earth as if he had been stitched to the ground, as if it was holding him tightly. Never letting him go.

Vines had wrapped around his neck. One had reached into his mouth and remained like a breathing tube anchored in the corner of his lips.

I found you.

When Amber first came to him, he could've come right to the garden. Wet heat poured down his cheeks again, tears pooling against the bridge of his nose.

"What did you do?" he whispered.

The memory of his mom's death, the live-action memory of holding Bo's hand and watching her take her last breath, the realization that she had gone gracefully with Drayton at her side... *that was you.*

The foliage shuddered as if it heard.

Anguish fueled the old familiar furnace of anger, red-hot and erupting. He slammed a fist on the ground and felt the world tremor. He punished the earth for his imperfections. His fears. Pummeling a divot, dirt spraying over Drayton's face, clinging to the whites of his unblinking eyes, a thin layer settling on his pale cheek.

Panting, sobs hitching his throat, he clawed at the soil until the heat and fury spilled into the spaciousness that had opened inside him. He swallowed the grief and sniffed back the fury. There was room for the pain and suffering, the guilt and confusion. He felt as endless and accommodating as the emptiness of space. It was not cold and unfeeling.

It was warm and accepting.

Everything existed because of space. And space existed to allow everything. Young experienced this expansion in his heart and head, as if the crown of his skull opened up to peer into the secrets of the universe. That the space was inside him.

And secrets too.

He rolled over and reached out, brushed the debris from Drayton's cheek, and closed his eyes. A beautiful man who gave everything, Young was there to bear witness. He deserved that much.

The ground thundered again. Branches exploded and vines ripped apart, foliage fluttering like confetti. The jungle was parted like giant waves. A path cleaved through the toothy thicket.

It reached all the way to the tree.

28

*M*ors was on all fours.

He understood. He was more than a companion to pass the centuries. He was a vessel, like Nassfau Rauttu.

Ambrogina needed him.

Umi laid him between the deep arms of buttressed roots. Aged beyond the limits of human life, unrecognizable—pale and parched, flesh hugging sharp angles, his mouth a desperate hole. Sadness was faint and fleeting. She would have preferred to keep him at her side. Fondness had found a place in her, a petty, human emotion, but how could she not feel something for her lifelong companions?

Raging currents bled from him, yet something was wrong. The garden wasn't responding. Ambrogina wasn't becoming more with Mors's sacrifice, and Umi didn't know why. And what she didn't know was a threat. Mors gasped a desperate breath of a drowning man.

She stopped the bleeding.

The tree had the girth of an inner-city building. Umi dragged her fingers over the deep ridges. Leaves cascaded, puffy seeds floating on a gentle breeze. Swaths of moss gracefully swayed as she ducked beneath massive branches.

"What are you hiding?" she whispered.

Mors attempted to lift his arm as she circled back around. Jowls slack, an excess of skin quivered as he attempted to speak. The words raked his throat.

"Shh, my love." Umi knelt beside him. "Save your strength. She will need the rest of you."

She pressed his hand to her cheek and kissed the dry, delicate flesh. His eyes, still razor-gray, held no malice.

You are death, love.

Umi pressed her cheek against the tree, closed her eyes, and felt a vibrant surge, a subtle pulse of energy ride down her spine. She slipped her arm between the corky ridges, the valley deep and glowing, fingers finding the tree's core soft and warm. The energy within was raw and dangerous, pure essence boiling out impurities of human imperfection.

She let her mind drift inward.

Mental fingers probing, she sought the center where Ambrogina's body was curled into a fetal position. There she gently stroked with her mind like a mother kissing the forehead of her newborn.

"There, there," she whispered. "Mother's here."

No longer a human mind, Ambrogina was easy to penetrate and manipulate. Umi gently plugged into a bubbling well of precious essence, delicious and raw; it filled her throat with ecstasy so boundless, freedom so pure, that she began weeping.

The expansion of her own consciousness extended out to the garden walls bulging to contain her. Once they came down, Ambrogina would race outward like an exploding star, swallowing the universe, consuming souls and slaking a thirst that would know no end.

A Big Bang.

And Umi would ride her like a steed—a wild and raw animal with very little understanding of what she was becoming. This new universe needed a god.

Ambrogina, her only begotten child.

The garden shuddered. A distant thunder without lightning. A disturbance foreign, a particle of grit rubbing beneath her eyelid, aching in her teeth.

How did I not see this?

Mind still plugged in to Ambrogina, she flicked her hand, bending the garden to her will. Vines as thick as pythons snapped like gunshots. Foliage ripped and roots unearthed, the impenetrable jungle parted. Mind sniffing the ground like a bloodhound, she found the trespasser next to Nassfau Rauttu.

It was the boy.

Umi couldn't understand how he'd gotten this deep into the garden without her sensing him. The personality that was Ambrogina had nearly completely dissolved into pure awareness. She wouldn't recognize the boy or care if she did. The human race was no longer a concern of hers any more than stepping on a bug.

Umi summoned him.

Vines twined around him and lifted him off the ground. In moments, he was passed toward the tree and delivered. Umi watched with curiosity as the tattooed boy was presented to her. Arms out, his shriveled legs dangled below him, feet just above the ground. His hair was wild and knotted, draped across his face. He peered down at her without fear.

A child.

He had been parked outside the grandmother's house, hardly a friend of Ambrogina's, barely an acquaintance. Why was he here?

And why don't I know him?

A ripple of concern went through her like a knotted rope pulled from her hands. Silence had fallen in the garden. Even the tree had stopped swaying. No groans in its mass. No essence to feed it. Everything stopped. Everything waited.

Umi took a step closer.

Her old and wrinkled form, the elderly Umi Eilif, transformed into the lithe and dangerous young woman. Sexual energy sizzled on her darkening flesh. The foliage around her quaked as she circled the boy, vines twisting around his arms and torso.

Her mind constricted around his thoughts.

He stiffened. Her invasion would feel like an adult squeezing into child's clothing, the seams pushed to their limits, threads popping. She was careful not to break him. His thoughts were easy to pick. His personality convenient to absorb.

Almost too convenient.

She felt the mystery beneath his mental construct. It was the same ruse Umi and Mors had presented to Nassfau Rauttu when he'd attempted to directly know them. It was how they hid their true identities until they were ready to reveal themselves. And now she was seeing the same façade in this boy. This tattooed and damaged boy.

"Who are you?"

She waited for an answer in thoughts or words. But he hung silently, his mind still presenting a cardboard cutout of a personality —handicapped all of his life, a young man angry at the world.

The vines coiled tighter.

He groaned at first. Then screamed. His flesh bulged between the green cords. His ribs popped like chicken bones. His head fell to the side. She willed him awake and soothed his suffering, deadening the nerves that told his brain that she'd broke him in nine places. If he didn't reveal himself, she'd let him feel it.

"Who are you?"

A string of drool hung from his lip. He peeked through strands of wavy hair. Was she mistaken? He didn't seem to know who he was any more than she did—a confused and paranoid young man with no purpose.

She dug deeper.

His thoughts were a brittle mantle of ordinariness. She was careful not to plunge through them like a drill in search of oil. She had no sense of what was below them. His true nature felt mysterious and empty. Perhaps he was special like Ambrogina, a rare human with the potential to become something more than human. *Did I miss him?*

She had been lucky to discover Ambrogina. Perhaps the girl had drawn the young man to her. That was logical. He didn't blink. He was brazen in his courage. Even daring.

He remembers Nassfau Rauttu.

"You don't know who I am," she said. "I see your thoughts and beliefs, who you think I am. But you are mistaken. I am beyond your comprehension."

The smell of fear oozed from him, pungent and sour.

"I will pull you apart, peel your skin, and let you feel every nerve ending your frail and human body contains. I will keep your heart beating so that you feel the full extent of your senses."

A vine fell out of the canopy and snatched a flower from the ground. It presented it to the boy.

"I will watch and listen as you experience the true depths of human suffering, for I am Life—I am all parts of it. I am its beauty and its joy; its pain and suffering. I will do these things not for the sake of torment, but for you to know your true nature."

She parted his hair.

"To reveal it."

It wasn't compassion that drove her to say these things—to know the true self was truly a gift and she would be a compassionate god. But he was a mystery to her. A mystery she needed to know.

Tell me who you are.

She explored him again, harvesting more thoughts, absorbing them like dewdrops, making sense of who he believed he was. His affection for Ambrogina was buried beneath layers of self-doubt and anger. Umi looked toward the tree. A slight grin fell across her face. An amused chuckle escaped her.

You're hiding him.

A trace of Ambrogina still remained, a faint ghost of personality that, despite her agitation and resistance to the boy, liked him. She was drawn to him, a magnetic reaction of affection. Perhaps she wasn't even aware of it.

You're protecting him, blinding me from him, sneaking him into the garden. And for what, Ambrogina? What did you expect would happen, that I would never find him? That you would keep him under a rock?

She was holding onto him for human reasons. Perhaps she knew how close she was to completely dissolving, that the personality that knew itself as Ambrogina was an illusion, and bringing Young into the garden would remind her of who she was. That she still existed.

That will pass.

If Umi was to be the mother and god of a new universe, she couldn't allow Ambrogina to hide. This was a show of power. The naughty girl.

Umi needed to take it back.

She heard the sound of tearing fabric. Young's clothes lay in shredded piles below him. Held up nude for her to see, the flesh on his arms turning purplish where the vines strangled the circulation, masking the tattooed vines. He was a canvas of ink, the artwork coursing around his midsection, running down his underdeveloped legs.

A rogue breeze rustled the tree.

I have your attention?

With a wry smile, Umi dragged the back of her fingers down his stomach and around his clenching buttocks. The vines lowered him closer. She frowned at the artwork down his back. A tree went from shoulder to shoulder, twisting branches down his arms and gnarly roots creeping down the backs of his legs. A coincidence or human premonition?

Have these two been drawn together all this time?

A face on his thigh, familiar eyes in a dark complexion. Umi stroked the remarkable likeness and, despite the imminent threat, a sheet of gooseflesh rose on his thigh. His useless legs responded to her touch as she scoured his thoughts, once again delicately prancing through his mind. His feet twitched as she found deep traces of Nassfau Rauttu in his memories.

"Was it Nassfau Rauttu who hid you?"

A stiffening wind blew his hair back. The boy didn't react. She felt another presence involved in this mystery besides Ambrogina. She suspected Nassfau Rauttu, but he was emptied of life.

Who else is here?

The boy's obsession with Nassfau Rauttu appeared true and seeking, no evidence of collusion. If Young was indeed his prodigy—just as

Nassfau Rauttu was hers—then he was an unwitting one. Young had no idea he was being groomed for this fate. That would have helped keep him from Umi's sight.

Perhaps, in his final moments, Nassfau Rauttu had drawn him into the garden and cloaked him with his final breath. That was why she'd found the boy at the body. But then why did she suddenly see him? Was it because she had hijacked the garden from Ambrogina?

Did I underestimate Nassfau Rauttu?

Leaves showered down like an autumn storm, swirling on the ground and whipping through the trees. Umi felt pressure all around, not just on her body but on her thoughts as well. Ambrogina was curious, too. She was attempting to look inside Young's mind as well. But Umi stood in the way, blocking her entrance. She needed to keep them separate; she needed to kill this curiosity before it strengthened Ambrogina's presence.

Before she did that, she needed to know.

What was this boy's true identity? What was below this personality veneer? A wave of excited discovery tingled inside her.

Did he hide essence in you? That's why he wasn't enough for Ambrogina to become. Nassfau Rauttu discovered what I would do with him and transferred a portion of essence into your being!

The boy could be a vessel with a hidden treasure capped with a mental lid. He wouldn't know that he carried lifetimes of essence and memories inside him. A smile slithered deep into her cheeks. Umi's eyes narrowed.

He brought you to the garden to retrieve it.

An angry burn lit Umi's cheeks. Perhaps she hadn't had to betray Mors after all, but it was too late for that. The pressure increased behind her. Ambrogina could sense it too. She was hungry. Mors would be enough for her to break down the walls, but Young would guarantee it.

The vines creaked as they lowered him. His legs twitched, toes brushing the soil. A newborn storm blew dust and grit against his cheeks as his hair fluttered back. Eye to eye, Umi drew him closer. Their lips brushing, she tasted his fear and confusion. A cool wisp escaped him. She stroked his cheeks and slid her fingers behind his head. Physical pain was no match for the discomfort of the mind.

She probed his thoughts once more.

Ambrogina's presence pressed against her like a child held against her will. Umi looked into Young's eyes with a seductive tongue between her lips.

"I want you."

She dug into him one last time, preparing to plunge deep into his subconscious and unearth what treasures hid below. His thoughts, however, splintered like thin ice. An oilfield of essence did not release. Umi began to withdraw.

It was too late.

Ambrogina's presence poured into Young. The dam had been broken, and nothing would stop the force she had become. Umi's mind was caught in the current and swept inside. She would not find thoughts below the façade of personality or anything of substance, no essence to feed the garden. Young contained nothing at all.

He was an endless void of emptiness.

2 9

I have no body to fear.

I am dissolved in a primordial soup where stars are born. I am not my senses, not my body, not my thoughts. I am all that ever will be and all that ever has been. I have no name.

I am the breath of existence.

I will become more. I will become what is beyond the walls. I will become the streets and houses, oceans and sky. I will become the place where I had a name, where I was bound by flesh. I will dispel that dream.

I will be its savior.

The one who is named Umi is with me. She is Life. She is the one who will break down the walls. It is her breast upon which I will feed, her who so selflessly gave me Death. It is Death who rests at my tree, who empties of essence that I may become. It is Death she has sacrificed.

And there is only Life.

But she pulls away; she leaves me hungry. There is something separate in the garden, something that is not me. Umi feels it too. She comes to me, and I allow her inside, feel her mind knit with cold needles into me, the sharp edges of her thoughts, the spiky corners of her mind take control. She saddles me and digs with spurs, becomes my eyes in search of what is separate. I allow her to ride me, allow her to see.

There.

A body lay stitched to the earth, heavy and dense. I know him. Drayton is a shell of his previous self, emptied and alone. Sliding through filaments, I assume his eyes, assume his ears and nose, assume his flesh.

He has nothing left to give.

It is the one lying next to him that Umi sees. He is the one who is separate. I know him, too. A memory rises. I knew him outside the walls, in the dream when I was Ambrogina and he was Young. He still is.

And I am still Ambrogina.

The hot breath of Umi's anger blows in the garden. Her agitation burns inside me. She is bothered by his separation. She does not know him. There is something within him. There is something he is hiding even from himself.

He does not know who he is.

She wrings pain from his body. So irrelevant, the human body. A shell to be discarded, a husk that imprisons the true self. So impermanent, the sensations. She seeks to discover his secret, opening herself up to penetrate deeper. This intertwining reveals her own essence and tugs on my desire to seek more. I want to feed but avoid taking from her. Instead, I see the reflections of memories skidding inside her, memories like colors across the skin of bubbles.

She contains so many.

These are the memories she has taken, but it is the ones at the bottom that define her. These are the memories that belong to her. These are the memories before she became Life. Before she was Umi.

When she was a child.

Dirty and frightened, she hides in a dark place. Her mother took her there and made her stay, struck her when she tried to follow. In fear, she hid. Even when the shouts came closer and the rocks clattered, when the women screamed and the men screamed louder, she did not move. She closed her eyes and held her hands over her ears.

She wet the ground.

It was when quiet came that she followed the light to find her mother. There were fires where her family cooked animals and shelter where they lay. Now they lay on the ground with open mouths and spilled bodies. There were strangers who stood among them, dragging them and taking the covers from her people.

Umi watched the strangers take what did not belong. A woman's legs lay strangely apart and her arm twisted. Her face was muddled and clotted with mud as one of the men mounted her, his buttocks clenching as he forced his way between her legs.

Umi recognized her mother's hair.

The pressure gathered within. And when she let it out, it shrieked like a great predator from above. The strangers saw her then. They did not come for her, did not cover their ears. Umi suddenly felt them like pebbles strewn across a shallow creek. The pressure was too much for her to contain.

When she opened her eyes, a man was standing over her.

He did not look like the strangers. They were lying where she last saw them, crumpled in awkward positions, mouths open, eyes staring into the heavens. The man was slender and elegant. His face smooth and familiar. He was the one who gave her the great expansion, took away her fear. She felt her mind open, felt the world around her. She became who she is today.

She became Life.

Young's pain pulls me out of Umi's memories. He hangs nude in the limbs, head limp as she searches his mind, picking his thoughts like fruit, poking at what lies beneath. He's hiding something, she knows. I know, too.

I am curious.

I contract from the walls that surrounded the garden and center in the tree. He contains something quite vast that draws me toward it. Curiosity becomes obsession that I cannot deny. I need to know him. Even the promise of essence begins to pale. There is something he possesses that will fulfill me. Inside the walls, I am becoming but am not satisfied.

What does he have?

Umi stands in my way, surrounding his mind. She feels me gather. His pain is palpable as she pecks the fabric.

And then breaks through.

The vacuum of empty space draws her into the void. She struggles to retract, to gather her mind into her body, but I am a current. I am the energy that flows, the water cascading through the hole.

I am unstoppable.

Together, we flow into the void. He is endless. He is formless. He contains the space to hold all of me and all of her. Hold all of everything. I bleed into him, where I am no longer becoming.

I just am.

Umi dissolves into this nowhere, her consciousness breaking apart. She is diluted in the void, becomes nothing and nowhere as her body dries into a leathery husk that falls at the foot of the tree.

I am still here.

Because I am the light. And he is the dark.

One cannot be without the other. Life and Death. The flow eternal.

With you, I am whole.

Without you, I feed and never fill.

We continue, one into the other, the snake eating its tail. There is no need to consume the world outside the walls. There is only here, where flames begin to rage and foliage begins to wither. The fire purifies and collapses until there is no light or dark. No pain or pleasure. No enlightenment. There is no me. There is no you.

There is only this.

3 0

The ocean was black and starless.

No thoughts of where she was or how she got there. Or where she had been. Every second brand new. Memory cleansed in the rise and fall of the black waves. Up the crest, down the valley.

Again. And again.

She didn't question being in such a place any more than one questioned a dream. It was just up and down and rock a bye baby.

Until the snow began.

Snowflakes like feathers. They landed not on the black waves of a moonless ocean but weaved a gray blanket on firm ground, giving rise to a memory.

It sprouted like a seedling.

It was the year snow had fallen in the Lowcountry. It was nighttime when it came. She sat in the window and watched the snowflakes melt on the driveway and road, a slick shine that gobbled them up. The grass was different. Puffy white snowflakes perched on winter blades and piled up on the branches of barren trees.

Halos glowed around streetlights.

The world grew soft and silent. Sound damp and cold. She twirled around the front yard with her tongue out, and her mom came out to join her, falling on the ground and waving her arms and legs.

A snow angel, she said.

When her dad joined them, they scraped the ground to make snowballs. They didn't have gloves, their fingers cold as steel. Amber had a pyramid of tiny ones, and her mom and dad were making a big one. Cheeks red and foggy.

Laughing.

She sat next to her pyramid and watched her parents make a snowman as tall as her knees with a baby carrot for a nose. Her dad wrapped up her mom and rolled on the ground, snow sticking to their sweaters and Mom shouting for him to stop but not really meaning it. Amber pretended to protect her. In a fit of laughter as warm as summer vacation, she fell between them.

A memory came from nowhere.

It was an apparition from the ethers, presented to her. She had been lost in the black ocean of forgetting—her identity dissolved in expanding spaciousness that had no end. She was nobody in a dream —a never-ending dream. But that memory... her mom's shampoo, her dad's whiskers.

I remember.

The black ocean was still rising and falling, but she could hear it now. The waves rose in shrill alarm and dropped slowly into a receding trough. Something fluttered. A moment later, it happened again.

She was blinking.

She dreamed her arms were branches that reached into the sky and her feet rooted deep into the ground. Now her head, heavy and full, was cradled in a deep pillow. The world was muffled. *Like snow.*

A sooty taste on her tongue, coating the hair in her nostrils. She pushed onto elbows and felt her flesh tighten in the cool air.

She was nude.

Her lower half was buried in volcanic ash. A gray blanket extended to the remains of a brick wall. Once there was a garden; now there was only ash. No trees or guesthouse. The Garden House was gone.

Houses across the street stared over the wasteland, and the wall lay in pieces on the sidewalk.

Waves shimmered above the road. A carriage was in the street. The horse lay on its side still in its harness. Nothing moved.

Nothing lives.

That thought seeped into her awareness, as if she absorbed the realization. Her body was light and strangely porous. Sensations moved through her from above and below like breath coming and going through her flesh. Her head was cool and weightless, her scalp smooth and hairless. Even her eyebrows had vanished.

The shrill rise and fall of sirens was in the distance.

Silence, though, had claimed the surroundings. She searched her memory but found only dreamy thoughts slipping through her fingers, the illogical memories of branching arms and rooted legs. She had come to the garden to draw.

Now there's nothing.

Young lay next to her. His back tattoos were visible through a light dusting. Puffs of ash blew from his nostrils, his head half-buried. His scalp was smooth, the earrings gone. She swiped the edge of her hand across his back, felt his breath sweep in a long stroke.

The tree.

She had never seen the extent of his tattoo, only the branches and vines that snaked out from his sleeves. A gnarly, twisted trunk reached across the shoulders and spanned the small of his back. Roots went over the hips and down the buttocks. Thorny vines twisted in branches draped with moss.

I am the dark.

The dregs of a deep and disturbing dream shuddered through her. She was the center of a universe, absorbing sunlight to fill her desire. Even now, she felt the omnipresent sensation of every organ in her body, every cell. Her bones like branches. But it wasn't sunlight she had absorbed. She had taken something cool and silky from the world, something pure and elemental.

"The light," she whispered.

Young twitched at the sound of her voice. His eyelids fluttered open but remained blankly calm. She sensed thoughts stir in his awareness. They felt like grit tossed into the wind. They sank through her porous body and presented themselves to her.

Where am I? he thought.

It echoed in her mind, not a sound but more of a vibrating image that developed in her awareness. She willed his thought to be softer. It had filled her head and flashed behind her eyes. She winced while watching him.

You are here, she thought gently.

He turned his head, eyes sliding toward her, studying. In the dead-quiet atmosphere, they stared. Strangely calm, the moment hung pregnant and wanting, drawing on them to be closer. Her hand on his back, a warm buzzy energy flowing.

He pushed off the ground, shedding a sheet of ash from his shoulders, shaking it from his scalp. His chest was smeared with soot. She hooked his arm to help him sit up when the ash fell from his legs.

He bent a knee.

The moment froze. They locked eyes. Something wasn't right. Scant memories told them so. His jaws flexed as his stare grew larger. His memories rose like tiny bubbles, a history in a chair, a life lived never knowing the sensation of standing, balancing.

Bending a knee.

The tattoos danced over a muscled thigh dimpled at the knee and curving toward his groin. His toes wiggled beneath the ash; his calf bulged and flared. He began shaking his head as the carbonated memories demanded attention; the top had been pulled off the clean slate and the past rushed in.

The garden was gone, the walls knocked down. This was impossible.

Moving my leg is fucking impossible.

A cold wave rushed through him. His hand quivered. Amber stood up, unabashed in nudity. No one was there to witness her climb out and expose herself. She reached down and took his hand. Eyes locked, he hesitated.

This is a dream, he thought.

She pulled him toward her before panic overtook him. He surged off the ground and overcompensated with newfound strength. Knees buckling, his doubt hit him. She threw her arms around him. Their bodies warm and smooth against each other, a current flowed between them. She held him upright, her cheek against his, emotions welling up hot and wet.

Slowly, she let go.

He stood alone, swinging his arms. His eyes glittered beneath smooth and hooded brows. He shook his head, fending off doubt and fear he would wake up and find himself napping in his chair. But the legs were strong and capable. His belief was catching up.

The sirens called from the corner.

They stood with only dust to cover them and watched lights flash against the houses. Police were the first to arrive. An ambulance was next. A fire truck howled a few blocks behind them.

Tentatively, they climbed out of their cars.

Their thoughts polluted the atmosphere like grit in a sandstorm. Dispatch had received calls about multiple and mysterious deaths in a large area of downtown. That was followed by an earthquake that shook all of the Lowcountry.

No one had reported the disappearance of the Garden House.

Nobody had yet ventured to the epicenter to witness it. Now the police and EMTs and firemen stared at a hairless couple of young adults covered in soot.

Ghostly color streamed around them, the opaqueness pulsing. Each person vibed a different spectrum. Amber could taste the colors on her tongue. Their emotions soaked through her skin, bitter, stringent and sour. Confusion tinted their thoughts.

You don't see us, she thought. *You won't remember us.*

The sandstorm of thoughts responded, drifting away and reorganizing. Moments later, their instincts kicked into action. The EMTs rushed to the bodies around the carriage. The police set up a perimeter.

Amber put her arm around Young.

He dragged his feet through the ash, his balance teetering as they stumbled toward the street. They didn't understand what they were doing or how.

No one stopped them.

* * *

SAMU'S HEAD was in the window.

She had been standing with her paws on the windowsill, had grown tired of waiting, wondering why no one had gotten out of the van. It had been running all this time in the driveway. She could see Amber in the passenger seat.

Young was on the floor.

Without the wheelchair, there was nowhere to sit. He drove using the hand controls, upright on his knees, a dirty towel wrapped around his waist. Amber had a blanket that smelled like wet dog, golden hairs scattered across it. They arrived without a word.

Sirens sang throughout the Lowcountry.

Her personality wrapped around her like a snug-fitting jacket. She was more Amber than she had been when they left the ash field. Memories continued rising, reminding her who she was before the dream.

It wasn't a dream.

She continued reminding herself what had happened. There were branches and roots, sky and moss. Life all around. Freedom in the air she breathed, where there was no separation, no fear. Otherworldly. And the more time that settled between her and the ash field, the more unreal it felt.

Just like dreams.

Her personality had begun to harden, feeling more like a shell than the soft fabric of clothing. The porousness she had experienced when first waking was now locked inside. She no longer felt thoughts of random strangers they passed in traffic or tasted their emotions. It allowed her thoughts to settle.

Young needed his own space. He didn't need her feeling his thoughts or knowing his emotions. In time, she knew, they might convince themselves this was all a dream, an unexplained accident. They only believed to have known each other's thoughts.

But the legs.

He continued staring, watching them occasionally twitch, his toes wiggling like someone pulling a switch. His thoughts were concealed behind a mental veil. If she wished to know them, she could simply reach out with a thought and feel the barrier between them, perhaps pull it aside. It moved like a thin membrane. He could feel the pressure.

"We should get inside," she said, "before the neighbors see you."

She reached for his foot, and he yanked it back with such force that the towel flew open. He didn't bother dragging it back over his lap. He buried his face in his hands. The sooty smear looked like war paint over tattooed tribal markings. He thumped the back of his head on the door, tapping his teeth and staring at the ceiling.

"I keep thinking we dropped acid," he said, "or iowaska or some shit. Maybe we set the garden on fire after we shaved ourselves and burned our clothes. Maybe we're still tripping."

He thumped the floor harder, punching the carpeted metal floorboard until he turned his frustration on the door then the steering wheel, growling and grinding his teeth. There were dents in the sidewall, and the steering wheel had cracked when she grabbed him. Sheets of flesh dangled from his knuckles, exposing wet tissue.

He buried his face again, this time sobbing, knees pulled up. The pressure was a slow build and was uncontainable once the thoughts began to pile up. Amber climbed next to him and leaned against him, shoulder to shoulder. He was still scared he would wake up.

"What the fuck is happening?"

She wanted to assure him that they weren't asleep, that this wasn't a dream. They sat until the shadows grew and the windows fogged.

The street was empty. The neighbors weren't outside, and no one looked out the window when Amber opened the passenger door. She came around to the driver's side and pulled him out, knotting the towel around his waist. They looked like a cult—hairless and smeared with dust. They could explain that if someone saw them.

But not Young walking.

Dev wasn't on the porch. They could deal with that explanation later. The chairs were straightened and the ashtray clean. Samu was swishing her tail at the door. Amber helped Young to the table and into a chair. He stared at the floor, digesting thoughts coming like shrapnel, spastically swallowing.

She went to the kitchen for a glass of water.

Samu was licking his hand when she returned. Amber put the glass in his hands and told him to drink, but he just stared at the studio. The floor was marred with paint. The canvases had been wrecked and torn, but they were neatly stacked up. Tubes of paint and brushes were neatly put away. It appeared a vandal had trashed the place and in a fit of remorse tried to put it back together.

Amber pulled a chair next to him. He was shaking. Another surge of panic was coming in. She took his hand and closed her eyes, wishing to soothe the current, to slow down his thoughts. Their hands began to warm.

The energy started to flow.

She felt the jagged edges of his panic leak into her and her calming, smooth energy trickle into him. An exchange took place that left him a little more settled, her a bit more agitated.

"I'll get us some clothes."

He nodded without looking away from the studio, his chin hanging, lips dry. Amber squeezed his shoulder instead of his knee and went to the back of the house, keeping her attention on him, feeling his presence on the chair. She went straight to the shower and quickly rinsed off. Gray, muddy streams trickled down her legs and into the drain. Her skin so smooth, so sensitive. She wondered if the hair would grow back.

If Young would keep walking.

She didn't care how she looked. She could always wear a hat or wrap a kerchief over her head. After the ash field, however, she didn't think anyone would notice if she didn't want them to. And then something unexpected happened. It came suddenly and out of nowhere.

She began sobbing.

The memory of Drayton was clear and present. His empty eyes. His sacrifice. He'd given everything to her.

I took it.

She was sobbing into her hands. Sobbed for Drayton, for her and Young, for the confusion and the suffering. The sacrifice. She hoped Young wouldn't hear it. Hoped he wasn't *reaching* for her to feel the rich flow of sadness that swept through her and then flow through him. It would be a steep drop if they both went down that emotional hole.

Drying off, she went to the bedroom. Two stacks of clothing were on the bed, neatly folded with shoes on top. She slowed, towel wrapped around her, and thought that was strange. She lifted shoes that were her size. The shirt, too.

Samu was looking out the front door. The chair was empty.

Amber stopped in the hall, a stack of clothes in her arms, and looked around before *reaching* out. She couldn't feel his thoughts anywhere until she pushed a little harder, imagining her mind a net to be thrown into the ocean. The noise of their surroundings scratched her mind like fingernails on a brick road—car exhaust, hungry birds, neighbors' thoughts and emotions that made her cringe. She closed her eyes.

The studio had been moved around.

Young had pulled paintings from the stack. Drayton's eyes looked out from a torn and broken mosaic. If she hadn't already purged the sorrow in the shower, she would have fallen on her knees right there. Instead, she squatted down and leaned closer.

The eyes were heavy with compassion and forgiveness.

There was another painting behind it. She shuffled it to the front and stood back. Knees suddenly weak, she searched for the chair Young had been sitting on. The paint was thick and textured, a mash-up of colors that funneled around a white and black vortex, as if this center was drawing everything toward it, mingling a thousand colors until they seemed to be inseparable.

Are you a painter? she'd asked Dev.

More of a creator.

She stood up and wobbled, shuffling closer, dragging her hands over layers of acrylics. The room slowly turned as she looked at the center. Remembering the tree. The way Umi stood over Mors. The way she poured into Young's mind with the urgency of Niagara Falls.

And finding a hole with no bottom.

Young was spacious. His mind an endless void. No form, no thoughts. Emptiness, cold and dark. Amber flowed into him, sweeping Umi inside, feeling her dissolve. Her memories unfolding. Amber absorbing them all the way to the beginning.

Umi's primal memory of looking up at the one who made her immortal.

* * *

THE PERSPECTIVE WAS ODD.

Young would describe it as floating above the ground on someone's shoulders. He could feel the steps as he climbed to the second floor, feel the burn in his calves as the muscles tensed.

Like operating remote control.

Two chairs were on the upper deck. Dev's pipes were on a small table between them, the one he sucked on while looking up thoughtfully, as if ideas floated in the blue cloud. A humorless grin spread across Young's face, a mirthless chuckle escaped.

Two chairs.

Young had only been up there once, on the day he'd visited the house with the realtor. Dev had carried him like an overgrown child. Young never came back up. The upstairs was Dev's pad. Still, there were two chairs.

Like someday Young would visit.

The curtains were drawn. Young tapped on the glass door overlooking the backyard. Dusty air slipped out of the dim room. The bed was in the corner, a bare mattress without sheets or pillow. The shelf above the stove was empty, the clock stuck on six o'clock. The battery dead.

Just like that first day.

A hint of vapor was in the air. Young quickly looked out on the deck, imagining Dev sneaking up behind him, but that was all it was. He turned to close the door.

A chair was pulled away from the table, one of those small tables for two. It was against the window where the blinds were closed. The apartment was barren, like someone had cleaned it out and moved on. But the truth was right there on the table.

He fell into the chair.

In the center of the table were two peppermint candies, one stacked on top of the other. The red and white spokes swirled around the center. Beneath them was a business card.

Young slid it out without tipping the candies and held it by the corners. A realtor's face was embossed on the shiny surface. Her hair was gray; wrinkles were bunched at the corners of her eyes. Selling houses was what she did during the summer. That was what she had said the day she showed him the house.

A shadow crossed the deck.

"She sold me this house." He looked up at Amber leaning in the open doorway and flashed the card. "One of those deals I couldn't pass up, she said. Not that money mattered. I just needed a place to stay, and this had the upstairs where Dev could live."

He wrinkled his nose and swallowed.

"He, um, he carried me up here. I had my arm around his neck and he, uh"—he shook his head—"climbed the steps without breaking a sweat. Same person whose only exercise was sucking on a pipe carried me up here hardly breathing, put me right over there."

He nodded at the bed.

"Ms. Bellinger"—he dropped the card—"did the realtor special for us, opened the doors and promised paradise on ice. 'I don't need much,' Dev said. I didn't even make an offer, just told her I'd take it. The old woman was counting dollar signs."

He stared at her picture, recalling the grin that had wrinkled her entire face.

"She put these right there." He stacked the candies on the card. "If we ever needed anything, her number was on the card. That was five years ago."

Five years and they were still there, exactly where she'd left them. The only difference a layer of dust. Nothing in this little room had changed. Not the bathroom, not the sink or the trash cans. The mini-fridge hadn't even been plugged in. All those nights Young had heard him in the little hours and he'd just assumed it was insomnia. But he didn't have a hard time sleeping.

He didn't sleep.

Young gritted back emotion. He'd already spilled enough. He tapped the table.

"You think…" he started then stopped. He tried again. "Was he ever even here, or did I…"

"He was here."

He shook his head. They both had a memory of meeting him, but that didn't mean anything. Maybe at one time it did, but not after the garden.

Memory didn't prove anything.

He pushed past her to find cooler air and escape the hint of vaping. The sun had fallen below the neighboring houses. Dusk was fast approaching. Insects sang. A cat wandered in a mulched bed where barren tomato cages leaned with last year's plants limp and brown. Dev planted them every spring, harvested the plump fruit, and left them in Young's kitchen, where they would draw flies.

"I don't understand."

He leaned on the railing. Amber stood next to him, their shoulders touching. His body humming where their bodies met. Bodies that had been incinerated in the dream, bodies now hairless and perfect. His body once crippled and tortured by Umi, now faultless and normal. He cringed when that memory came into focus and pushed it away.

Maybe I don't want to understand, he thought.

"Umi and Mors weren't human," she said. "They'd been around a long time, you proved that."

He recalled the research he'd done, the reasons that led him to find Amber.

"Umi wanted something. She wanted me to become..." Amber waved her hand, as if capturing the abstract nature of the dream. Her energy waned. Guilt slumped over her shoulders. "I don't know what she wanted, Young, or what she was doing to me... to us... but..."

He felt gentle pressure inside his head, a friendly invitation to open his mind. He took a deep breath and let it out, relaxing and letting go. Images seeped into his thoughts like his mind was a semi-permeable membrane. He felt Amber's memories of curling up inside the tree, spreading out and becoming everything in the garden, how space had seemed to unfold and expand. She had been unfettered and fearless.

And hungry.

The cool flow of life had fed her. She didn't know where it was coming from or how, just that she wanted more, and those walls were the only thing stopping her. When they came down, she was going to gobble this universe up. And Umi would be holding the reins.

She took his hand. "You stopped her."

It was his turn to recall being strung up, how Umi had forced herself inside him and the unexpected feeling when she couldn't escape. The cool flow pushing her in. He cringed and pulled the memory back, the strange sensation of absorbing energy, the endlessness inside him difficult to comprehend.

"What am I?" he said.

She shook her head. She didn't know what they were or how they became this, only what had happened.

"Dev knew," she said. "I saw him."

Amber continued staring at the backyard.

"It was when... she was..." She sighed and frowned, her smooth brows crimping together. She gave up trying to find the words and offered the memory instead.

She held both his hands and squeezed, as if he might fall. A quiver of fear accompanied the pressure. Reluctantly, he opened like cracking a faucet, allowing her thoughts to trickle in at first. He saw them from a distance, the details faint and bleached. When he had been strung up. When Umi had pressed against him.

When Amber had flowed in.

Umi had been dissolved along with all of her memories. Amber had seen the primal memory, all the way back in the beginning, the one where Umi had become an immortal. It had been prehistoric days when she was human, when someone had discovered her.

Dev.

"It was him," Amber whispered. "He made her that."

"What are we?"

She turned his hands over.

His knuckles were no longer raw and scuffed. The tantrum he'd thrown in the van left not a trace. His flesh was brand new. He studied it with distant curiosity, careful not to analyze what it meant. The foundation of reality was still soft and unreliable. If he really thought about it, it would turn to quicksand.

"Maybe you were right," she said. "We're just cattle raised for the slaughterhouse. It's just… you and I were pulled out of the line."

Young had said that when he was talking about vampires. *Is that what we are?* He closed down his thoughts, but it was too late. A shudder passed through them as the memory of Drayton's blank eyes looked out from a shriveled human shell—a body drawn dry by a hungry garden that only wanted to become more. And did so with the essence of others.

"You didn't take it," Young said. "He gave it."

She nodded. Not because she understood or agreed or was fine with it. She nodded because that was all she could do. Maybe Umi needed to end and Drayton helped do that. Or maybe he couldn't stop her.

She sat in one of the chairs. Young chuckled drily. He realized now why Dev had left two chairs on the deck. It wasn't for him and Young to pass a pipe.

He sat next to Amber.

They remained there until night fell, the sound of distant sirens reminding them of the dream and the ashes left behind. They sat quietly as their thoughts settled.

The mosquitos weren't interested in them.

He thought of the painting left behind, the one with the vortex inhaling all the colors, and the wigwam who consumed the world to find endless spaciousness and the acorn safely stored in his belly. The painting and the story were the same thing. It was difficult to capture the dream with words. Perhaps the meaning of all of this was like a koan that just couldn't be explained, a concept beyond the human mind. A direct experience that had no past or future.

The wigwam.

All of those colors swirling around a vortex intermingling with black and white. Life and death needed each other in this universe. One cannot be without the other. Life without death was a vampire with an endless appetite.

Umi never believed she really needed Mors.

The birds began singing before the sun appeared. Dew settled on the grass, and steam rose from sunbeams. Young reached over and took her hand. She turned to him and opened her mind. They shared a thought, each a mirror of the other. Maybe they'd never know exactly what had happened or if Dev was the one who made them this, or where he'd gone. If he was ever really there. They only had this moment. The light and the dark.

One cannot be without the other.

31

The rooftop was nearly full.

Trish pushed her ticket across the bar. A year ago there wouldn't have been room for her to take a break, and Sal wouldn't have had time to fingerfuck his phone.

Sal grabbed her ticket with both hands. "I don't have this."

"Check the pantry," she said, "next to the coffee."

He was annoyed. The lazy bastard took the ticket like he might forget what he was looking for.

Soccer was on the television behind the bar. Trish channel-surfed since no one was watching. She stopped randomly on a news station and watched lips move as music played over the words. She didn't need to hear it. It had been the same story for a year now, everyone starting with the drone footage.

Looks like a charcoal dumping ground, her dad would say.

The blame for the recent tourist recession went to the Eilif family. The elderly couple was personally responsible for chasing money out of the Lowcountry. *Faster than hard-ons fleeing a carpet-muncher wedding,* her dad would say. She didn't think the analogy worked, but he made his point.

The bones of the elderly couple were found in twenty-four inches of uniform ashes. The wealthy weirdos had somehow managed to level the first house ever built in Charleston and everything on their lot in magnanimous fashion. A glorious fucking suicide, social memes coined it. How they did it, no one would ever know.

And that was the beauty of it.

The added conspiracy bonus was that Mors had died on the rooftop almost two years earlier. Trish wouldn't believe it if she hadn't seen the old bastard eat it right there on the floor. He'd stopped breathing with a whole crowd of onlookers snapping pics.

Stranger still, Trish always thought, was that Mrs. Eilif sat by his side the whole time without shedding a single salty tear. In fact, she'd looked bored. Trish never forgot that. Maybe that was how you said goodbye after a lifetime of marriage. Or maybe she had a side hustle going on.

That would explain the bones next to her.

How do you vaporize three houses and an entire garden without making a sound? There were a lot of theories. Even if they'd lit everything up with a mysterious fuel source, no one could explain the mass deaths that had surrounded the place. Toxic fumes or poison gas were at the top of the list, but if you drew a line on a map, the area made a perfect circle. A compass couldn't outline it any better.

What does that?

"Let me check downstairs." Sal waved an empty box. "Hold down the bar."

Trish nodded. Her customer wasn't in a hurry. She was surprised they even had a box of what he was asking for. It was an oddball request.

News footage showed people decked in hazmat suits working in one corner of the ash pit. There was no trace of poison in the soil or radioactive residue, but an event that horrific without explanation required a hazmat.

On the day the bodies were found, no one had heard anything. No sonic boom, no ball of fire. A tremor had been registered at the fault line running through the Lowcountry, but earthquakes didn't trigger mass suicides any more than crop circles.

Tourists had fled the Lowcountry like Noah's Ark had arrived at the port with a message to burn all newcomers. On the other hand, conspiracy theorists and reality television producers couldn't get there fast enough. Problem was they didn't come with bags of money like the tourists. They were there to discover alien genocide or uncover government treachery, not collect sunburns on the beach. If Trish wasn't divorced with kids, she would have up and moved.

Probably not.

"Oh, I'm so sorry." She had been so caught up in the television that she hadn't noticed the woman sitting at the bar. "Can I get you something, ma'am?"

"What do you have on tap?"

Trish recited the beers as she went around the bar, wondering if she'd just committed the royalest of all fuckups. The customer's face was so smooth and pretty.

She took the customer's order and slid a pint across the bar. "Start a tab?"

The customer put bills on the bar instead of a credit card. So much for seeing a name such as Janet or Harry. *Hello, my name's Trish. Are you a man?*

She decided he was a man instead of a woman based on how he sampled the beer's aroma first then took a sip. Not that women weren't beer snobs, but Trish's experience went with the odds.

"Anything new?" He gestured to the television.

"Just more ash," she said. "Like they're digging for treasure. Shame it happened."

He shrugged so dismissively that she bristled.

"Seven hundred thirty-two people in that neighborhood are dead and no one knows why." She shrugged back. "No big deal, huh."

"Not if it saved seven billion."

"What?"

"Perspective, that's all I'm saying. What if a tragedy like that kept the world from imploding? Not a bad deal."

He presented a wry smile. She wasn't sure if he was serious, but it reminded her of her dad looking for a fight.

"Look at you, making lemonade." Trish wiped the bar in front of him. "You might want to tell them your theory. It would make everyone breathe a little easier, bring back the tourists."

He shrugged again, this time a little more playfully.

"Do you make a living as a therapist?" she said. "Because I'm feeling better already."

"Shepherd."

"You're a shepherd?"

He nodded.

"You forgot your cane, Mr. Shepherd."

"It's called a staff."

"Shouldn't you be with your flock instead of drinking beer?"

"I check in from time to time. You know, when the wolves get a little greedy."

"Keep them from eating all the sheep."

He tipped the pint toward her.

Sal circled around the bar, slightly winded, peeling a wrapper off a brand-new box of tea. He wasn't much of a stair man, but the elevator wasn't working. Management didn't seem to be in a hurry to fix it.

"Steep exactly four minutes," Trish said. "That's what the customer wants."

"I'll count with my fingers."

Sal disappeared into the back room, where he'd nuke a cup of water then scroll through his phone until it felt like four minutes. Customers on the rooftop couldn't tell the difference.

"He's particular."

Trish turned toward her beer-drinking customer. "Sal? As long as the tea is sweet, that's all that matters to him. Earl Grey is a little foo-foo-lala."

"Your customer, the one who ordered it, his palette is a little sophisticated. He'll know you used the microwave."

"Serves him right. Rooftop isn't a tea snob hotspot."

He pulled a vape pen from his front pocket.

"Can't use that here. Sal will lose his mind."

Sal didn't care about much, but he liked working on the rooftop, and management had made the rules clear: vaping was the same as smoking. The customer put it on the bar after a toke.

The tea-drinking customer was leaning on the wall overlooking the city. He looked more South African than Lowcountry. Ethiopian, maybe. Somewhere Trish thought of as famished or malnourished. His accent, though, carried hints of Gullah. Or maybe it was Jamaican. She still couldn't tell the difference.

"One of your sheep?" Trish leaned toward the customer.

The pint hung lazily in his hand as he cast a gaze across the rooftop. Lost in wonderful thought, he mused, "He's a beautiful man, Tristen. A savior."

Okay, got it. He's gay. She felt more comfortable leaning closer to him and teasing, completely unaware that he just used her birth name.

"Well, maybe you should introduce yourself to him."

Wistfully, he took a swallow. "Maybe another time."

"How old is he?" she asked. "And is he into forty-year-old single mothers?"

"He's not into people. More of a sheep guy."

Trish waited for the punchline. When he smiled without even blinking, she tossed the towel on the bar and laughed too loud, snorting. "You're super weird."

He pointed the vape pen at her. A light glowed as he took a drag. Thin streams of smoke fired from his nostrils. It smelled a little like marijuana. When he offered it to her, she looked around before hitting it, blowing the smoke into the hand towel.

Definitely weed.

"Tea up." Sal delivered the cup on a tray.

Trish jumped back then giggled, hiding her laughter behind her hand.

"Hell is so funny?"

He didn't say anything about the smoke or even look at the customer pulling another drag, winking as he did it. Sal changed the channel back to soccer.

That was weird, too.

She was off to deliver the tea. It was nice having someone to shoot the shit with, especially someone funny like that. Someone with a weed pen that Sal didn't notice. Someone gay she didn't have to fend off.

The other customer sat down as she approached. He crossed his legs and folded his hands on his lap. She put the teacup in front of him.

"Earl Grey," she said. "Four minutes."

"Thank you."

Delicately, carefully, he lifted the cup and closed his eyes, inhaling the aroma. A single, barely perceptible nod of approval. Sal must have used a stopwatch. She found herself staring at him unacceptably long by social standards, captivated by something in his expression, remembering what the customer at the bar had said. It was the pain in his eyes, the frailty. She had the urge to sit down and weep.

A savior.

"Can I, uh, I get you anything else?"

He shook his head. She wanted to stay and talk, to ask him if he was okay, if he wanted any company but not exactly sex. Just sit there with him. Instead, she went back to the bar. Her lip was quivering. She sighed heavily and wiped her eyes. Her period must be coming.

"Did he leave?" She gestured to the empty barstool.

"Who?" Sal said.

"The guy sitting there."

Sal shook his head and frowned. The towel was still wadded up where she'd left it, but there was no condensation on the bar or empty glass. Trish rubbed her face and sighed. She glanced across the rooftop. At least the other guy was there drinking his tea. She hadn't imagined everything.

Maybe don't get high at work.

EPILOGUE

"**W**elcome."

Millie Sprague handed a trifold leaflet to a man in shorts and flip-flops. His wife, who was wearing oversized sunglasses and a hat wide enough to shade half a team of little leaguers, took one, too.

"If you have any questions, just ask the docent by the pond. Enjoy the tour."

Not a minute went by before the next guests arrived, and Millie handed them a leaflet along with the same friendly smile. She didn't mind handling the gate duties. It was boring (no one ever came out to the gate to ask a question), but it was easy, and no one ever complained. A retired middle-school teacher now master gardener, she was happy as long as they were.

Everyone had a gripe.

The Lowcountry Garden Tour had always been her favorite. She'd been a volunteer long before she retired. In fact, her kids were still in diapers when she got her first gig. She had seniority over the other master gardeners. That was why she picked the Miller Residence— thirty-thousand-gallon koi pond, manicured knot garden, and wandering gravel paths brought all the tourists to the yard.

The Miller Residence was bringing back the gazing ball, with half a dozen of them strategically placed throughout the garden. Although Millie never called it that. *Gazing balls* sounded too kitschy.

Butler ball was more fitting.

She'd rather be watching the koi—three feet long and gliding like angels—than handing out trifolds and saying the same thing over and over. But she took turns with the others. She was considerate that way. As long as she had something to do.

An occupied mind leaves no room for thoughts.

And thoughts she had plenty. Her husband of thirty-two years had a late-life crisis. Or maybe he'd had a mid-life one too, did she dig that far back. All she knew was that he was currently fucking a harlot their granddaughter's age, and everyone knew about it. A root canal without sedation would've hurt less.

Millie could sue his ass into poverty, but what good would that do? She preferred to stay busy. What better way than to wander the raked gravel paths of the Miller Residence, the largest residential garden in downtown Charleston for the past five years?

That honor had previously gone to the Garden House.

The lot was still a tourist attraction but for different reasons. Five years and still an ash pit. Not like Millie or any of the other master gardeners had gotten to see it before it was turned to ash. The Eilifs had never put their garden in the tour. And now it was gone.

The whole event was sad for a lot of reasons.

It was nearly lunchtime. Millie had brought a snack and would eat it next to the pond and watch the koi. She was a bit hungry when her back started hurting. There was pain in her jaw as well. She'd been on her feet all morning. It was time for a break.

She put the trifolds on the ground and left her post without telling anyone, following one of the raked paths around the side of the house. The yellow butler ball was on her right. Her distorted reflection was approaching when a giant hand reached into her chest.

She didn't feel the ground.

All the strength dripped out of her legs. Gravel was grinding into the back of her head as she stared through live oaks and resurrection fern. Short breaths stabbed her.

Surprisingly, she felt relief.

Her parents had died of heart attacks. Neither one of them had reached sixty years of age. Millie was almost seventy. She'd beat them both by at least ten years, long enough to see her life fall apart. Maybe they knew what they were doing.

There would be no need for an ambulance. She just wished she didn't have to do this alone. If she was honest, even her lecherous husband would be preferable to dying in a stranger's backyard all by herself.

She had closed her eyes. When she opened them, someone approached. They didn't seem alarmed that she was sprawled halfway in a flower bed with drool wetting her cheek. They knelt next to her. A firm hand cradled her head so that it wasn't grinding into the gravel.

It was a young couple.

Strange, though, they didn't panic. Maybe they realized an ambulance wouldn't do her any good. As her breaths grew sharper, there was no bright light drawing her up to heaven, no angels coming to escort her, either. She felt comfortable. The bitterness that had gripped her insides since her ex-husband left had finally let go.

Peace wrapped around her.

Her body vibrated as a silky ribbon coolly slid through her. The young couple hadn't said a word until she floated above them, drifting through the branches and resurrection fern, a feather finding a summer breeze to carry her home.

"Thank you," they said.

WHAT TO READ NEXT?

Get the novellas of Drayton in the Lowcountry in *The Drayton Chronicles*.
bertauski.com/drayton

REVIEW DRAYTON!

If you enjoyed this ride, please drop a review on your favorite vendor. It doesn't have to be long and complicated. Throw some stars on it and write *Loved it!* or *It was really, really okay!* or *Meh.*

Reviews make the difference.

Find all vendors links at
bertauski.com/drayton

BERTAUSKI STARTER LIBRARY

FREE!

* * *

bertauski.com

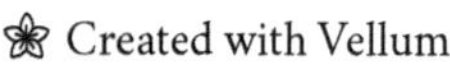 Created with Vellum

9 781951 432584